"Jana?"

"How are you real?" Tears filled her eyes and she shook her head, wiped them away with a ferocity that surprised him. "This isn't right. You aren't supposed to exist. Men like you..." She let out a little sob as a solitary tear escaped to roll down her cheek. "Good men like you aren't supposed to exist."

"I exist. And I'm here." He wrapped an arm around her shoulders and pulled her against him, feeling an odd sense of pride when she held him, too, and cried. "I'm not going anywhere." He pressed his lips against her hair, rocked her gently. He hadn't lied. Not about any of it. Not about her or what she'd been through or...

Or what he thought of her. He smiled, shocked and stunned to realize he was doing the one thing he never expected to do again.

He was falling in love with Jana Powell.

Dear Reader,

Some characters arrive in my head fully formed. I know precisely who they are and what they're all about. Silas Garwood was not one of those characters. Nor was his soon-to-be heroine, Jana Powell. Until I sat down to write, they were names on a page, and other than Silas being a single father to his challenging five-year old daughter, Freya, their histories and situations developed with each word I wrote.

Silas's journey through single fatherhood exemplifies the kind of devotion and love every child deserves. Jana, through her own life struggles, has overcome every obstacle placed in her way, including a battle with cancer. If there are two characters of mine who deserve a happily-ever-after more, I honestly can't think of them. Surrounding them with Ohana, the family both of them need and long for, only made their story all the sweeter.

Welcome back to Nalani.

Anna

THE SINGLE DAD'S PROMISE

ANNA J. STEWART

If you purchased this book without a cover you should be aware that this book is stolen property. It was reported as "unsold and destroyed" to the publisher, and neither the author nor the publisher has received any payment for this "stripped book."

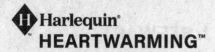

ISBN-13: 978-1-335-46006-6

The Single Dad's Promise

Copyright © 2025 by Anna J. Stewart

All rights reserved. No part of this book may be used or reproduced in any manner whatsoever without written permission.

Without limiting the author's and publisher's exclusive rights, any unauthorized use of this publication to train generative artificial intelligence (AI) technologies is expressly prohibited.

This is a work of fiction. Names, characters, places and incidents are either the product of the author's imagination or are used fictitiously. Any resemblance to actual persons, living or dead, businesses, companies, events or locales is entirely coincidental.

For questions and comments about the quality of this book, please contact us at CustomerService@Harlequin.com.

TM and ® are trademarks of Harlequin Enterprises ULC.

 Harlequin Enterprises ULC
22 Adelaide St. West, 41st Floor
Toronto, Ontario M5H 4E3, Canada
www.Harlequin.com

Printed in U.S.A.

Bestselling author **Anna J. Stewart** honestly believes she was born with a book in her hand. After growing up devouring every story she could get her hands on, now she gets to earn her living making up stories and fulfilling happily-ever-afters of her own. Her dreams have most definitely come true. Anna lives in Northern California (only a ninety-minute flight from Disneyland, her favorite place on earth) with two monstrous, devious, adorable cats named Sherlock and Rosie.

Books by Anna J. Stewart

Harlequin Heartwarming

Hawaiian Reunions

Her Island Homecoming
Their Surprise Island Wedding
A Surprise Second Chance
A Hawaiian Christmas Romance

Butterfly Harbor Stories

The Bad Boy of Butterfly Harbor
Recipe for Redemption
A Dad for Charlie
Always the Hero
Holiday Kisses
Safe in His Arms
The Firefighter's Thanksgiving Wish
A Match Made Perfect
Building a Surprise Family
Worth the Risk
The Mayor's Baby Surprise

Visit the Author Profile page
at Harlequin.com for more titles.

For Jessica Bogard.

Extraordinary friend. Honorary little sister.
Awesome single mom.

My life would be far less exciting without you in it.

CHAPTER ONE

SILAS GARWOOD HAD survived seven years as a San Francisco patrol officer. He'd handled muggings and burglaries, car accidents, and hit and runs. He'd walked into convenience store robberies and uncertain domestic disturbances, searched for his fair share of lost dogs, cats and, in one odd occurrence, a runaway lizard. He'd worked crowd control, concert security. For one very long summer, he'd pulled the unenviable patrol of Golden Gate Park on the night shift.

Yet with all of that, nothing could have prepared him for the six-hour flight to Hawai'i with his very tired, very cranky five-year-old daughter.

"I want Roscoe." Freya scowled and folded her arms across her chest. It didn't matter that the last of the other passengers were disembarking the plane or that he was already stressing over retrieving their luggage from the carousel at Hilo International Airport. Freya had a way of inserting attitude into just about every statement she made.

"You brought Fred." He pointed to the over-

8 THE SINGLE DAD'S PROMISE

size, smooshy pillow in the shape of a carrot complete with a worn, green, curly yarn top. Fred had served as both Freya's comfort object and Silas's peace of mind. Given the battles Fred had witnessed and survived, Silas was this close to submitting Fred for a commendation medal. "And Winnie's in your treasure bag." He indicated the quilted, sunshine-yellow bag looped across her chest, which contained, among other things, a one-eyed plastic chicken with a missing foot. "Roscoe was too big to fit in the suitcase." Instead, Roscoe was on guard duty back in their three-bedroom, Potrero Hill home in San Francisco.

Silas had been determined to make this two-week trip with one checked bag and one carry-on, and neither was large enough for the bigheaded moose with giant googly eyes. "He'll be waiting for us when we get home."

"I want him now." Tears filled her bright green eyes as her lower lip trembled.

Sensing a coming meltdown, Silas glanced at the pair of flight attendants waiting for them to deplane. He grabbed their carry-on from the overhead bin, lowered it to the floor and crouched beside his daughter. "Freya." He touched a hand to her shoulder and waited until she looked at him. He could see the fear, the uncertainty of being away from home. His little girl was strong in many ways, but this was the first time they'd ever gone anywhere far away. It had to be overwhelming for a child who was steeped in schedule and routine. "We talked about this being an adventure, right? That we were going to have to go out of our comfort zones and try new things. That means spending some time away from Roscoe and Evie." His neighbor/part-time housekeeper/babysitter had, in her grandmotherly ways, attempted to prepare Freya for the upcoming trip, but it was apparent her gentle guidance hadn't quite taken hold. "Come on, sweetie." He nudged Freya gently. "You'll be happier once you see where we're staying and we get something to eat." Even as he said it, his stomach rumbled.

The snacks he'd packed hadn't lasted the two of them half the flight, even if Freya hadn't spilled most of her popcorn all over the carpeted floor.

"Roscoe really wanted to come to Hawai'i," Freya grumbled but she finally unclicked her seat belt and dropped out of her chair.

"Maybe he can come next time and Winnie can stay home," Silas suggested, amazed he could even think about repeating this journey. At the moment he would be happy never to leave the house again. "Hang on." He caught her arm and pivoted her back around. "What's the Garwood family saying?" He pointed to the crumbs on the floor.

Freya sighed in a way that made him dread her teenage years. "We don't make work for other

10 THE SINGLE DAD'S PROMISE

people." Rolling her eyes, she fell in line and together they cleaned up their mess.

Whatever impatience he'd seen in the flight attendants' eyes earlier was gone when, after carefully picking up every bit of popcorn they could find and placing it in a baggie to throw away, Silas and Freya made their way to the front of the plane. Freya hugged Fred tight, the carrot's fraying green top wedged under her chin.

Silas offered an apologetic smile as they exited. "Sorry we took so long."

"Totally okay," the younger, male flight attendant assured him. "First trip to Hawai'i?"

"Not for me." Silas could already feel himself sinking into the fond memories of that one carefree summer after college graduation. Well before his life got seriously complicated "It's good to be back." Even now he recognized that familiar warm breeze blowing through the open cabin door. He could smell jasmine, hibiscus, the ocean and the clean March air. "Thanks again for everything. Come on, Frey."

Giving her another nudge, he walked behind her down the gangplank. The hot terminal air collided with the humidity, filling his lungs with a hint of diesel and heat. Hilo International might be the biggest airport on the eastern coast of the Big Island, but it still had its limitations. Personally, he preferred smaller airports like this one, airports that had a bit of character. He noticed the display of the work of local artists, including stunning murals and a beautiful metal sculpture of a trio of dancers.

"Daddy, I have to go potty." Frey grabbed hold of the hem of his wrinkled T-shirt and gave a gentle tug.

"Right. Okay." He hoisted the strap of his carryon higher on his shoulder. "I bet there's one on the way to baggage…" His thought trailed off upon catching sight of a familiar face all but standing guard near the automatic doors to the terminal. Tall, dark-haired, muscles bulging beneath the expensively tailored dark suit he wore. Only one person Silas knew could look borderline menacing and welcoming in equal measure.

"Mano." The tension and turmoil of the past few hours faded as his mind filled with some of the happiest memories of his life. The second he slapped his hand into Mano Iokepa's, emotion welled inside of him. The greeting of a brotherly hug sent the past few years careening in his mind. "I figured I'd find you at your office tomorrow. I didn't expect you to meet us here."

"I'm part of the reason you came all this way." Mano stepped back, kept a hand solidly on Silas's shoulder. "And unless your sense of direction's gotten any better, I couldn't take the chance you'd get lost on your way to Nalani."

Silas rolled his eyes and wondered if that was

12 THE SINGLE DAD'S PROMISE

where Freya had picked it up. "That was more than a decade ago, man. Let it go."

"Never," Mano chuckled. "Aloha, brah." Mano squeezed his shoulder. From the collar of his dark gray button-down shirt, Mano's tattoos eeked into sight, trailing up and around his neck, highlighting his brown skin. *"E komo mai."*

"Mahalo, Mano." Silas's heart twisted as he sighed. "It's good to be home."

Mano looked at him for a long moment, and for an instant, Silas wondered if his college friend was trying to see who he'd become since they'd last seen one another in person. It wasn't, Silas thought as he glanced away and down at his daughter, an examination he was ready to partake in. Not yet, anyway.

If Mano noticed his reluctance, he didn't let on. Instead he stepped back and crouched down, resting his arms on his knees. "You must be Freya." He reached into the pocket of his suit jacket and pulled out a thick strand of shells. "Aloha, Freya. Welcome to the islands." He held the necklaces out, patiently waiting when Freya turned her confused face up at Silas.

"It's a welcome present," Silas told her. "This is my friend Mano. I told you about him, remember? We went to school together."

"When you were little like me?" Freya asked, still eyeing the shells with suspicion.

"It's hard to believe we were ever as little as

you, but it was definitely when we were younger," Mano said with a smile. "Would you like to just hold it?"

Silas touched Freya's shoulder, squeezed gently in silent encouragement. She took a step forward and ducked her head so Mano could slip the shell necklace over her head.

"Thank you," she whispered, touching uncertain fingers to the shells.

"In Nalani, we say mahalo," Mano said easily.

"Ma-ha-lo," Freya repeated carefully. "They're pretty. Daddy, can I keep them in my treasure bag?"

"It's your treasure bag," Silas reminded her. "You can keep anything in there that fits."

She stepped back and stood beside Silas, clutched at his leg and lifted her head to watch, wide-eyed, as Mano rose to his full height.

"I have someone collecting your bags," Mano said as he led the way out of the terminal. "I've got a car—"

"Daddy," Freya almost whined. "I really gotta go."

"Right. Ah, bathroom?" Silas asked Mano.

"There's a family bathroom just down there." Mano pointed beyond them, then lifted the bag off Silas's shoulder as they picked up speed. "Take your time." He pointed toward a kiosk selling snacks, reading material and those moon-shaped travel pillows, indicating he'd be waiting there.

14 THE SINGLE DAD'S PROMISE

They rejoined Mano and headed to the car, a large black SUV parked at the far end of the pickup area. A young woman wearing a bright yellow flowered shirt and beige shorts emerged from the terminal wheeling their bag. Her long dark hair was pulled into a high knot on her head. "Just one bag, sir?" she called and Silas nodded.

"Traveling light," Silas said to a surprised-looking Mano. "Figured we could pick up anything we forgot. Luanda's still across the street from the resort?"

"Always will be," Mano assured him. "Mikayla, this is Freya and her father, Silas Garwood. Silas is an old college friend. He went to school with me and Remy."

"Aloha," Mikayla said with a quick wave at Freya. Silas touched his daughter's shoulder and she moved closer. Freya hadn't been around a lot of women under fifty.

"Mikayla's just finishing up her internship at the management program I've started at the Hibiscus Bay," Mano said. "She suggested having someone on site at the airport to welcome resort guests."

"Be careful what you tell the boss," Mikayla said with a laugh. "He'll make you test it out to prove it works." She loaded the bags into the trunk. "We have another couple arriving in about an hour," she told Mano as he walked around to the driver's side. "I'll be back at my desk once they're on their way."

"Sounds good." He offered a quick wave with his key fob. "Thanks, Mikayla."

Silas got Freya settled into the expertly installed car seat in the back and had her choose one of her favorite storybooks from her treasure bag. When he climbed into the front passenger seat, Mano shifted into Drive and took off toward the freeway.

"Good flight?" Mano asked and Silas resisted the urge to groan.

"I survived," was all he said. "Thanks for the tickets. You didn't have to—"

"You're the one who's been keeping tabs on Golden Vistas even after I thought the threat of a takeover was gone," Mano said, keeping his voice low as Freya hummed to herself in the back seat. "Least I could do is bring you out for a one-on-one conversation about what they might be up to. Besides, I'm going to make you work for it."

Silas bit the inside of his cheek. He'd done a bit more than keep tabs on the struggling business that had its parasitic eyes fixed squarely on Mano's hotel and at least one other Nalani business. But details like that could wait. "What did Sydney say when you told her about Golden Vistas taking another swing at buying out Ohana and the resort?" Silas asked.

"It wasn't so much what she said as the vehemence with which she said it," Mano said of the owner of Ohana Odysseys, the local tour and excursion company that had been making a serious name for itself in the island tourist industry. The company that had been built from scratch by one of the best friends Silas had ever had.

Mano went on, "Sydney has a bit more personal insight into Golden Vistas Incorporated than you or I do."

"Because she married one of their former accountants?" Silas found himself smiling at the idea of Remy's younger sister being all grown-up and now, as of this past New Year's Eve anyway, a happily married woman to the aforementioned accountant, Theo Fairfax. The photos he'd seen had made him regret not making the trip out sooner. He'd have loved to attend, but between work and Freya, last-minute trips just weren't possible. "I'm looking forward to meeting Theo face-to-face." Silas paused.

"He's anxious to meet you, too. I think you'll make a good team, keeping GVI out of our hair and off our island." Mano said. "And we have lots of support, both with friends around the islands and in Nalani. We're ready for whatever GVI throws at us."

The absolute confidence in Mano's voice eased Silas's nerves about the situation. "Did Don Martin show up like I said?"

"He's scheduled to check into the resort late tomorrow afternoon," Mano confirmed, glancing into the rearview mirror before he merged lanes. "Booked himself into one of our suites for five days. He asked for tour company recommendations."

"Trying to stay under the radar, I bet," Silas said. "Considering Ohana Odysseys is the only tour company in town." Silas's information on Don Martin pinned him as GVI's one-man reconnaissance team, sent to scout businesses the investment firm was focused on buying out or taking over. Somehow, some way, they needed to either show Don Martin that Nalani wasn't worth GVI's time and attention, or prove Nalani wasn't going to give in without a serious fight.

"The staff knows to notify me when he gets here." Mano smirked. "He'll hopefully see their added attention as a perk of his stay rather than viewing it as surveillance."

That was what Silas was here for. Partially, at least. "You told your staff about GVI circling back around to attempt another takeover?"

"Of course." Mano didn't blink. "The Hibiscus Bay is family—it's Ohana, as we like to say. What affects one of us, affects our livelihoods, affects all of us. If GVI is taking another run at us, I want everyone on high alert."

"The details Theo emailed me gave me a great place to start." The wealth of nonproprietary information Silas had been able to gather on Theo's former employer and how they operated gave Silas an entry point for a deep dive into GIV's operating history. "Keep in mind, I'm not here in any official capacity," he reminded Mano. "And Don Martin isn't doing anything illegal by coming here."

"Noted. I've spoken with Alec Aheona Malloy, our chief of police. He's aware of what's going on." Mano glanced at him. "I also told him you were coming in. Wouldn't hurt for you to touch base, just so you're both on the same page."

"I don't want to step on any toes," Silas said without hesitation.

"Alec doesn't have toes," Mano said seriously. "And when push comes to shove, he'd welcome more help. It's only him and one deputy, and with Nalani gaining in popularity, things are getting… well, let's say they're stretched a bit thin these days. I told him because I wanted him prepared for any eventuality. In case things get ugly with GVI."

"Understood." Silas looked over his shoulder at his daughter. "I'll just need some help with the Freya side of things." He couldn't very well run surveillance on someone with a five-year-old tagging along.

"Mr. Martin reached out to Ohana Odysseys for their tour and excursion options," Mano informed him. "Tehani's going to book you on the same ones as soon as he decides."

"Sounds like a plan. Theo's up to date on what's happening? Martin is going to recognize him." Theo Fairfax had, after all, worked for GVI for years before moving to Nalani last spring.

"Not necessarily." Mano's voice carried a bit of levity. "Other than his glasses, our recent mainland transplant has seriously embraced island life right down to the most horrendous Hawaiian shirt collection you could imagine."

Silas grinned.

"As for Freya," Mano went on. "We've got a few options for you to consider. We've just remodeled our day care center at the resort. Or, if you'd prefer something more structured, our pre-K and kindergarten teachers at the elementary school said they could find a place for Freya while you're here."

Silas wasn't entirely sure structured was ideal, given her initial pre-K experience back home had been...problematic. Freya was scheduled to start kindergarten in the fall but...maybe the pre-K class in Nalani was worth a shot. If for no other reason than to keep her preparation moving forward.

"I'll stop in and check the daycare facility out," Silas said in compromise. "I'm sure your staff is great but just for my peace of mind..."

"Of course. No need to decide right now," Mano said. "Schools let out by two, so there will be plenty of other kids for her to play with in the afternoons. Daphne said she's happy to keep an eye on Freya if you'd prefer more one-on-one care. Cammie and Noah have some after-school activities—there might be some Freya is old enough for."

"You're right. That's a lot of options." And he was grateful for them. Silas wasn't entirely sure how any of those would go over with Freya. She was…particular about how she spent any time away from Silas. It had taken her months to get used to their neighbor being around. Still, the world and life couldn't revolve around one five-year-old. Freya could easily amaze him. She always did.

Silas looked out the window, surprised at how familiar everything felt despite the thirteen years that had passed since he'd been on the Big Island. The foliage and greenery never failed to impress. The islands were otherworldly in their beauty even with all the modernity surrounding them. This was how things should be, he thought, as he watched the island zoom by.

The closer they got to Nalani, which was only about a half hour south of Hilo, the more he felt at peace. Not unlike the first time he'd been here. There was something about the islands and Nalani in particular, with its small-town, personal touches and its dedication to tradition and community that made it a home away from home no matter how much time had gone by. It had been a long time since he'd been here, since he'd felt those sensations. Now he'd only been back minutes and the feeling had returned stronger than before.

"Speaking of support." He eyed Silas. "We've a lot of catching up to do."

"Yeah." Putting aside the emails, video chats and phone calls, plus one brief visit for Mano's wedding, thirteen years was a lot of time to go between visits. And Silas had lived a lot of life in those years. As had Mano. "Thanks for putting us up at the resort. We don't need anything fancy or big. A broom closet will be fine as long as we can get some beach time."

"The Hibiscus Bay Resort does not do broom closets," Mano said with a touch of disdain in his voice. "And while my original idea was indeed to put you in a suite at the resort—"

"A suite?" Silas barely got the words out before he felt his wallet scream. "Mano, that's not nece—"

"You're Ohana," Mano cut him off easily, as if he'd been prepared for the argument. "We've got you, brah. But as I was saying, that was my original idea. Sydney had a better one."

Silas pressed his lips together. What was better than a resort suite?

"Before Christmas, Sydney had remodeled the second beach hut that Remy had bought," Mano told him. "We used it as a test run during the surfing championship Nalani now hosts. This time she wants to test it out for family rentals. She's anxious for practical feedback, so there will be critical discussions required in exchange for you staying there. It's a two-bedroom cottage right on the beach." Mano flashed one of his happy island smiles. "She thought Freya might enjoy being right near the water. Daphne's kids added special touches for her in the smaller bedroom."

Silas's heart tipped a bit in his chest. Freya might be distrustful and suspicious about everything else on the planet, but when it came to the ocean, it was as if she were a little mermaid looking for her way home. Discovering her love of the water shortly after she'd turned two had been one of the biggest joys of Silas's life. Finally. Something of himself he saw in his daughter. "Being that close to the water should make her feel a lot less anxious," Silas confirmed. "Please let Sydney know I appreciate the consideration."

"If you're up to it, you can tell her yourself tomorrow evening." Mano did a quick lane change and they cruised into town. "It's Keane's birthday, so Marella is throwing a luau for him on the beach around sunset."

"I don't remember Keane as being particularly impressed with birthdays." If anything, Silas recalled Keane Harper thinking birthdays were a grim reminder of his rather bleak upbringing.

Mano shrugged. "Keane's changed a lot since

you last saw him. And even more since he met Marella. He's also trying to get in as much party time as he can before the baby gets here."

"Baby?" Silas couldn't blink his shock away. "Keane's going to be a father?"

"In about three months," Mano confirmed. "I told you. He's changed."

Silas shook his head in disbelief. Who would have thought it? Keane Harper on the precipice of fatherhood. Given the man's complicated past with family relations and parenting, Silas would have bet big that becoming a dad was the last thing on Keane's list of things to do. Apparently, Marella, Keane's wife, had worked some serious island magic on the man.

"Freya?" Mano glanced into the rearview mirror.

"Yes?" Her tiny voice was almost drowned out by the near-silent hum of the car's engine.

"Do you like birthday parties on the beach?"

Silas looked over his shoulder as Freya's forehead furrowed.

"I don't know." Her big eyes met her father's and he saw rising trepidation in their depths. "Daddy?"

"It'll be fun," he encouraged her. "I know you've only been to a couple, but this one is on the beach. And there will probably be kids your age there. Right?"

"Absolutely," Mano reassured.

"If you don't like it, we can leave," Silas added

24 THE SINGLE DAD'S PROMISE

to ease his daughter's concerns. She'd attended two birthday parties so far and neither had been a rousing success for his very solitary-minded child. That said, the longing to see friends he hadn't connected with in years, the guilt he felt at having lost the chance to speak to Remy Calvert one last time before his friend had passed, slightly overrode his usual inclination to give in to Freya's reluctance.

He'd been trying to work on pushing her out of her comfort zone. It was his job as a parent to get her ready for the real world, to get her to see all of what life had to offer. No better place to push her boundaries in than Nalani.

"We'll have all kinds of food and music," Mano said, as if sensing Freya's discomfort. "I have no doubt you'll make new friends."

"I don't have any friends," Freya said matter-of-factly. "No one likes me."

"I'm sure that's not true," Mano countered even as Silas sighed.

"Her first days at pre-K were not exactly a triumph," Silas muttered under his breath. "For either of us." The number of calls he'd gotten from the school, from Freya's teacher personally, had left him wondering if he was completely failing as a parent. Things had settled down since, mostly. But those first few weeks had been stressful for both of them.

"Well, I like you, Freya," Mano said easily.

"That means you will have at least one friend at the party. That's one more than you had when your plane landed."

Freya's mouth twisted as she considered that.

"You can wear your new swimsuit and sandals." Silas had become a master cajoler in recent years. While he tried not to push her too hard, he knew how to get around that inherent reticence she possessed.

"Can I bring my treasure bag?"

"Of course." Silas shouldn't have felt as relieved as he did, but man, he would be really, really grateful for a kind of break right now. "We'll make sure you have everything you need."

"Okay." She heaved a sigh of adult proportions. "I guess I'll go. I don't want to eat any fish, though. Fish are our friends."

"Right." Mano nodded as if he not only understood, but completely agreed. "Thank you, Freya. I think you'll find you like my Ohana very much."

"What's Ohana?"

"Family," Silas said before Mano could reply. "Ohana means family."

"Oh." Freya began to hum to herself and returned her attention to her worn storybook.

"We figured we'd leave you alone tonight," Mano said easily. "Let you guys get acclimated. We don't want to all land on you the second you're back."

"Appreciate that." Still, he was looking forward to reconnecting to friends he'd lost touch

26   THE SINGLE DAD'S PROMISE

with. Silas felt his lungs relax. Freya needed a nap and they both needed something to eat. Once again, his stomach growled. "Please tell me Seas & Breeze is still there."

Mano grinned. "Nalani wouldn't be Nalani without our shave ice shop." The sweet and icy treat was an island specialty and featured dozens of different flavors in a softer version of a sno-cone. Eating a shave ice was like eating the lightest, airiest flavored snow imaginable. "As for other food, we've got the kitchen stocked and waiting for you," Mano said. "You want anything else, call Luanda's. They'll deliver and you can put it on my account."

"That's not necessary," Silas protested.

"You're Ohana, remember?" Mano said as if he didn't plan to remind Silas again. "We've finally got you home and I'm not giving you any excuse to leave again." Mano paused. "At least, not until you have to."

JANA POWELL STEPPED onto the porch of the rented beach cottage and, taking a deep breath, closed her eyes against the late afternoon breeze. The air lifted the hem of her knotted flower-patterned sarong and touched her bare stomach with the tempting promise of a refreshing dip in the ocean.

The best thing she'd done in her entire life had been to keep a promise. Not to a family member— she didn't have much family. Not even to a friend—

she'd always led a very solitary life. No. The promise she'd made had been to herself. And here she was, in the ocean in Hawai'i, making it happen.

The absolute peace she'd found since arriving in Nalani a little over a week ago had been overwhelming in its perfection. The problems and fears plaguing her not only for the past six months, but what she now realized had been most of her life, had evaporated the instant her feet touched the soil.

Well, not so much soil as concrete. She'd almost dropped to her knees and kissed the ground when the plane landed at Hilo International. Not because the flight had been particularly bumpy, but because she felt grateful for the opportunity to step out of the life she'd only recently realized she felt trapped in.

It was a series of impulsive choices that led her to booking this trip only days before departure. For years, her success as an inventor and a scientist had meant she was caught between the demands of a company she'd invested in and the burnout generated by her creativity. Isolation had become a way of life for her, leaving her locked away either in her office, trying to one-up herself professionally, or at home...doing the same thing.

It had taken a lot to get here, but she now knew what so many others had discovered: life was too short not to be lived.

It was as if she'd been hit by a summer light-

ning bolt. She wanted—no, no, that was wrong—
she'd *craved* something, anything, everything
beyond what she already had. What she'd quietly settled for.

Adventure and excitement had bumped everything else off her to-do list. She needed unexpected options and relaxation and a place for her
mind to reset and refocus, to discover where she
went next. What she did next. She'd eliminated
no from her vocabulary, even when *yes* scared
her all the way down to her currently bare toes.

Typing all that into a search engine online
along with the word *paradise* had resulted in a
list of suggestions. In the middle of that first page
on her screen had been the mention of a small, unexpected and unheard-of town called Nalani. The
name had all but glowed with an aura of promise
around it that had her clicking "Book now."

Six months ago, even just a few weeks prior,
she couldn't have conceived of standing where she
stood now, feeling the trade winds blow across
her face, catching her short hair in a fluttering
current. For the first time in her life, she felt em-
powered at having given in to a whim that last
year would have seemed foolhardy and reckless.

She took a step off the porch, her feet sinking
into the warm sand. Her heart skipped to a now
familiar beat.

Gratitude. It filled nearly every moment of
every day. She'd been shoved into a new phase

of her life against her will. So much still felt completely out of her control, but not this. Not today.

Impulse had become her new best friend. She'd left behind a lifetime of caution, practicality and the mistaken belief that there was always a tomorrow.

She'd been reborn these last six months. Cancer had a habit of doing that: resetting one's life in new and unexpected ways. While she might still be figuring out who the new Jana Powell was and what the future might hold, she found herself consistently excited about the journey she was on.

Celebrating her thirtieth birthday had once seemed like an impossible goal. But she'd celebrate it here, in Nalani, in only a few short days. It was shocking to realize that after three decades of living, she had very little to show for it. On the personal side at least. She might have a healthy and substantial bank account, but her heart wasn't remotely full. She couldn't recall the last time she'd felt joy or even a little fulfilled. She'd simply been…existing, chasing one project after another.

Now? She touched her hands to the stomach exposed by the first bikini she'd ever bought. A stomach that displayed the trio of scars serving as a reminder of how close she'd come to not having this moment. Stepping onto that plane last week had been a defiant step into independence after living in a fog of routine, depression and fear.

She'd left everything behind to live in the moment.

No excuses. No fear. Just...living.

She unknotted her skirt, tossed it onto the sand and raced down to the shore. She didn't stop until she was knee-deep in the foamy surf that danced and swirled around her in tempting waves.

She laughed, spinning until she was dizzy, arms outstretched as if she could absorb every ounce of the sun's healing rays.

Jana held her breath and fell back, dropping into the water only to surface with a gulp of air that felt yet again like the start of a new life. She floated on her back, bouncing and bobbing along the waves. In the distance, she heard a car door slam, then another. Muted voices drifted toward her on the wind.

The new tenants had arrived.

Her vacation cottage landlord, Sydney Calvert, had dropped by yesterday morning to let Jana know about the new arrivals in the other rental. Sydney had wanted to make certain Jana was all right with neighbors given the fact Jana had been looking for peace and quiet during her stay.

Of course Jana hadn't had much of either as she'd dived headfirst into the plethora of activities Ohana Odysseys had to offer any visitor to Nalani. Tehani Iokepa, the scheduling manager at the increasingly popular tour and excursion company, had been more than eager to help Jana plan out her days and evenings. As a bonus, Jana was surprised to find she'd made not only one friend in Tehani, but several, including Sydney.

She'd learned quickly the tour company took its dedication to the Ohana part of its name seriously.

Jana's easygoing agreement to the new neighbors had eased Sydney's mind. It seemed the friend was in town to help Sydney with a bit of a business problem that had cropped up, but Sydney also wanted him to enjoy his return to Nalani in the same peace and quiet Jana had craved.

In truth, Sydney's cursory explanation had piqued Jana's curiosity about the visitor. Whoever the friend was, it was clear they were well thought of. Who was Jana to stand in the way of that? Sydney's subsequent invitation for Jana to join them for Keane Harper's upcoming birthday luau had Jana leaning back into the familiar and comfortable territory of refusing. She'd managed to sidestep giving an actual answer. Parties made her nervous. Anxious even, despite not having had much experience with them.

Some fears were harder to conquer than others.

She knew Keane, of course. She'd toppled and tumbled her way through her first few surfing lesions. Once upon a time Keane had been a professional surfer and swimming competitor, but Jana was convinced his main gift in life was unending patience with people who honestly had no business being anywhere near a surfboard.

Example A: Jana.

32 THE SINGLE DAD'S PROMISE

Marella, Keane's wife, was a frequent witness to Jana's sunrise tumbles and assured Jana that she was not the only one in Nalani without aquatic talent. It was a comment that eased Jana's nerves considerably.

Marella was a marketing expert and executive from New York who had turned most of her attention to the promotion side of Ohana Odysseys. But she was also preparing for her most important job to date: becoming a mother.

That information had left a forced smile on Jana's face, while a longing she'd only recently realized she'd had—a longing that would never be fulfilled—settled painfully around her heart.

Jana had pushed away as much of the negative as she could and chose instead to focus on something she hadn't admitted she'd been starved for: friends. Attending a party that was for family felt like a particularly high mountain to climb. The last thing she wanted was to be some kind of intruder, especially if the invitation had come from sheer politeness. Still, everyone Jana had met in Nalani was a hoot and had made her feel included. She had no doubt another opportunity to join in would present itself.

"That's right," she murmured and blinked her eyes open against the fading sunlight. "Only looking forward. No more looking back."

She righted herself in the water, slicked back her hair and treaded as she watched two men climb out of an SUV. The one guy she recognized from the Hibiscus Bay Resort, Mano Iokepa. The part owner-manager always seemed to be there whenever she walked past or had gone to the lovely restaurant with a perfect view of the marina. Mano looked as if he'd stepped out of the pages of Hawaiian history or one of their many island legends. Tall, strong, determined and fiercely loyal, she'd gathered.

The man with Mano was nearly as tall. Not nearly as broad-shouldered perhaps, but even from a distance, his physique spoke of good health and vitality. All of which Jana had only recently begun to regain. She found herself unusually intrigued watching from a distance. For an instant, she felt tempted to hurry out of the water to introduce herself.

She quickly reined in that impulse. Obviously, she still had to work on her self-confidence.

When Mano's friend opened the back door, he bent down and held out his arms for a small girl who instantly wrapped her arms around his neck.

Jana's smile faltered. The hitch in her chest she'd wish would go away forever, reappeared and stopped her breath. The girl's bright red hair practically glowed beneath the sun as she tucked her head beneath her father's chin.

Such trust. And innocence and...love.

Jana stared, heart pounding. The moment was beautiful, but at the same time she felt as if she was intruding on something she wasn't meant to see.

She watched them disappear around the corner of their cottage. She took a deep breath, looked up at the sun until spots left her blinking. Then she sank beneath the waves to let her tears mingle with the ocean.

CHAPTER TWO

"WHAT DO YOU THINK?" Mano asked Silas. "Does this place pass inspection?"

Silas was so surprised he had to blink several times before answering Mano's question. "More than." Better than that, Freya had let out a bit of a squeal when she'd seen her mermaid-inspired room, complete with a beautiful quilt featuring waves draped over the foot of her bed and a collection of seashells sitting on the window ledge.

The beach cottage was deceptively small on the outside. Or maybe it was the way the interior was laid out that gave the impression of it being incredibly spacious. With a cozy seating area, a practical kitchen and the two bedrooms there was more than enough room for him and Freya. It was quiet, which was a definite bonus. He'd been wondering about how best to deal with Freya's anxieties when it came to dealing with strangers, and new, untested situations.

Staying here would ease his concerns exceedingly. The cottage was mostly decorated in soft

36   THE SINGLE DAD'S PROMISE

blues, greens and yellows, and pops of brighter color came from various plants as well as personal, artistic touches. From the bright, pink-and-orange flowered crocheted throw on the back of the love seat to the hand-carved wooden bowl on top of the coffee table.

He'd bet his last dollar the living flora had been courtesy of Daphne Mercer...no. Silas frowned. That wasn't right. She'd gotten married last year. It was Daphne Townsend now. She'd definitely have added her special horticultural touch.

So much had changed since he'd been here last and yet...somehow a cottage he'd never stepped foot in before felt like home. His throat tightened with emotion.

"Have to admit." Mano wandered through the seating area, which, with its large bay window and bamboo straw mat, was only steps away from the shore. "I gave Remy a bad time when he bought these cabins. I saw them as complete teardowns. Even considered taking that project on myself, but he had other ideas and beat me to it. Didn't have much time to spend on it, though."

The mere mention of their college buddy— one of the best friends Silas had ever had—had the grief Silas struggled to control surging to the surface once more. It had been Mano who had called last spring to tell Silas of Remy's unexpected passing. It hadn't seemed possible—still didn't seem possible, in fact—that Remy Calvert was gone. Especially since Silas could still feel his friend's presence. It made a mystical kind of sense, of course. Remy had been the heart and soul of Nalani, Hawai'i. It was logical that his spirit could still be felt everywhere.

"I'm sorry I wasn't here." The guilt he'd carried for over a year had Silas swallowing hard. "I'm sorry I didn't come out for the service. For Sydney. For all of you."

Mano met his gaze, but the other man's expression was unreadable, leaving Silas struggling to wonder what his friend must think of him.

"Freya is your primary concern," Mano finally said. "As she should be."

"Remy was Freya's godfather. I should have made the effort." But honestly, he knew the reason he hadn't. He didn't want to admit his friend was gone.

For the first time since arriving at the airport, Silas saw a cloud pass across Mano's features. "Should-haves won't get you anywhere, Silas. Trust me on that. No one, least of all me, blames you for staying away. You've had your hands full raising her on your own." Mano retreated into the galley-style kitchen and opened the fridge door. He got two bottles, held one out and waited patiently for Silas to take it. "I'll confess your lack of communication left more than a little to be desired." Mano twisted the cap off his beer. "I'd be lying if I didn't say we've all been worried

THE SINGLE DAD'S PROMISE

about you. But you're making up for that now. You can only do your best to deal with things as they come. No one can blame you for that."

"I blame me." The self-pity irked him. Still, he hadn't had anyone to talk to about the guilt he felt over mistakes he now saw that he'd made. Granted, that was a situation of his own making: communication worked both ways. But until Mano told him to shut up, he needed to keep going so he could get it all out. "Remy was on a plane ten minutes after I told him Caroline left. He camped out so long in my guest room I considered naming it after him." The foggy memory of those weeks had never really cleared, something Silas considered a bit of a blessing. Being left to care for a preemie baby alone had been the hardest thing he'd ever had to come through. Best he couldn't recall all the drama and chaos that had happened outside the NICU. "The least I could have done—"

"You aren't the only one who has issues regarding Remy's passing. Consider yourself part of the club and let's move on. Don't add that unnecessary load to your shoulders on top of everything else." Mano gestured for Silas to follow him out onto the front porch. The screen door bumped closed behind them. They each took possession of a rocking chair and, as Silas sat, he felt those last tendrils of uncertainty fade.

The questions Silas had about Remy's death

had been piling up but now that he was here, his intention to ask them faded. The answers wouldn't change anything. Remy was gone and while Silas would always regret that he'd allowed himself to lose touch, he wasn't so far removed from the situation that he didn't understand Remy being gone had done the impossible.

It had brought him, brought *them*, back to Nalani.

Mano's cell phone buzzed from inside his suit jacket pocket. He pulled it out, glanced at the screen, put it away again.

"If you have to go—"

"I don't." Mano rocked in the chair, took a long drink of his beer. "I'm no good to anyone if I don't take a break every now and then."

Silas's brows went up in a big enough action that Mano's expression shifted from passive to glowering.

"I am capable of change," Mano defended himself. "Or, at least I'm working on it. I'm a bit slow on the uptake according to Tehani. But I'm doing my best."

Silas wasn't used to walking on seashells, especially around Mano, but there were times it couldn't be avoided. "Do you ever see her?"

"Tehani?" Mano's tone was filled with forced amusement. "I see my sister all the time. I'm on rotating babysitting duty for my nephew Kai.

40 THE SINGLE DAD'S PROMISE

Even got him his own crib for my office." Mano was nothing if not an expert deflector.

"I meant Emilia." Silas had only met Mano's former wife once, but she'd impressed him with her calm, rational and steadfast demeanor. Mano Iokepa wasn't an easy person in any way. He had more baggage than most people took with them on an around-the-world cruise. He was, as Remy had described Mano, a brick wall with feet. And yes, Mano was capable of incredible acts of kindness and generosity; he was also incredibly ambitious and focused on work. Sometimes, maybe most of the time, to the detriment of his relationships.

Mano examined the label on his locally brewed beer. "I haven't seen Emilia since she decided to stay on the mainland, so…a little over four years." The wince he tried to hide told Silas the split still hurt.

"I'm sorry." The end of any relationship was never cause for celebration. "That must have been difficult."

"We'd just met and jumped into marriage," Mano said in a somewhat defensive tone. "Neither of us really thought things through despite being head over heels for each other. I'd chalk it up to us being kids, but we were both old enough to know better."

Silas refrained from commenting. The Mano he knew could think a problem down from a tree trunk to a splinter. Personally and businesswise, that quality worked well. When it came to personal relationships?

"Hindsight is usually crystal clear." Mano shrugged. "Communication wasn't my greatest skill. Obviously, I missed the signals that she was unhappy. She went back home when her mother got sick. A few weeks later she called to say she planned to stay and that was that."

"You ever think about trying again? The relationship thing?" Silas asked. "Not with Emilia," he added at the frown on Mano's face. "With someone else?"

"I learned my lesson." Mano shook his head. "I won't inflict myself on anyone else." His smile was quick this time, but there was no mistaking the shimmer in his eyes. It was an expression Silas had seen in the mirror far too often. Loneliness was a difficult road to travel, especially when it was purposely chosen. "What about you? It's been a while since Caroline left."

"I'd be lying if I said I didn't think about it," Silas admitted. "It would be nice having someone to share my life with, but I wouldn't be the only one involved, would I? Like you said earlier, Freya always comes first and she's not the best at adjusting to new people, as you bore witness to at the airport."

"She seemed to do pretty well with me," Mano said, concern marring his furrowed brow. "Children are individuals. They deal how they deal.

Personally, I think your daughter is charming and unsurprisingly stubborn. Much like her father." He toasted Silas with his bottle.

"Relationships involve risk." Silas shook his head even as he accepted the compliment. "And risk came off the table the second Freya was born. Maybe it was the weeks she was in NICU, the weeks I did little else other than sit in that room with her, willing her to keep breathing." How he wished those memories would fade into the fog along with those of Freya's mother, his ex-wife. It was a very particular kind of trauma that was difficult to deal with. Or treat. "We do all right, just her and me. I'm not willing to change that. Not now. Maybe when she's older." Even as he said it, he didn't see that happening. He'd made a lot of deals with himself when he'd been terrified of losing Freya, including how he'd devote every moment he could to making her life the best it could be. He wasn't going to go back on those promises now. "Besides, unlike you, I'm not in a position to change anything about our lives, so…" He shrugged.

"Careful issuing challenges like that to the universe," Mano teased.

Silas smirked. "The universe stopped listening to me a long time ago."

Mano pursed his lips, tearing at the label on his bottle as he stared at the ocean. "You know you've always got a place here, with us. In Nalani."

He'd been wondering how long it would take his friend to bring that up. "You're talking about Remy's email wanting me to become a partner in Ohana Odysseys. The email he never got a chance to send." The email Remy's sister Sydney had sent after finding it on Remy's computer after his death.

The email that brought Silas's memory all the way back to that summer after college graduation. The only summer Silas had spent in Nalani. The summer Remy had announced he planned to begin a local tour company and that he wanted them—Keane, Daphne and Mano, to run it with him. They'd laughed about it then. They'd even gone so far as to tease Remy about his penchant for living in a dream world; but there had been a light in his late friend's eye that Silas had never been able to forget. The light of hope, certainty and determination.

"Remy wanted you, wanted all of you home, with him." Mano shrugged. "There was some selfish aspect to his wanting that, I suppose. The change in him when Daphne moved here was remarkable, but he still missed you and Keane."

"Probably because other than you, we kept him in check," Silas tried to joke.

"Remy took Ohana very seriously. The people and the business. He never gave up on you changing your minds."

44 THE SINGLE DAD'S PROMISE

"He was right since two of us did, clearly," Silas added.

Mano smirked, nodded. "True enough."

"I give Remy a lot of credit for not pushing the idea on me when Freya was born." The last thing Silas could have managed was the idea of moving, on top of everything else.

"He knew when to push," Mano agreed. "His plan was to make Ohana Odysseys the best tour company on the Big Island. Then he was going to circle back around and ask you and Keane."

"It already was the best tour company," Silas reminded him. "It's why GVI has renewed their intention to get their hands on it. And your resort." The San Francisco–based equity and investment firm had already attempted one buyout of Ohana shortly after Remy's death. Sydney's eventual refusal to sell had, according to what Silas had learned, left the increasingly struggling company willing to skirt the edges of legality in a new bid to win ownership. "Do you want to get into this now or—?"

"Daddy?" Freya's soft voice spoke from the other side of the screen door. "I'm hungry." She clutched at the shell necklace around her neck and tilted her head back as Mano got to his feet.

"It's waited this long. You two should settle in and get some rest." Mano flashed Silas a smile as he walked by. "Starting tomorrow you're going to be overwhelmed with the attention of a lot of people who have missed you. Have a good evening, Freya." He offered a little wave and earned a confused smile and wave from her in return.

Freya pushed open the door, poked her head out enough to watch Mano leave. She blinked back at Silas.

"Do you like your room?" Silas followed her inside, set his bottle on the counter before heading to the fridge to check out what they had to eat.

"It's not like home," Freya said matter-of-factly as she wedged under his arm to peer inside. "What's that?" She pointed to a tub filled with brightly colored fruit.

"Let's see." He pulled out the clear container. "That's mango and pineapple. Like a salad. You like pineapple. Would you like some?" Hopefully he could distract her with that first while he threw something else together.

"Yes."

He looked at her until she glanced up. He inclined his head and sent subliminal dad waves into her thoughts.

"Yes, please," she corrected herself.

"Okay, then. Take a seat." He motioned to the square table under one of the front windows. She climbed into one of the two pale yellow bucket chairs. In the cabinets, he found a nice selection of plates, cups and serving bowls. Practically arranged. The dedicated coffee cabinet, complete with a large stash of Kona coffee, nearly

46 THE SINGLE DAD'S PROMISE

set his system to zinging all on its own. Morning couldn't come fast enough for that first cup of Hawaiian coffee.

He added a handful of pineapple chunks into a bowl, added one piece of mango and, after finding papaya at the bottom, added a slice of that as well. He grabbed a fork and set the fruit in front of her. He popped a large cube of mango into his mouth and closed his eyes in bliss. Nothing like the sweet taste of island fruit.

Freya purposely pushed the mango and papaya well out of the way before stabbing the pineapple. The smile that curved her mouth when she tasted it definitely lightened his mood.

"Pretty good, huh?" Silas said. "Everything tastes sweeter here, especially the pineapple."

"It's yummy." She ate another piece, frowned at the mango.

"You just have to try it once," Silas urged gently. It was a new challenge for them, getting her to try different foods. She had her favorites, but life was filled with more than chicken fingers and French fries. "If you don't like it, you don't have to eat it again."

She sighed, stuck her fork into the mango and brought it to her lips. She licked it. Considered. Frowned. Licked it again. Then took a teeny-tiny bite that wouldn't have choked an ant.

"Huh." She seemed surprised before she nibbled again. Then again. The rest of it vanished. "That's good, Daddy! More!"

He gave her the look again, wondering when she'd started to backslide on being polite.

"More, please." She rolled her eyes and collapsed on the table. "I'm starving!"

By the time he'd added more mango to her bowl—he definitely took that as a win since she wasn't a big fan of the papaya—he was ready to dive face-first into the other containers in the fridge. Memories flooded through him as he read the distinctive red lettering: Hula Chicken. The place had been a staple in Nalani since long before he'd first visited. Pretty soon he had his plate filled with roasted, spiced chicken, macaroni salad, some lomi-lomi salmon and a heaping spoonful of tuna poke, which he'd never had the inclination to eat anywhere outside the islands. The raw fish was seasoned with sea salt, soy and thin threads of chopped, dried nori. He didn't even wait to sit down before he'd scooped a big portion onto his fork.

Eating with Freya at times rivaled the Indy 500. He had to race to get finished before she was off and running. Sure enough, before he was halfway through, she was stretching her foot down, ready to leave the table at any second. His daughter was nothing if not predictable. "You want to go put your suit on? We can take a quick swim before bedtime."

48 THE SINGLE DAD'S PROMISE

"Okay."

"I can help you if you can wait for me to finish my dinner."

"I'm a big girl," she declared as her feet hit the floor. "I can do it."

"All right." He continued eating as she disappeared into her bedroom. He heard her unzip her suitcase, which she'd helped him pack. She was quite particular about how she liked things and possessed an attitude that shifted into place and demanded she triumph.

Despite the five years that had passed since her birth, there were times parental uncertainty reared its irritating head when it came to how he handled Freya's manner of doing things.

He second-guessed himself constantly, but he did his best not to show weakness. His daughter, much like most kids, could definitely smell fear and had no qualms about pouncing on it. He prided himself on not being a pushover and instead chose his battles with care.

He finished eating standing by the sink, decided to clean up after they got back, then headed in to change into his own swim trunks. On the other side of her half-closed door, he heard Freya singing quietly to herself. It was all he could do not to poke his head in and check on her progress, but they'd reached the stage where he waited for her to ask for help if she needed it.

The linen closet at the end of the hall between

their bedrooms also stored a stackable washer and dryer. Towels, bedding and other items were neatly arranged on the various shelves alongside cleaning and laundry products. He chose a dark blue beach towel for himself and quickly sighed in relief. Freya was quite certain about her favorite colors and yellow was at the top of her list. It had taken a tantrum or two before he'd learned that if yellow was an option, it was the only correct choice to be made.

Towels tucked under his arm, he returned to his room, slipped into a pair of flip-flops—"slippahs," if his long-unused island vocabulary was still correct—then gently knocked on her door. "Freya?"

"Yes."

He did push the door open. She had carefully unloaded her suitcase, lining everything up in precise rows on her bed. The straps of the yellow-and-pink flowered swimsuit were twisted and the fabric around her butt sagged as if it needed to be tugged up. "You ready to hit the waves?"

She looked intently at the drawers of the small dresser she'd pulled open. "I can't decide where my things should live." She frowned, as if facing the prospect of solving world peace. She'd displayed a keen desire for order and organization from very early on.

He felt safe in challenging the universe to show him a more disciplined and tidy child. It had thrown him for a bit of a loop at first; personally, he'd never quite outgrown his slob-like tendencies, but together they'd learned through trial and error how to cooperate. One thing he never had to ask her to do was clean her room. Everything had its assigned place and woe to whoever attempted to make a change.

He set the towels on the chair by her door, picked up the clear plastic travel bag containing her brush and hair items. Silas motioned her over for "hair time," one of the few rituals that never caused a fuss. They'd agreed that as long as she wanted to keep her hair long, she needed to accept his help with it. Otherwise, her curls and waves turned into a seriously tangled mess.

He slipped off the yellow plastic headband, set it aside, then gently pulled the no-tangle brush through it. "Maybe you can put your things away in the same order you have them at home." He tugged gently at the knots, but quickly had her hair smoothed out.

She frowned at him in the dresser mirror. "But we aren't home."

Logic from a five-year-old was oddly daunting. He collected all her hair into one hand, held it firmly while he wrapped a band around it. "You can always change things if you aren't happy with them."

She made a silent O with her mouth, as if she'd forgotten that was a possibility. "Maybe I put them in order of how I put them on." She clasped her hands together and rocked back on her heels, up on her toes, a familiar indication of impatience. When he was done, she touched her hands to the smoothed hair. "Pretty."

He bent down and kissed the top of her head. "Very pretty."

She immediately picked the short stack of her underwear, set the pile in the drawer and stood back to evaluate. She nodded, then returned to the bed for her shirts. Since they weren't quite straight the first time, she scooted them over an inch. Back a half inch. Nodded again.

The process continued until she'd filled the two top drawers with her pants and shorts, and then socks. She lined up her shoes on the floor in a line so straight he could have walked across it. She stood back, hands twisting together. "Is that okay?"

"It's okay with me if it's okay with you." Outside, the sun was beginning to set. "You can check it when we come back from our swim. If you want to change things then, you can."

"Okay." She placed her empty suitcase in the space between the dresser and the wall, then gently arranged Fred, the stuffed carrot, and Winnie, the one-eyed, one-footed plastic chicken, on her bed. "I left space for Roscoe." She pointed to the gap between them against her pillow. "That's where he goes at home."

"I'm sure he'd be happy about that," Silas said.

52 THE SINGLE DAD'S PROMISE

"You ready for a swim? I've got your floaties. I just need to blow them up."

She grabbed her treasure bag that was beginning to show its age with frayed seams, thinning fabric and a long-ago broken zipper. Dresser dilemma resolved, she walked out the door.

It took Silas a moment to follow. There were times his love for Freya was so fierce it robbed him of breath. She wasn't always easy—no child was. But the pride he felt whenever she tackled and mostly conquered what she considered to be a problem was a never-ending source of happiness for him.

She was waiting for him by the door. He handed her the yellow towel and earned an ear-to-ear smile as she accepted it. Freya rubbed her cheek against the material. "Mmmmm. Soft."

Silas pushed open the screen door and nudged her outside.

The warm evening breeze welcomed them, drawing them away from the house and toward the tumbling ocean.

"It's bigger than at home." Freya's voice trembled and when he looked down at her, he saw the fear in her wide eyes.

They'd made a few treks to the beach in San Francisco, but...the water didn't beckon as it did here. He'd wanted her to get used to the sounds and smells and feel of the tide, but as they stood ankle-deep in the still sun-warmed sand of the islands, he realized that other than sand and water, there was no way to compare the two beaches.

Despite her misgivings, Freya pointed her foot out in front of her and dipped her toe into the frothy tide. She giggled, did a little jump and faced him, the fear just about gone. "It tickles! And it's warm!"

It also soothed in ways nothing else could. There was little that was more healing than the island waters.

"Remember what we talked about," Silas reminded her. "You don't come out to the water without me or another adult."

She turned that scrunched expression up at him again. "What other adult?"

"Any other adult." He knew when to use his no-argument tone and, fortunately, Freya understood it. "I've got a lot of friends here and there might be times I'm not around. I don't want you in or around the water without someone bigger than you, okay?"

"But where would you go?" She dropped her towel, turned and grabbed hold of the waistband of his board shorts. "You aren't going to leave me, are you?"

Silas's heart cracked open.

Sadly, this wasn't the first time she'd expressed this worry, and for the millionth time since Caroline left them, he silently chastised his ex-wife. It was easier than blaming the obnoxious student in her pre-K class who had made it clear Freya was "different," not only in some of her behaviors, but because she had no trouble admitting she didn't have a mom.

Everybody had a mom, she was informed, and if Freya didn't, then something was wrong with her.

Silas hadn't known he could feel so much anger. The school principal and teachers had done their best to mitigate the emotional fallout and had even called a meeting with the student's parents, but it was now two months later. No reprimand could undo the fear of being abandoned that had been fully instilled in his little girl. The damage was done and had left Freya rather anxious every morning when she had to go to school.

"Freya." He dropped his towel beside hers, crouched down and caught her tiny hands in his. "I'm not going to leave you. Ever. We're always going to be together. But it's like when I go to work and you go to school. You stay with another adult who cares about you and will make sure you're okay. That's all that might happen here. I'd leave you with people I trust. And if I trust them, then you can, too."

"You mean like Mr. Mano?" Her eyes narrowed as they always did when processing new information. "He's really big. He wouldn't let anything hurt me."

"No, he wouldn't." It meant the world that she saw Mano in that light. "He's someone you can always go to if you're in trouble or scared and I'm not around. And tomorrow, you're going to meet more people who will become your friends. Maybe even some kids close to your own age." Nicer ones than in her pre-K class.

She didn't look completely convinced, but she did seem to relax a little.

"How about we get your floaties blown up and we take a swim?"

"I don't need them if you carry me." She locked her arms around his neck in a way that did not give him a choice. He picked her up as he stood, hefted her onto his hip. Pretty soon she'd be too big to be carried. She almost was now. All the more reason to embrace the moment.

He strode into the waves, pushing himself forward, and as the waves splashed up and around his hips and her legs, Freya's hold tightened. She squealed, rose up a bit as if trying to avoid the water, but he kept moving.

It had been more than a decade since he'd last walked into these waters, but his body remembered. It wasn't magic so much as the instant reconnection he felt to who he'd been at the time along with the peace and promise he'd found here. Carrying his daughter into the waves now felt almost like a rebirth, a return to what truly mattered. Just the two of them, doing the best they could, together.

"You okay?" He tucked his chin into his chest

56 THE SINGLE DAD'S PROMISE

to get a look at her face. Those big eyes of hers were taking everything in. The tension he'd felt in her body as he'd stepped into the water had eased. She still clung to him, but not as tightly. "Want me to hold you out?"

She nodded and he pulled her off his side and, keeping his hands solidly around her waist, let her drift a bit away from him.

"Don't let go!" she squealed even as she kicked and splashed. He hopped at the oncoming wave and earned a genuine laugh this time. "This is fun!" Silas turned her a bit so he could walk while she play-swam. He had no doubt she could do it on her own, but as glorious as the ocean might be, it wasn't always kind. Next time, definitely floaties.

"Do you want to go under?"

She surprised him by nodding. "But quick!"

"Okay. Real quick. One, two, three—" They each took a deep breath and he pulled them under, just for a count of three. The world went almost completely silent except for the dull roar of the water. When they surfaced, they were both sputtering, but the smile and joy on Freya's face lifted a weight off his heart.

"Again, Daddy!" She squirmed in his hands, but he held firm. He had a good grip on her—he didn't want that to change. "Longer this time."

"Okay." A five count, then again at seven, but he added in a bit of movement that had her grabbing hold of his forearms. This time when they surfaced, she spit out seawater and dragged her hands down her dripping face. "Too long that time?" he asked.

She shook her head. "I got scared but then it went away. Daddy, I love the ocean." She pivoted and latched on to his neck again. "I want to do this every day until forever!"

He held her close. What he wouldn't give to make all her wishes come true.

"Oh my gosh, Daddy, look!" Freya squealed into his ear.

Wincing, he turned, almost losing his footing in the sand as he looked to where she pointed.

"It's a mermaid, Daddy! She's so pretty! Her hair is so shiny!"

Silas blinked the salty water out of his eyes, clinging to his daughter as, a few hundred feet away, a woman dipped down then resurfaced in the water. Her close-cropped, blond—almost platinum—hair did indeed glisten a bit. The bare, pale skin of her shoulders as she rode the waves definitely gave her the effortless look of a water nymph. Minus the long, cascading hair. And tail, of course. "Mermaids are only in stories, Freya."

She frowned, glanced at him for a fraction of a second before looking back to the woman. "Don't you see her, Daddy? What else could she be?"

He did see her, moving through the water as if it were nothing more than air. How she spun and

58 THE SINGLE DAD'S PROMISE

dove and rose up into the fading sunlight streaming across the waves. She was mesmerizing, as if she were pulling him into the water with an energy that sparked and hopped across the lapping waves.

"I see her," he whispered even as he admitted his daughter might be right.

He may very well have just seen his first mermaid.

CHAPTER THREE

"Eeeeeee!" Jana gripped the overhead leather loop so tight her fingers went numb. "I can't believe I'm doing this!" Not one part of her wasn't buzzing and it took all her willpower not to squeeze her eyes shut as the helicopter swooped and tilted, rounding up and over the cliffs' edge just beyond Hilo on the Big Island.

"You said you wanted some thrills," Sydney Calvert laughed as she steered the chopper with astounding ease. "Ohana Odysseys is always willing to oblige."

The roar of the blades created a kind of white noise that felt oddly comforting. Jana concentrated on relaxing, but the idea was much easier than the execution. Cool air wafted in through the small triangular window that was tilted open near her legs.

"Look!" Sydney's voice came through loud and clear in Jana's headset. "Down there." She tilted the chopper a bit to the right and Jana looked out her window, blinked even as she gasped.

A pod of dolphins leaped and arced out of the water in near perfect synchronicity. Jana's eyes misted at the sight and she wanted nothing more than to...

The helicopter dipped again and rotated around, then slowed as the pod made their way into the depths of the ocean. Excited, Jana leaned forward, pressed her hands against the windshield. Logic told her there was no touching them, no reaching them, but that didn't stop her from trying. Or dreaming.

"Amazing." Her breath caught in her chest as Sydney lifted the nose once more and set them to soaring back over the cliffs toward the densely forested area. Sydney had explained it was one of the many protected areas of the islands. "I can't believe you get to do this every day." Jana turned wide eyes on her new friend.

"I don't get to do *this* as often as I'd like," Sydney teased. "Most of the people who fly with me don't ask for the added thrills."

"Then they don't know what they're missing." Now that she'd acclimated and no longer feared the very real possibility of physics working against them, Jana couldn't stop twisting and turning in her seat. There wasn't a speck of space that wasn't filled with absolute natural beauty. "This really is paradise."

"Not going to argue with you." Sydney shifted her grip on the controls and her wedding set glinted against the midmorning sun. "It's tough to say goodbye to this place. There are times I tease Theo that he married me in part so he had an excuse to stay in Nalani. Oh, hang on." She turned again and the helicopter all but brushed against the treetops as it raced forward. "I think there's something you'd like to see."

Jana couldn't think of anything she wouldn't want to see. She had a break today from any of the scheduled activities—something Tehani had suggested working into her daily routine. It was a good idea to keep herself busy, but there was also something to be said for taking a day here and there to just relax and appreciate all the things surrounding her.

She couldn't recall the last time she'd slept as well as she had last night. She'd felt oddly invigorated after her third swim of the day; it was as if a charge had struck her while she'd been in the water. A charge that left her both exhilarated and exhausted.

She'd barely had the energy to change out of her suit before she'd crashed into bed. This morning when she woke up, that charge was still there. Inspiring her. Energizing her. Leaving her unable to sit still or relax.

With the ocean behind them as they continued to coast through the sky, Sydney sustained their low altitude over the trees, slowing when they reached a clearing filled with an astonishingly beautiful waterfall that tumbled and dropped into a pristine lake.

"We, or I guess, I call this Remy's mauka—his mountain," Sydney told her through the headset. "My brother used this place as a retreat when he needed to get away."

Jana blinked back tears. It was impossible to spend more than a minute in Nalani without hearing about Remy Calvert, Sydney's older brother. Thinking of this place as his struck Jana. She could never have imagined a more perfect tribute.

"Tehani and I have talked about adding a special excursion up here," Sydney said. "But I prefer to keep it as sort of a secret."

"Yes," Jana said, finally finding her voice. "It should remain special. Untouched." Personal. So much of the islands seemed to be just that. But the idea that there was a secret hideaway with a special place in Sydney's—and her friends' hearts—felt right. "Thank you for sharing it with me."

"Haven't been by in a while myself," Sydney admitted as she steered the chopper in a slow circle. "Might need to do a trek, the group of us. We could do most of it by vehicle, then hike the rest." She paused, inclined her head. "Maybe for Remy's birthday. It's coming up in a few weeks. You should stick around for it."

"We'll see." One thing about being impulsive for a change was that it gave Jana an excuse not to commit, especially to what she perceived as a family event.

On the other hand, the impulse to explore the main drag of Nalani was what had caused her to run into Sydney this morning. After chatting a bit outside Seas & Breeze, the shave ice shop that had turned into a daily indulgence for Jana, they realized they both had the day off—Sydney from work and Jana from tours. The offer of a personal helicopter ride around the Big Island wasn't something Jana even thought about refusing.

The idea of it had both terrified and thrilled Jana, which was why she'd eagerly accepted. She'd spent far too much time doing what she should do, rather than what she wanted to do.

Now, as they crisscrossed over the treetops before doing a quick flyby of Kona, they headed back to Nalani.

It was only when they landed on the platform at the top of the hill above Ohana Odysseys that Jana glanced at her watch. The morning was completely gone. Time had literally flown by.

"You really do have the best job in the world," Jana said on a sigh as the engines and blades slowed down.

"What's the old saying? Do what you love and you'll never work a day in your life?" Sydney flipped switches and clicked buttons. The blades gradually stopped spinning and Jana took off her headset. "If I'd listened to my brother, I could

64 THE SINGLE DAD'S PROMISE

have been doing this for years. Thanks for coming along with me. Theo never says, but he worries when I fly alone."

Jana glanced down at the rings on Sydney's finger. "Your husband doesn't like to fly with you?"

"He does now." Sydney grinned. "It's still not his favorite pastime, but he's a lot better than when he first got to the islands. You'll understand when you meet him. He's definitely the kind of guy who is more comfortable with his feet on the ground. He probably would have been willing to come with me today, but he had a meeting with Mano at the resort." She hung up her headset and shoved open her door. They walked across the landing platform to the short staircase leading down to the road. "It didn't escape my notice you didn't give me a firm answer on coming to Keane's birthday celebration tonight."

"I appreciate the invitation." Nerves jangled in her belly. Jana hated to disappoint anyone, especially a new friend who had been so generous with her time and helicopter. "I really don't want to impose." That said, the promise of one of Nalani's famed luaus—even a small one—definitely intrigued her, although she wondered if her crowd-induced anxiety might also show up.

"Hey." Sydney stopped on the bottom step and gently reached for Jana's arm. "There's no such thing as imposing in Nalani. While you're here, you're Ohana. You're family. Not only because you're one of our clients, but because it's the Nalani way." Sydney squeezed her arm and nodded. "Okay?"

"Yeah." Jana's throat tightened with emotion as her resolve weakened. "Yeah, I'll definitely think about it."

"Think all you want," Sydney said and took the last step down. "As long as it gets you to yes. I'll come push you out of that cottage if I have to."

"Noodles might not appreciate that," Jana said of her island lizard roommate, an unexpected addition to her vacation cottage. It had taken a bit of getting used to, sharing the space with a charming little cartoon character of an island dweller, but so far Noodles had kept to the patio and spent most of his time sunbathing. And eating the fruit Jana left out for him after reading the menu and instructions that had been pinned up in one of the cabinets. According to Tehani, there was also Noodles's girlfriend Zilla, but Zilla was more leery of strangers and took a little longer to acclimate to new cottage residents. Jana had never related to a reptile more.

Sydney gasped in a way that had Jana looking around for trouble.

"Oh my gosh." Sydney let out a little cheer and hopped before she ran flat out toward the man and little girl heading up the hill. "Silas! You're here!" She leaped into his arms and laughed as he swung her around.

66   THE SINGLE DAD'S PROMISE

Jana recognized the man, of course. Along with the little girl standing close beside him. Jana's heart did its own little jump as her observations about him yesterday proved more than true. There was also a presence about him she hadn't been able to pick up on long distance. Nor had she seen how his blue eyes twinkled when he smiled.

Suddenly fidgety, Jana quickly looked around for an escape route. She shouldn't be watching the emotional moment. She could easily just make her way around them, but when she took her first step, she found her gaze caught on that of the little girl's.

The expression on her small face was all too familiar to Jana. There was fear. And confusion. Adjusting to a new situation. New people. New… experiences. Uncertainty rolled off the child in waves and had Jana longing to hold her close and rock away the anxiety. The child hugged her arms around her torso and squeezed, as if trying to shrink out of sight. Jana pushed out a painful breath. Oh, how she could relate.

The girl reached for the strap of the threadbare bag she carried crossbody-style across her torso as she took a short step away. She didn't seem to notice Jana, though. All her attention was on her father.

Jana's heart squeezed as she watched the man hold Sydney at arm's length, looking at her as if she were a kind of lifeboat in a storm.

"Look at you, all grown-up and married." He touched her face, regret shining in his eyes. "I'm sorry I wasn't here for your wedding. Or for Remy. I am so sorry about Remy."

Sydney shook her head, but when she glanced back at Jana, tears shimmered in her eyes. "You're here now. That's all that would matter to him."

Jana shifted on her sandaled feet, hands twisting together at the mention of Remy who had passed away unexpectedly last spring.

"Still." The man's voice broke and Jana's heart cracked a bit more.

"It's okay." Sydney touched his face. "I promise. You didn't take long to get back into the island spirit, did you?" She dropped a hand to the shoulder of his dark blue Hawaiian shirt. Jana took the opportunity to finally make her move and stepped around them.

Sydney's hand shot out and grabbed Jana's arm before she could leave. "I got so caught up I forgot about you. Silas Garwood, this is Jana Powell. She's on an extended stay here in Nalani and is Ohana Odyssey's newest best customer."

Jana felt her face warm at the introduction. "Hi." She offered a quick wave before she twisted her hands together again.

"Hello." His smile was just as warm for her as it had been for Sydney.

"Silas and his daughter, Freya, are staying in

the cottage near yours," Sydney said. "He's the old friend I told you about."

"I'm not that old," Silas joked as his cheeks went a bit pink. His dark brown hair was trimmed neatly and his clean-shaven appearance made his skin glow a little. Her assessment yesterday had been spot-on. Fit and tall and more than slightly swoon-worthy, if Jana's thoughts were so inclined to travel there. "Always nice to meet a fellow visitor to Nalani. This is the aforementioned Freya."

Jana wobbled as she accepted his offered hand, butterflies taking flight inside of her. She pressed on her stomach in a futile attempt to calm them.

"It's nice to finally meet you, Freya." Sydney braced her hands on her thighs and leaned down. Her long, strawberry blond hair fell over her shoulders. "You're even prettier than in your pictures."

"Thank you." Freya twisted back and forth, her hands clutching the strap of her bag.

"Silas, Keane, Remy and Daphne all went to college together." Sydney stood up, looked between Silas and Jana as if following a pickle ball match. "They also spent one rather eventful summer out here in Nalani the year they graduated."

"It wasn't that eventful." Silas rolled his eyes. "And before you start in on me, it was a shark I saw and nothing anyone says will ever convince me otherwise."

ANNA J. STEWART 69

"You saw a shark?" Jana was suddenly rethinking every step she'd taken into the ocean.

"A real shark, Daddy?" His daughter looked both amazed and scared.

"That's up for debate," Sydney clarified. "I wasn't there to witness it myself. Word is you practically ran across the water getting back to shore."

"That's an…exaggeration."

Jana stifled a laugh at Silas's discomfort, thoughts of possible sharks nipping at her own ankles forgotten.

"It really was a shark," Silas defended himself to Jana.

"Uh-huh." Sydney smirked. "Benji still calls you Shark Boy, by the way. He loves telling that story to tourists."

"Benji's still around?" His blush deepened and so did Jana's enjoyment.

"Benji is definitely still around," Sydney confirmed. Jana had heard the name mentioned before and how he was one of the most senior members of the Nalani community. Evidently, he put-putted his way around town in a seasonally decorated golf cart. "He's got a long-distance girlfriend named Pippy, and Kahlua, a pet pig who is learning to surf."

"No way." Silas didn't look convinced.

"Yep. Kahlua's been taking lessons for about

70 THE SINGLE DAD'S PROMISE

four years now." Sydney nodded firmly. "Apparently not all pigs have a great learning curve."

The confusion in the little girl's eyes intensified, probably because, like Jana, she was trying to imagine a pig on a surfboard.

"Benji should be making an appearance at Keane's birthday luau," Sydney told them.

"Will he be bringing his pig?" Silas's laughter set his blue eyes to dancing while Jana's insides did a happy jig of their own.

She couldn't bring herself to look away from him. He had a warm aura about him, one that Jana felt surprisingly drawn to. Strange how her thoughts were moving into territory she wasn't normally inclined to explore. But she had told herself to take chances. The fact that she wondered if Silas was going to be one of them threw her completely off-balance.

"Nope, no pig," Sydney confirmed. "Kahlua doesn't particularly enjoy luaus."

"How come?" Silas's daughter asked.

"Ah." Sydney's suddenly obvious discomfort now had Silas grinning. "Let's just say she's not a fan of the menu. I'll let your father explain that to you further."

"Chicken," Silas accused.

"You bet." Sydney's wry smile proved she wasn't offended.

"I should be going." Jana made a second attempt, but Silas stepped into her path.

"I'm sorry. This is going to sound…" A confused smile curved his full lips. "I've got this strange feeling we've met before."

"Wow," Sydney said and snort-laughed. "You think that line up all on your own? He's not married by the way," she told a rapidly blinking Jana. "You probably should have led with that considering…" She inclined her head toward his daughter.

"It wasn't a line." The sudden seriousness in Silas's voice captured Jana's complete attention. Looking directly into his eyes had her feeling a bit hypnotized. "You just seem really familiar."

She flexed her hands at her sides. "We haven't met." She'd have remembered. She tilted her head, winced against the sun.

"Daddy." The little girl moved in and grabbed the edge of her father's shirt. Her green eyes had gone saucer-wide and the smile on her lips sent tingles down Jana's spine. "Daddy, we saw her last night. She's the mermaid!"

Jana automatically looked down at her legs as if expecting to find fins and a tail, then at Sydney, who seemed as surprised as Jana. "Mermaid?" Jana asked Silas.

Silas's cheeks flushed again. "We went for a swim yesterday and…" He pointed to Jana's flaxen, short-cropped hair. "I think you might have been glowing in the sunset. Freya was convinced you were a mermaid."

"Did you go swimming yesterday, Jana?" Sydney asked.

"I've been in the water more than I've been out of it." Perhaps that qualified her as a mermaid? "So yes, I was." She dropped down so she was eye to eye with the child. "I'm sorry, Freya, but I'm afraid I'm not—"

"Yes, you are! I know you are." Freya stepped away from her father, touched a hand to Jana's as if testing to see whether she was real. She then touched Jana's short hair. "I saw you swimming."

"Well, I have been called part-fish, I suppose." Jana cast a quick glance at Silas, who appeared shell-shocked at his daughter's interest. "But you know what, Freya? If I was a mermaid, I couldn't tell anyone because mermaids are secret." She pressed a finger to her lips. "That's how we— how *they* stay safe while they're on land. We're very solitary creatures." What a pleasure it was to fall into fantasy and make-believe for a moment.

"I knew it! Oh my gosh, Daddy! A real-life mermaid!" Freya jumped up and down, grabbed her father's hand. "Isn't that the best thing ever?"

Jana felt her entire being fill with joy. She wasn't one to lie, but there were times little fibs could be forgiven. Besides, it wasn't as if they were ever going to see each other again.

Freya's eyes dimmed a bit as she looked more closely at Jana. "What does solitary mean?"

"Alone," Silas said at the same time Sydney said "lonely."

It took Jana an extra beat to realize Sydney's definition was probably more accurate. "It just means I'm on my own," she said in an effort to sound less woeful.

"Makes me sad." Sydney heaved a heavy and far too dramatic sigh. "You in the cottage all by yourself while the rest of us are at a big party this evening. It would have been really cool to have a mermaid at Keane's birthday luau."

Jana glared at Sydney before she thought better of it. "No fair."

Sydney only grinned as Freya's mood brightened. "But we're going to be there, aren't we, Daddy?"

Silas inclined his head. "You weren't too keen yesterday." Silently, he mouthed, "I'm sorry" to Jana in a way that had her heart tipping toward him.

"That was before I knew a mermaid would be there," Freya said simply. "I want to go now. I really do. Please can we go, Daddy?"

"How can I say no?" Silas feigned surrender. "We'll definitely go." He grinned at Jana. "If the mermaid does."

It was the way his voice dropped, the way he looked at her, as if suddenly they were alone beneath the pulsing island sun. The butterflies in her stomach picked up hurricane speed. "I—" She cleared her throat. "I really don't want to—"

74 THE SINGLE DAD'S PROMISE

"If you say impose one more time I'm going to cancel your zip lining trip," Sydney warned. "Imposing is not a thing here, Jana. I promise. You're Ohana, remember?"

"Ohana means family," Freya announced. "Mr. Mano said so. Are you scared of people, too?" Freya asked, suddenly very concerned. "I get scared around strangers sometimes. Like when I went to school." She clasped her tiny hand around Jana's so gently tears clogged Jana's throat. "We can be scared together. And you won't be…" She looked up at her father.

"Solitary," Silas murmured.

"That," Freya said and nodded firmly.

There wasn't any other response to give. It had taken less than five minutes for Jana to fall completely under the spell of this little girl. And her father. "Okay. I guess I'll have to come." If Freya's father couldn't resist his daughter's pleas—and he'd had practice!—Jana certainly couldn't.

"Yay!" Sydney pumped a fist and danced in a circle. "Freya, you and I make a fabulous team."

Freya beamed up at Sydney even as she squeezed Jana's hand.

"Things'll get rolling around six," Sydney told Jana. "We'll be at the beach near Maru's malasada stand."

"Malasadas," Silas groaned. "I almost forgot about those."

"She's expanded her menu since you were here

last," Sydney told him. "Which makes you obligated to try all of them before you leave."

"What are mala…mal-a." Freya heaved out a frustrated sigh that had Jana lifting her free hand to cover her amusement, even as the nerves attempted to grab hold. "What are those?"

"They're like doughnuts," Sydney told Freya. "Only they're filled with all kinds of yummy things like coconut or chocolate or pineapple."

"Pineapple?" The last of Freya's trepidation vanished upon that reveal and she released her hold on Jana. "Ooooh."

"You just said the magic word." Silas smiled. "I sense many a malasada in our future."

"You can work them off swimming away from sharks," Sydney teased. "I'm joking, Freya," she added quickly at Freya's gasp of concern. "We haven't had a shark sighting around these parts since your father was here."

"It just gets funnier the more we talk about it, doesn't it?" Silas said and turned his attention on Jana while Sydney asked Freya about the bag she carried. "I'm sorry if you feel backed into a corner," he said under his breath.

"It's fine," Jana said, surprised to find that she meant it. Her whole body relaxed as she felt the warmth of his smile. "She's hard to say no to." She wasn't sure if she was referring to Freya or Sydney.

"It's cute at first," Silas chuckled. "Freya doesn't

76   THE SINGLE DAD'S PROMISE

usually do well with strangers, but she's taken with you."

"The feeling's mutual," Jana admitted. "You do know I'm not really a mermaid, right?"

He pressed a finger to his lips. "That will be *our* secret."

"Daddy, you were right," Freya announced. "I'm making friends. First, Mr. Mano and now Miss Jana and Miss Sydney. That's three whole friends!"

"Look at you go." Pride shone on Silas's face. "I guess we'll see you tonight, Jana." He held out his hand for Freya to take before they started following Sydney down the hill to the Ohana Odysseys office. "Six o'clock." As Freya began to skip, Silas looked over his shoulder and shot her the most beautiful smile she'd ever seen in her life. "Don't be late."

CHAPTER FOUR

DON'T BE LATE.

Wow, Silas thought. Sydney was right. He really was out of practice. Not that he wanted to practice anything with Jana Powell. Or did...

He shook his head, pushed his feet into his slippahs and willed his mind to maybe, hopefully, move beyond the memory of the beautiful blonde with huge gray-blue eyes and a smile that erased the clouds from the sky. A vacation romance was the last thing he needed, especially with a woman who had so completely entranced his daughter.

Not that he could blame Freya.

He'd never seen his daughter react so immediately to someone before. It always, always took her time to warm up and, well, trust. Jana's apparently instinctive reaction to his daughter had touched a part of Silas's heart he'd long given up hope on.

Maybe the mermaid story was responsible, but whatever it had been, Freya had been the one to initiate contact with Jana and that was definitely a big leap forward for his little girl. He wished he could credit his hard work getting Freya acclimated to school as the reason for the change, but he suspected it was more of a meeting of kindred spirits that had Freya opening like one of her beloved storybooks.

"Is this okay for the party, Daddy?" Freya walked into the kitchen while putting the strand of shells Mano had given her back around her neck. She was wearing the new yellow, flowered sarong they'd picked out at Luanda's after lunch. The bright pattern went perfectly with her bathing suit that Silas was beginning to think might be the only thing she wore for the duration of their stay.

"It's more than okay." He motioned her forward and smoothed a bump in her braid and then tightened the flower-topped elastic resting against her back. "You look perfect."

"I want to look pretty for the mermaid," Freya announced and had Silas silently warring with himself once again. He could sense her fixation beginning, both on mermaids and Jana Powell. Hopefully he could spin a way toward positivity and use this as a teaching moment about boundaries and expectations.

"I know it's a secret," Freya went on. "That she's a mermaid, but maybe if I'm really good and nice she'll take me to her undersea world. I bet it's really pretty down there."

Given things with Freya often took a bit of

extra work, the need to keep a solid line between fantasy and reality—especially when both practically involved strangers—wasn't a complete surprise. She'd had her difficulties since birth, but her mind had always seemed to be ahead of the rest of her. Her current reading ability was far beyond that of her fellow pre-K students, one of the things that had instantly set her apart. She plowed through books faster than he could supply them, but she also often clung to fiction as if it was fact.

He wanted to embrace the imagination she obviously had, but he also worried that doing so would make the real world feel more harsh than it actually was.

Their local library was close by and the librarians knew Freya by name. It had become one of her safe places and Silas had never once said no to a visit when she asked. While he tried to steer her into different types of stories, she wasn't about to give up on her fairy tales. Anything that featured magical, mystical, imaginary worlds endlessly fascinated her. Possibly because she spent a lot of time in her own head, she wanted it to be a happy, beautiful place.

Still.

"You know mermaids aren't real, Freya."

She dismissed the idea with a very small shrug. "Are they not real because they aren't real or because you never met one before?"

"I..." Silas's mind went blank. "They aren't real

80 THE SINGLE DAD'S PROMISE

because...they aren't real." There simply wasn't another way to say it.

"Jana said mermaids are secret. She's a secret, Daddy. I don't think we should tell her she isn't real." The frankness in her young voice was accentuated by the determination in her eyes. "Can we go now?"

"Yesterday you weren't sure you wanted to go. Now you want to go early? You sure you're okay being around a lot of people you don't know?" He wanted her prepared for the crowd. "You have to have your polite manners in place."

"I know." Freya frowned and looked at the floor. "But they won't all be new. Mr. Mano will be there. And Miss Sidney." She lowered her voice, as if afraid to say, "And the mermaid."

"Right." Now Silas did sigh. The mermaid. Something told him that by the end of this evening he was going to owe Jana Powell a very big apology. Even as he thought that, his heart bounced a bit at the idea of seeing her again. She'd seemed so shy, but he'd also detected a spark of excitement in her eyes. "Maybe you should just call her Jana, okay?"

"To keep her secret." Freya nodded before looking up at him seriously. "I think you're right. I want to change my shoes." She raced off, her long red braid bouncing against her back.

"Last thing I expected to have to deal with in Nalani were mermaids." Silas waited patiently by the door, watching the ocean tumble over itself. The heat of the day was behind them, although he wasn't entirely sure the mideighties equated hot in this region. The humidity was something, though, but hey, he was in Hawai'i. Not much to complain about given that situation.

"All ready?" Silas asked as Freya finally joined him, her treasure bag slung across her body. He'd started to plant the seed that it might be time to get a new bag, one that didn't look as if it wasn't going to fall apart at the seams at any second. So far his suggestions had been brushed aside. His daughter, much like him, had selective hearing when it came to things she didn't want to consider.

He made certain they left well before six, wanting to arrive ahead of most of the crowd. Easing her into a large group situation tended to go better than abruptly joining the fray. He'd misjudged their arrival. He counted at least a couple dozen people moving tables, arranging food, setting up the makeshift tiki bar on the far end of what was shaping up to be a huge buffet.

Freya moved closer and grabbed his hand.

"It's okay." He squeezed gently. "They're all friendly." Unfamiliar, but definitely friendly. They were both greeted with smiles and alohas, but Freya didn't seem completely convinced.

She tugged on his hand and lifted her other arm, a sign she wanted him to pick her up. He bent down and scooped her into his arms, moving her bag out of the way with practiced ease. Silas tried to focus on Freya rather than the memories that bombarded him. It had been years since he'd stepped foot on this beach and yet…

And yet if he closed his eyes and listened, he could almost hear Remy calling to him over the gentle lapping of the waves.

He really missed his friend.

His hold on Freya tightened, but she didn't protest. Instead, the hand on his back gently patted him, as if she could sense his emotions. Love swamped him, dragging him into that familiar tide of pride and gratitude. What a lucky man he was to have this little girl in his life. Whatever else went on, Freya was, and always would be, his constant.

Back on the mainland, it had been easier to deal with Remy being gone. But now that he was here, now that he'd been welcomed back by Remy's sister, the feelings of loss he'd locked away for so long surged afresh. Their friendship had been steadfast from the moment they'd met in college—the only time Remy had lived anywhere but the islands. It was the kind of friendship that had remained strong despite the distance. The kind of friendship where they could pick up where they left off, no matter how much time passed.

But Nalani…

Silas rested his forehead against Freya's warm cheek. This place just sank into your soul.

He'd only spent that one summer here and he'd been barely an adult, yet he couldn't recall a more perfect time in his life than those few months of absolute freedom he'd found in Nalani. With his friends. With his Ohana.

"Are you sad again, Daddy?" Freya asked as he navigated through the ankle-deep sand to keep out of the way.

"Not really." Hope remained, but it seemed to be tied to him keeping an eye out for a certain blond-haired mermaid. He'd seen the panic in her eyes when Freya had been talking to her. A panic and also a little fear. But he'd also seen her battle it back, as if determined not to let whatever was causing her doubt to stand in her way of having fun.

Maybe she'd change her mind and not come. He hoped that wouldn't be the case.

Freya leaned over so she was the only thing in his field of vision. She poked a finger into the dimple on his left cheek and pressed up. "Smile, Daddy."

"I'll try." He didn't lie to Freya. Ever. But he always strived to be gentle with the truth. "I just really miss your Uncle Remy."

"He was funny." But Freya's smile was one of joy as she dropped her hand on his shoulder. "He mailed Winnie to me. That's why I brought

THE SINGLE DAD'S PROMISE

her. Because she came from here." She frowned. "I didn't think Roscoe would have to stay home, though."

Determined not to let her slide back into the regret over leaving one of her stuffed besties behind, Silas hugged her, faced the ocean and prayed for inner peace. "Your Uncle Remy really loved you, Freya."

"He loved both of you." Sydney spoke from behind them. "Sorry for eavesdropping," she said when they turned around. She carried a cooler and under her other arm was a stack of reusable tablecloths. "I miss him, too, Silas. Every day." The grief he'd carried was reflected in Sydney's eyes.

"We probably always will." Silas immediately set Freya down so he could relieve Sydney of the cooler. The ice inside rattled. "But he's here." Silas said as he motioned out to the ocean. "I can feel him. And if I'm not mistaken, he's telling me to suck it up, buttercup, and lend a hand."

"Suck what up?" Freya's question made Sydney laugh and the tears vanish from her eyes.

"Come on." Sydney pushed them ahead of her. "We'll put you two to work."

Freya stayed close to Silas as he helped unload not only Sydney's cooler, but the additional barrels and buckets with ice and drinks. They got into a rhythm of him handing her the bottles and cans and Freya burying them in the ice. It was a nice distraction for her as more people began to arrive.

The buffet table gradually filled with overflowing platters and bowls, from hot, roasted and shredded Kahlua pork, laulau, which consisted of fish or chicken slow-steamed and roasted in taro leaves, various salads including a pineapple one that definitely caught Freya's eye, and of course a huge offering of haupia, the traditional island coconut pudding. The aroma of all the fresh food made Silas's stomach rumble to the point of Freya noticing.

"I'm hungry, too," Freya admitted but then she went silent as she took a step back and tilted her chin up so high she nearly toppled backward. Her mouth made a silent O as she looked up and reached for Silas.

"'Bout time we saw your face around here." Keane Harper didn't wait for Silas to respond before he pulled him in for a huge bro hug, slapping a hard hand against his back. "Best birthday present I've gotten yet. You've been missed, brah."

Most of Silas's trepidation over his long-delayed return to Nalani evaporated at his friend's welcome. "You, too." When he felt Freya's hand tugging at his shirt, he said, "Keane, this is my daughter, Freya. Freya, this is Keane Harper." He paused, long-banked emotion swelling inside of him. "One of the best friends I've ever had."

Keane seemed a bit surprised at that declaration, but he quickly turned his attention to Freya. He crouched, reached back for the hand of the dark-haired woman standing behind him.

Sydney had sent Silas some of the wedding photographs. He immediately recognized Keane's wife, one of Nalani's latest transplants from the mainland. Silas had yet to hear the entire story, but word had it she and Keane had met under unexpected and entertaining circumstances. Circumstances that led to a surprise island wedding and Marella's permanent relocation to Nalani.

"Aloha, Freya," Keane said. "Welcome to Nalani."

"Hi." She half hid behind Silas but offered a little wave and a smile.

"This is my wife, Marella."

"It's wonderful to finally meet you both." Marella held out a small lei strung with bright yellow hibiscus flowers. "We thought you might like this, Freya. I hear yellow is your favorite color."

Silas looked down as Freya's trepidation eased. "It's very pretty," she whispered and glanced at Silas as if asking for permission.

"It's okay," he urged, but let her take her time approaching the couple. "They're two of the people I told you about."

"What did you tell her about us exactly?" Keane eyed Silas as Marella carefully draped the lei over Freya's head.

"He said you're safe." Freya gently touched

the flowers. "Thank…ma-ha-lo." Each syllable sounded like she was pulling it out of her memory.

"Okay, now you're in the way." Sydney laughed and knocked a knee into Silas's leg as her arms were full with more aluminum containers filled with food. "Go play with your friends for a while, Silas. We'll call when dinner's ready."

Silas blinked, falling so quickly into the past he wasn't sure he'd make it out.

"What?" Sydney asked, her expression innocent.

"You just…" Silas shook his head, the memory fierce. "You reminded me of your mom just then. She used to say that to us when we hung around the house too long." His smile was quick. Sydney and Remy's parents had died unexpectedly in a plane crash on Molokai shortly before Sydney graduated from high school. Silas had just graduated from the police academy and couldn't get the time off to attend that funeral, a regret he carried to this day. "Sorry. Getting caught up in things, I guess." Given the way all the emotions were cycling through him he'd been suppressing them even more than he thought.

"Mom and Dad would be glad you're back, too." Sydney planted a loud kiss on his cheek before pushing him away. "Now, get going, would you? We've got more food coming. Including the birthday boy's cake. Freya, do you like cake?"

She nodded, considered. "Is it chocolate?"

"A kid after my own heart," Keane announced as he grabbed two bottles of beer, then dug through another bucket. "Wouldn't be my birthday cake if it wasn't chocolate. Aha!" He held up his find and earned a warm smile from his wife. "Just when we ran out at home."

"What is that?" Freya asked in a way that eased Silas's concern about her acclimating to the crowd.

"It's lychee juice," Marella told her. "Lychee is a tropical fruit. Looks a little like a fat raspberry before it's peeled. The doctor took me off all caffeine, so this has become my new daily habit." She cracked open the lid, held it out for Freya. "Would you like to try it? It's a little sweet and to me it tastes like a strawberry and grape got friendly."

Silas grinned at Marella's description. Even if Mano hadn't spilled the beans, Marella's rounded stomach beneath the flowing, orange, thin-strapped dress, and her restrictions on caffeine certainly would have given their impending parenthood away. He looked to Keane. So many questions and all he could do was shake his head in dismay. Keane shot him a casual shrug and sheepish grin in response. What a ride his friend was in for.

Freya accepted the drink, not looking particularly thrilled at the idea. She sighed and earned an amused smile from Keane. "Daddy says I should try new things at least once."

"Sounds like your daddy is very smart," Marella agreed.

Freya took a sip, frowned. Took another. "I like it!" She turned to Silas. "Daddy, it's good!"

"Here." Keane handed Marella another bottle.

"You can keep that one, Freya," Marella insisted.

Freya stayed close to Silas as they journeyed through the growing crowd. People shouted at and greeted Keane with warm wishes for a happy birthday, then did double takes when they recognized Silas. Only a few, thank goodness, called him Shark Boy.

Familiar faces he couldn't always put names to welcomed him back to the point Freya got confused. She tugged him down to her level, whispered in his ear.

"Daddy, you have so many friends."

"It looks like I do," Silas agreed even as he wondered how one summer in Nalani could have resulted in his being remembered so well. "That means you do, too. Speaking of friends." He stood up as a familiar redhead approached. Tall and lithe, Daphne Mercer hadn't changed one bit. Not physically, anyway. Emotionally? She had always struck him as a bit sad. Lonely. Much, he realized, in the same way he considered Jana earlier. Silas couldn't have missed the glowing aura of

90 THE SINGLE DAD'S PROMISE

happiness that surrounded Daphne now, though. Like Keane, her circumstances had changed as well. Just a few months ago she'd reunited with her high school sweetheart Griffin Townsend and become stepmother to his two kids, a boy and girl. Now they were building a life together, in Nalani.

A new start for all of them. And Daphne's sadness had been replaced with what looked like absolute contentment.

"Sorry we're late," Daphne said as they drew near. "*Somebody* lost their shell sandals and we could not come to the party without them." She brushed a hand across Marella's arm as she passed but made a beeline for Silas. *"Welina hou."* Welcome home. She didn't hesitate to hug him. "I don't want to let go," she murmured so only he could hear. "I don't want you to disappear on us again."

"I'm here for a little while, at least." Daphne had always been a calming influence for Silas. They'd met in a required biology class in college and, after quickly determining there was no spark between them, immediately become fast friends. When she finally released him, he saw tearstains on her cheeks.

She kept a hand on his shoulder, but before Silas could comment, she shifted her focus to Freya.

"Well." Daphne shook her head in amazement.

"You must be Freya. What a little lady you are. And so pretty in yellow."

"It's my favorite color." Freya beamed.

"It's one of mine, too. And look." Daphne reached back and whipped her long braid over her shoulder. "We match!"

Freya giggled. "Daddy does my hair."

"Does he?" Daphne looked impressed. "Well, it's good to know you developed some important skills since I last saw you. Silas, this is my husband, Griffin, and our children Cammie and Noah."

"Griff, please. Pleasure." Griff's offered handshake was firm. Daphne's husband gave off island vibes for sure, with his dark green patterned Hawaiian shirt, board shorts and slippahs. He carried a square camera bag at his hip. Silas heard he never went anywhere without it. The man was an award-winning photojournalist who had recently taken on an editor role with a new media outlet. "Good to meet you finally, Silas," Griff said. "Daphne's told me a lot about you."

"Don't believe half of it," Silas tried to joke. It was taking some getting used to, seeing his friends happily married, settled down with kids—or with kids on the way.

Daphne motioned to the boy with serious sunstreaks in his brown hair, then tugged a young girl over and rested her hands on her shoulders.

92 THE SINGLE DAD'S PROMISE

"Guys, this is an old friend of mine from school. And his daughter, Freya."

"Cammie of the lost sandals fame, I suppose?" Silas asked and earned a giggle from the young girl. She appeared to be a little older than Freya, a few inches taller, but with far more innocence in her gaze than his daughter.

"I'd left them outside by the flower bed," Cammie announced. "Hi!" She offered a quick wave to Freya. "Pretty lei. They're hibiscus, right, Mama D?"

"Yes, they are," Daphne, ever the flower-fanatical botanist, confirmed.

"We're going to go check out the food," Griff said. "And hopefully I can keep Noah from eating all the Spam misubi. Freya, would you like to come with us?"

Freya's nose scrunched the way it always did when she was uncertain about something. Her hand tightened on the hem of Silas's shirt.

"Come on." Cammie, unwilling to take no for an answer, reached out and grabbed Freya's free hand. "I can tell you what everything is. It's okay," she said when Freya still held back, feet planted firmly in the sand. "My mom and your dad are friends. That makes us Ohana. Right, Mama D?"

"That's right," Daphne confirmed. "But Freya might not want to—"

"I'll go. Can I go, Daddy?" When Freya met

his gaze, he saw so much in her eyes. Fear, more than a little uncertainty, and sheer excitement. Much, Silas thought, like he'd seen in Jana's eyes earlier. "Mr. Mano said Ohana means family, so I'll be okay." It was a test Silas hadn't anticipated needing to pass: letting go of her long enough to test those wings he'd been trying so hard to help her build.

"I'll be right here if you need me. Go have fun." He put on a brave smile even as he felt a bit like a mama bird pushing his chick out of the nest. Cammie stood beside Freya, keeping her hand locked securely in hers. Noah and Griff followed the girls, kicking up sand as they made their way to the ever-growing amount of homemade celebratory food.

Silas swallowed hard. He didn't know how to process watching his little girl walk away from him. It was like crossing the threshold in a story, when things weren't ever going to be quite the same for the characters in question.

This was what he'd always wanted: for her to feel safe and secure enough to take some chances. Of course, it would finally happen when they arrived in Nalani. The place was, after all, pure magic. A gift that kept giving.

"She's beautiful, Silas," Daphne murmured from beside him. She reached down and took hold of his hand, squeezed hard. "She's perfect."

Silas beamed with pride. "She is to me."

"I'm still a little angry with you, you know," Daphne went on as Keane begged off to welcome his guests and Marella led them to a bank of picnic tables away from the crowd. "Don't let the hug and smile fool you. It shouldn't have taken you this long to come back."

"You're right." Silas sat beside her. "It shouldn't have."

"You didn't have to do it all on your own," she chided. "We could have helped you with Freya. Especially after what happened with Caroline."

"No." He shook his head. "You couldn't have. I wasn't ready to come back. Everything here…" He couldn't quite explain it. "Nalani is out of the ordinary. When you're here it doesn't feel quite real and I couldn't risk losing myself in that. I needed to stay grounded. And I was right. Even now this place feels…like a dream." And was one reason it was hard to get a grip on all of the emotions spiraling inside of him. Emotions he really didn't want to address. Not yet, anyway. "It's a different kind of life here. I needed to deal with Freya's birth and Caroline leaving. It sounds strange, I'm sure, but I needed to know I could stand on my own."

"I guess I can understand that." She rested her head on his shoulder as Marella sat across from them. "Now that you've come back, you'll have to do so more often."

He knocked his head against hers gently, earned

a little laugh. "I definitely plan to do that." If for no other reason than to keep Freya moving forward socially. She was already far more comfortable here than she'd ever been back in San Francisco. He couldn't help himself. He turned around, looked almost desperately for Freya, unused to her being out of his sight.

"She's fine." Marella gestured to the left with her bottle of lychee juice. "I can track her by her hair. Same as I do this one." She looked to Daphne, who laughed.

"Appreciate that. Congratulations," he said to her. "When is the baby due?"

"Mid-June." Marella sat back, tilted her dark head down and stared at her belly. "Guess my days of hiding it are over."

"You couldn't hide it three months ago," Daphne teased. "Pippy called her out at Christmas before Marella could even tell Keane."

"Benji's girlfriend Pippy?" Silas drank some of his beer. He wished he'd sat on the other side of the table. Not only so he could keep an eye on Freya, but so he could watch for Jana.

"Pippy's my grandmother. She's tough to keep track of, too." Marella waved her hand in the air. "She should be here this weekend. Fair warning, she's talking about moving to the island permanently," she told Daphne.

"She says that every time she visits," Daphne countered.

THE SINGLE DAD'S PROMISE

"True," Marella said. "We've got the guest-house for her if she decides to. In the meantime, I think we're going to need another table. There you are!"

Marella stood to welcome another familiar face, one that had Silas rising. Tehani Iokepa, Mano's younger sister. Just the sight of her had Silas falling back into that tide pool of memories.

She and Remy had been childhood sweethearts right up until he'd died. Like her brother, Tehani was a vision with her long, straight, obsidian hair, and deeply tanned skin. Hawaiian perfection. He was relieved there wasn't a heavy cloud of grief in her eyes.

Silas had heard through Mano that Tehani had recently fallen in love again, this time with Na-lani's most reputable handyman, Wyatt Jenkins. Wyatt, Silas recalled from his visit, was one of Remy's closest friends; he'd been quiet, really good at fixing things, and even back then, the type of person everyone could rely on.

Given the caring expression on Wyatt's face, Silas couldn't think of anyone better to now cherish and protect Tehani's once broken heart.

Tehani stood still, a baby snuggly situated on her sarong-clad hip. The dark orange top of her two-piece accentuated her full figure and glistening skin. Her dark eyes glowed against the setting sun. Eyes filled with so much emotion, Silas almost couldn't look at her.

"Silas."

"Aloha, Tehani." The words barely got out.

Tehani didn't respond for a long moment. She simply stared at him, her gaze shifting briefly to the ocean behind them as if she, too, could hear Remy's laughter on the breeze.

Wyatt, standing beside her, touched her arm. "T? You okay?"

"Sorry, yes." She nodded, offered a weak smile. "I'm fine." Her arm tightened around her son, Silas noticed, the way he'd clung to Freya earlier.

Silas hadn't been so out of touch that he didn't know about Kai, the child Remy had never met. The son he'd always dreamed of having. As he looked at the baby, with his mass of dark hair and dark eyes, it was the facial structure, the nose and that amused grin tilting the baby's lips that felt like a complete gut punch of recognition.

Tehani came closer, tears filling her eyes. Standing in front of him, she lifted a hand to touch Silas's cheek. "What took you so long?"

Her question broke the dam of swelling emotion, and she stepped into his arms, crying against his shoulder as her embrace welcomed him home.

CHAPTER FIVE

IN BETWEEN VISITING one shop after another and exploring the wonderful local items Nalani had to offer, Jana spent the rest of her day deciphering the odd sensation that had clung to her since meeting Silas Garwood earlier that day. She thought she'd done a good job of ignoring the feeling by spending more than an hour in The Hawaiian Snuggler, speaking with the owner, Shani, about the intricate handmade quilts and other fabrics she spotlighted in her store. But nope. The second she'd walked outside, there it was again, sending her insides into some kind of frenetic yet badly choreographed dance, even as it put what she assumed was an uncharacteristically goofy smile on her face.

It wasn't until she added a small sketch pad into the messenger bag that already contained a hastily wrapped birthday gift for Keane, along with her sandals, that she'd finally realized what the feeling was.

Excitement.

Yes, that was it. Excitement.

She'd forgotten what it felt like, to be amped up and anxious. At least, in a good way. And not in the all too familiar "my life is about to fall apart" way she'd experienced the last few months.

Not even the anticipation of her trip to Nalani had registered as more than a blip on her pulse meter, but that was probably because the journey was more like a determined escape.

But the thought of tonight, the promise of attending a birthday party that was described more like a town celebration, being surrounded by people she was learning to call friends? The idea of seeing Silas and his beautiful, shy little girl?

The inerasable smile she'd had on her face all day could definitely be called progress.

She closed the cottage door, released a deep breath and, taking a moment to center herself, offered a quick thought of thanks to the universe before she turned toward the ocean. Reveling in the warm evening air, Jana was determined to keep any anxiety at bay. She wasn't going to let fear or irrational worries stop her from enjoying herself.

And if that enjoyment included seeing Silas Garwood again, who was she to fight it? Just thinking of his name brought an image to mind that sent unexpected chills of anticipation coursing through her. It didn't make any sense, her reaction to him. The last thing on her mind these past six months had been men or...anything re-

100 THE SINGLE DAD'S PROMISE

motely connected to dipping her toe back into the very shallow dating pool in her suburb just outside Meridian, Idaho.

Apparently, one brief encounter with Silas had changed that completely.

It wasn't just that Silas was handsome. It had more to do with the presence he possessed of being grounded, being real. No affectations or performances or signs of a giant ego, three things she was more than familiar with given the male-dominated industry in which she worked. Add those sparkling blue eyes and his obvious devotion to his little girl, not to mention his affection for Sydney, and it had thrown Jana into a complete—well, to use a word from her escapist romance novels— tizzy. He made her want...

She sighed. He made her want so much more than what she had.

In fact, her newest acquaintance may very well have done the impossible: he'd awakened her longing to connect, the promise of which made her feel more alive than she had in a very long time. The scientist part of her was curious, too. New experiences provided new data and the potential for new possibilities. Talk about a win-win.

Attraction hadn't been the only thing Silas had sparked. The loss of creativity she'd struggled with since before her diagnosis surged back with the force of a tsunami. It was that, on top of trying to outrun unfamiliar emotions, which had her bopping all around Nalani searching for the art supplies she needed.

The internal switch that had flipped off in her doctor's office blasted back on suddenly, leaving her energized in a way she'd longed to feel again.

Was that Silas's doing? Of course not. But Jana couldn't help but tag him as the catalyst.

Watching him with his daughter, seeing how easy and calm he was with her made Jana think he possessed a special kind of magic. It was that magic that had Jana—as if she were Dorothy landing in Oz—taking that final step back into a world filled with color.

She'd laughed at herself when it took her over thirty minutes to decide what to wear; then another half hour spent in an attempt to manage her thin, white-blond hair into something it used to be. The butterflies had returned and brought feistier friends, but she was keeping them caged, determined to ignore them and take actual chances the second she stepped outside the cottage.

She couldn't fathom why the mere thought of a man she'd only just met elicited such nerves and fluttering, but she didn't necessarily want it to go away.

"Just don't get ahead of yourself." Sydney's not so subtle info dump about Silas's marital status aside, the self-warning banked her nerves. "Take things a day, an hour, even a minute at a time. One meeting does not a future make." But the idea she was even thinking like that again was a definite improvement on her mental state.

Jana walked along the shoreline, doing her best to keep her mood high and her expectations low. She'd only been in Nalani for a week, but it already felt comfortable. She'd discovered early on that she preferred the circuitous route into town. Nalani might be small, but she found Pulelehua Road a bit overwhelming at times. It made sense, of course, for the town to come alive, especially as the sun set.

With the dozens of shops, eateries and businesses welcoming locals and visitors alike, there was a cacophony of noise that included everything from ringing bike bells to shouts for more malasadas. All that to say the hustle and bustle was a big part of Nalani's charm and she was beginning to enjoy it as much as she did the peacefulness of her cottage.

Though it was the water that offered her the calm she'd sought. She hadn't realized how much she needed it until she'd come here, of course. There wasn't an ocean back home to run to no matter how loudly it called. There were rivers and lakes of course, but…

There was something almost healing about the ocean that had instantly improved her state of mind. Even now the gentle rush of the tide washing up and over her feet tamed the butterflies that continued to quiver as she walked to the party.

The ruffled hem of her pink sundress she'd bought at Luanda's this afternoon fluttered around her legs. The thin straps allowed the sun to kiss her skin with its continued presence. Another form of healing. The lower temperature also helped, but the humidity remained, eased somewhat by the water lapping around her ankles.

She heard the party before she saw it.

Her already rapid heartbeat increased.

The faint plinks of ukuleles, the undeniable happiness composed by laughter and cheer. Given the salty, meaty aroma in the air, the Kahlua pork must have already been removed from the imu, the underground roasting pit that was the traditional way to prepare the pig. Her appetite before coming to Nalani had been next to nil, but since she'd arrived? She'd been expanding not only her knowledge of local cuisine but also her culinary taste buds. That should help her start to regain the weight she'd lost during treatment.

Jana rounded the corner scanned the faces, looking for any and all familiar ones.

There were…so many people.

She stopped. Her toes curled into the sand, the grains scraping against the soles of her feet.

It seemed to her most if not all of the town had turned out to celebrate Keane's birthday. She lost count of the picnic tables that had been set up, expanding the party area to a significant portion of the beach. She could barely make out where the path through the overgrown trees led back into town. Some people stood in groups chatting, others were seated and focused on their food, while even more served and directed people to various dishes.

A number of celebrants moved through the crowd carrying pink and orange drinks with turquoise paper umbrellas in plastic, pineapple-shaped glasses.

The nerves she'd been fighting abated slightly as she took in her surroundings. Corners of multicolored tablecloths flapped gently in the breeze, held in place by platters and containers of food. A trio of ukulele players stood strumming island music while a hand-drummer kept time. Guests were making their best attempts at the hula. But it was the joy and goodwill that, like the food being consumed, permeated the air and filled Jana's lungs with hope. She breathed out her unease.

"You came!"

The excited words barely registered before Jana spotted Freya racing for her, her cute feet kicking up castles of sand. The same bag she'd carried earlier banged against her waist, putting a strain on the already fraying fabric. The unabashed smile on Freya's face had Jana blinking back an unexpected rush of tears.

Freya locked her arms around her waist and squeezed. Jana looked down into Freya's upturned face, her heart stuttering as if trying to remember how to beat.

"Hi, Jana."

"Hello, Freya." She touched a gentle hand to the girl's head. What had she done to deserve such an incredible welcome? "You look very pretty tonight." Movement at the table furthest from the crowd caught Jana's eye.

She relaxed. The entirety of the Ohana Odysseys family looked over, but it was Silas who captured Jana's attention. He'd risen, surprise evident on his face, even from a distance. He wore a button-down Hawaiian shirt similar to the one he'd had on when they'd met. Jana smiled at the thought that father and daughter had their preferred color schemes.

"I told Cammie you'd come." Freya grabbed hold of Jana's hands and held on tight, swinging them back and forth. "But I didn't tell her your secret," she added in a loud whisper.

"Our secret." Jana crouched down, squeezed the little girl's hands. "Are you having a good time at the party, Freya?"

"Yes." Freya's face scrunched in confusion. "Cammie said I'm her friend now. Her Ohana. I've never had a friend before. It's kinda neat."

"Friends are definitely neat." Jana looked over Freya's shoulder. Silas drew closer. "And you can never have too many." Only now did she begin to appreciate that theory.

106   THE SINGLE DAD'S PROMISE

"Can you be my friend, too?" Freya asked. "I already have four now! Five, if you count Noah, but he's a boy. Maybe six because of baby Kai. He's so cute! I've never seen a baby up close before."

Jana nodded, though she chuckled silently at the boy comment. "I would be happy to be your friend, Freya." She glanced up again and smiled at Silas. "Hello."

"Hello again."

There was something in his tone. An undercurrent that had chills racing up her spine and led her to believe he was as happy to see her as she was to see him. That hope and anticipation she'd been attempting to quell seemed poised to break free.

They headed toward the table. "We were starting to take bets on whether you'd turn up or not." Keane's always-there charming grin told her he was joking.

"I'm sorry. I lost track of time. But Freya and I had made a deal," she said. Freya linked their hands and swung them back and forth. "I couldn't very well not hold up my part of the bargain, now, could I?" Freya giggled in a way that said whatever worries she'd had about attending the party had disappeared.

"Daddy, can Jana sit with me and Cammie?"

"I think Jana would prefer to sit at the grown-ups table, don't you?" Silas said. "Why don't you give her some adult time first? Have you decided what you want to eat?"

"I guess." Freya didn't look thrilled. "I didn't see any chicken nuggets. Or French fries."

At Keane's wide-eyed horror, Jana pressed her lips together to stop from laughing. *Behold your future, Keane.* From what Jana understood about youngsters, chicken nuggets and fries were always their number-one food group.

"I saw a whole tray of pineapple. Let's check it out." Silas held out his hand to Freya, smiled at Jana. "Glad you made it."

"Thanks." And that, she thought as father and daughter strode away, was that. Regret tangled with disappointment. She dug into her bag, found the package and held it out to Keane. "I wasn't sure if gifts were in order. Happy birthday." She shrugged and tried not to blush at his surprise. "I hope you like it."

"Thank you." Keane beamed and made her think that was what he must have looked like as a kid at Christmas. "Gifts are always in order. Why don't you go grab a plate? I'll do my best to stop from opening this until you join us."

"Sure. Yeah, okay." The nervous habit she had of tucking her hair behind her ear never failed to remind her how much things in her life had changed. "I'll be right back." She walked over to the buffet tables, relieved to find the crowd had mostly dissipated. Since most folks were already eating, she didn't feel rushed to choose what to eat, but one look at the immense offerings had her feeling overwhelmed and uncertain.

Her hands trembled as she picked up a plate. Her gaze was immediately pulled to the end of the table where Silas and Freya stood admiring the pineapple selections.

As if sensing her eyes on him, Silas looked over, an amused smile curving his lips. "Need a food guide?"

Her cheeks went hot. She pushed her bag behind her, shrugged and forced a laugh. "Not really sure where to start."

Freya took the opportunity of her father being momentarily distracted to load another spoonful of fresh pineapple onto her plate. "I'm done, Daddy."

"You…are?"

"Uh-huh." Freya walked around him to join Jana. "What are you going to eat?"

"That is a very good question." The large, tossed green salad looked tempting. She'd been in the islands long enough to recognize some of the local fare: the Spam and rice misubi, a huge amount of fried rice. Steamed sweet Hawaiian bread rolls, some purple and flavored with taro. She wasn't a fan of raw fish, so she bypassed the salmon and ahi poke, but she did take a good amount of the Kahlua pork and macaroni salad. "I think that's enough."

Freya frowned. "What about dessert?"

"I can come back for that." Honestly, Jana wasn't sure where she'd put it, either on her plate or in her stomach.

"Come on, Freya." Silas steered his daughter away. "You can talk to Jana later, all right? Let her eat her dinner in peace."

It was on the tip of Jana's tongue to tell Silas she didn't mind. She wouldn't have come if she didn't want to spend time with Freya. Honestly, after that friend comment Freya made, Jana couldn't imagine anyone else in Nalani she had more in common with. With that thought in her head, she made her way to the Ohana Odysseys table, pushing herself out of her comfort zone to join a very established, close-knit group.

"Hi, everyone." She offered a quick wave and smile when they all greeted her. "Thanks for including me."

"So glad you came." Sydney was on her feet and hauling her into a one-armed hug before Jana could blink. "Sit." She pointed to the empty space next to Daphne Townsend. "You know everyone, don't you, Jana?"

"I think so. Hi." Jana's cheeks went a bit warm as she looked around. Daphne's husband, Griff, sat on Daphne's other side while across the table she spotted Keane, Marella and Tehani. It was, Jana realized, the first time she'd seen Tehani without her baby boy, Kai. "I don't see Theo or Mano. Are they not coming?"

110 THE SINGLE DAD'S PROMISE

"They'll be here later." Sydney looked tense. "They had a meeting about GVI issues."

"GV...?" Jana didn't have a clue what they were talking about. "Is that some kind of disease?"

Keane smirked before sipping his beer. "There's a thought."

"Golden Vistas Incorporated." Tehani flipped her long black hair behind her shoulder. "It's a financial company on the mainland that's trying to get an investment foothold here in Nalani."

"Theo used to work for them," Sydney told her. "Actually, that's how we met. He came out here to do a financial audit on Ohana Odysseys for a possible buyout."

Jana's hands froze while unwrapping the bamboo utensils from the napkin bundle. "You were going to sell Ohana?"

"She thought about it," Tehani muttered good-naturedly.

"For about five seconds," Sydney defended herself. "I was...spinning a bit after my brother died. But it all worked out in the end. And I got Theo because of it." The smile on her face was contagious. "Only now, word is GVI is gearing up for another attempt and this time they're coming after the resort as well. Don't worry," she added at Jana's apparent shock. "Mano is on top of things. No one's taking over anything if he can help it. That's the reason Silas is here. He's been investigating GVI back in San Francisco."

Jana poked her fork into the freshly roasted pork. Finally. An opportunity to learn more about Silas without sounding overly nosy. "What kind of investigating does he do?"

"The kind with a badge," Daphne said. "He works for the SFPD."

Well, that was unexpected. "He's a police officer?"

"Tangentially." Silas's voice joined from behind.

Jana looked over her shoulder, found him standing behind her, smiling. She smiled back. "How can you tangentially be a police officer?"

"Good question." Sydney grabbed Silas's arm and tugged him over, pushed him into her vacated seat. "Why don't you explain that to Jana while I go get her something to drink. Jana? What would you like?"

"Ah." As tempting as one of their mai tais was, she said, "Anything without alcohol would be great. Thanks." She hadn't been a big drinker before her treatment and since then, she'd lost the taste for it. Besides, she was warm enough with Silas suddenly sitting beside her.

"You've got it."

"I'm going to load up on those banana lumpia." Griff picked up his empty plate, reached for Daphne's, then got to his feet. "You want another of the guava cupcakes?" he asked Daphne, who beamed up at him. "Shouldn't have bothered to ask." He laughed, bent down and gave his wife a quick kiss before he moved off.

"He does come in handy sometimes." Daphne watched her husband walk away. "Dessert gives him an excuse to check on the kids."

Jana looked to the smaller picnic table where Wyatt Jenkins sat, baby Kai strapped to his chest, apparently being thoroughly entertained by Freya's new friend Cammie and her brother Noah, along with a dozen other children. Sure enough, Griff stopped long enough to see what his kids were up to, but they were so engrossed with Wyatt and Kai they barely noticed he was there.

Jana's gaze fell on Freya, who seemed inordinately attentive to her plate full of pineapple.

"She's doing okay." Silas's voice dropped so only Jana could hear. "It's all I can do not to sit on the other side of the table so I can watch her."

Jana turned back around, tried to focus on what she was certain was a delicious meal. If only she wasn't so distracted by...everything. "Making friends isn't easy," she said.

"Sometimes it's easier than we think," Silas countered as he took a long drink from his frosty bottle of beer.

"Okay, I've waited long enough," Keane announced. "Jana brought me a present." Across the table from them, he got to his feet. "Which is more than any of you can say, I might add."

"Our presence is present enough." Daphne toasted him and winked at Jana.

"Exactly," Silas said and mimicked the toast. "I got on a plane for you. With a five-year-old."

"Silas wins," Tehani teased.

"Open it already." Marella poked at the wrapping. "I can't wait to see what it is."

Jana pressed her lips together, keeping a hold of her confidence by a thread. "It's just something that popped into my head," Jana admitted. Keane, as expected, ripped off the paper like an unruly toddler. "It's not really that big a—"

"Oh. Wow." Keane blinked as he looked at the sketch turned painting. The expression on his face had Jana's pride surging. "This is amazing!" He turned the eight by ten canvas—that she'd found at Luanda's—around to show off the picture she'd drawn of Keane riding the waves. "I thought you work in tech," Keane said. "I had no idea you were an artist."

"I'm not. But I am in tech," Jana said with a forced laugh. "I just draw and sketch and paint to relax when inspiration strikes."

"Keane is nothing if not inspiring." Marella took the canvas from her husband's hand to examine it more closely. "Jana, this is beautiful. It's like a photograph. A moment in time." The awe in her eyes softened Jana's heart. "I can't wait to get it framed." Marella straightened suddenly.

"We're going to put it in the baby's room. It'll be our first addition."

"You don't have to do that." Jana blinked back another rush of tears this group of people kept triggering in her.

"Yes," Marella murmured. "Yes, I think we do."

Pleasure that she didn't know she could feel surged through her as the picture was passed around. The compliments came at her like the waves on the ocean. Fast and rejuvenating. She'd meant to capture Keane's connection to the water, in the way the waves cascaded over his back, the way his feet were planted on the board as he'd ridden across the top of the ocean.

She hadn't brought any art supplies with her. She hadn't touched the ones she had at home in months. The desire to paint had disappeared the day of her diagnosis and the impulse hadn't returned until...

She glanced at Silas.

Until today.

The second her hand had picked up the pencil, then the paints...something had broken free inside of her. Something she hoped to never let go of again.

"I'm glad you like it." Jana felt the tension in her body ease. "I practically bought all the art supplies Luanda's had."

"You ever walk away from science and the tech

world, you could have a serious career as an artist," Daphne said.

Jana had no doubt they were simply being kind. But that didn't explain the interest she saw on Tehani's and Daphne's faces as they each examined the painting.

"Be glad none of you got me any gifts," Keane told the table as he took the canvas back. "No way you could top this."

"Sugar rush time." Sydney returned and handed Jana a tall plastic pineapple filled to the brim with a pink straw and tiny turquoise umbrella. "Daphne's neighbor Pua makes this punch. We call it the Paradise Splash. No booze. But it'll have you hopping back to the cottage."

Jana accepted the drink, sipped, and sipped again. "It's delicious." Not too sweet, just the right amount of tart. "Passion fruit?"

"Good guess. Along with mango and pineapple. And a little soda. Enjoy." Sydney motioned to the others at the table. "Keane, Polunu and Akahi are here."

"They are?" Keane frowned at Sydney. "I thought they were on Oahu meeting with Akahi's specialist?"

"Don't worry," Tehani added at Keane's obvious concern. "Word is the appointment went well and she's been approved by her insurance for in-home nursing help." Tehani told him.

Sydney grinned. "They moved her appoint-

116 THE SINGLE DAD'S PROMISE

ment up so they could come back in time for your party. And you said no one else got you a gift. Polunu called me a couple of days ago, asked if I'd make sure Hori was at the airport to pick them up. Surprise!"

Jana had never seen so many emotions shift over a person's face. Keane's throat tightened, as if he couldn't quite manage to swallow. "I—"

Marella touched her husband's face, an action so tender Jana felt as if she were intruding. "We should go see them."

"Yeah." Keane rose. "I, yeah, we'll be back." He nearly tripped over the bench as he and Marella hurried off.

"Polunu and Akahi are kind of Keane's honorary parents," Sydney explained to Jana. "Keane worked on their boat during the summers when he visited. Now it's his boat. Well, Ohana Odysseys' boat, I guess." she added.

"The *Nani Nalu*." Jana had taken the cruise only a few evenings ago. It had been one of those must-do things she hadn't been about to pass up, and the experience had exceeded her expectations, from the food to the scenery, to watching the sun set. Keane had definitely put on a great show for her and the rest of the vacationers.

"Akahi was diagnosed with fibromyalgia a few years ago," Tehani said. "They're still looking for the right medication regime for her. It's been challenging."

Jana had no doubt. Rarely was there a one-treatment-fits-all solution for chronic illnesses.

"Hopefully an acute care nurse can help her manage better," Daphne said.

"Makes for a nice surprise for Keane. You've gotten better at keeping secrets." Silas toasted Sydney with his beer. "Well played."

"Thank you very much." Sydney did a little curtsy. "Daphne, I think we should go see what's keeping Griff with those desserts."

"What?" Daphne's brow furrowed.

"Come on." Sydney grabbed her arm and tugged. "You, too, Tehani. Let's check if there's anything new on the tables."

"Oh. Okay. Sure, yeah. Right." Tehani fell in line behind Sydney and eventually Daphne. "Might take us a while to, um, decide," she tossed over her shoulder as Sydney dragged her away.

As she sat beside Silas at a now-empty table, the butterflies Jana thought were under control fluttered back to life.

"Sydney might have gotten better at keeping secrets," Silas shifted so he could face her. "But her subtlety needs a lot of work." A nervous smile played across his lips. A smile Jana suspected matched her own.

She took a bite of macaroni salad, not because she was hungry, but because it gave her an extra few seconds to think of something to say. "So." She covered her mouth, cleared the frog out of

THE SINGLE DAD'S PROMISE

her throat. "What kind of work do you do as a tangential police officer?"

"I'm in the records division mostly. Desk work. Research, that kind of stuff." He glanced behind him to where Freya sat munching on pineapple. "Not exactly what I had in mind when I joined the force, but..." He shrugged. "It gives me a lot of flexibility where Freya's concerned."

"They mentioned you were helping with this GVI thing. And that's why you're here."

"Partially." He seemed amused at the idea. "I've been doing some digging into GVI for Mano, talked to a few people about the company and their plans. Theo gave me names of people to approach. Discovered most of them are not being treated well there, so they were more than eager to share what information they could."

"Charmed it out of them, did you?" Despite her nerves, she found him rather easy to talk to.

He chuckled. "Sure, we could look at it that way. It all worked out for the best, though, since GVI sent someone new out to evaluate the businesses and I decided to follow. So it brought me back to Nalani. And my friends." He took a long, deep breath. "I always knew I missed this place, but I didn't think it would feel as if I've come home."

Jana found her appetite fluctuating but tried another few mouthfuls of the delicious offerings. It wasn't that the food wasn't good—it was spectac-

ANNA J. STEWART

119

ular. Her stomach just wasn't in a receptive mood. She did, however, down her drink in record time.

"What about Freya's mother?" She picked up a sweet roll, broke it in half and nibbled at the corner. "Sydney said you aren't married. Where does she fit in for you and Freya?"

"She doesn't."

It surprised her to hear no hint of bitterness in Silas's voice, but then she realized there wasn't any emotion in his response. "I'm sorry." She pushed her plate away, giving up. "I don't know why I asked that. It's none of my business."

"It's okay. It's a natural question." He stared beyond her for a moment, then shifted his attention back to Jana. "Caroline and I were married for two years before she got pregnant with Freya. It wasn't an easy pregnancy and it took a toll on us, I suppose. When Freya was born at thirty-one weeks, Caroline..." He trailed off. "She always said she had doubts about becoming a mother. Frey's early arrival only seemed to worry her more. Turns out, I wasn't wrong. After she was discharged from the hospital and while I was with Freya in NICU, she packed up and left." His smile didn't quite reach his eyes now. "She sent me divorce papers a few weeks later, relinquished all her parental rights. It's been me and Freya on our own ever since."

"I am so sorry." Jana tried not to judge anyone, but walking away from a newborn baby, a frail one at that, was a difficult circumstance to understand.

"Don't be." He countered her comment easily. "Freya and I have done pretty okay. We've had our issues, of course," he added with a little laugh. "She's had her challenges and I'm not sure how Caroline would have handled them. Freya rallies through, just like she did when she was born. There were moments I wasn't sure I'd get her home. But she's kept me running ever since."

The affection, the absolute love she heard in Silas's voice melted through whatever nerves or unease Jana continued to feel. "She's lucky to have you."

"I'm the lucky one."

What it must feel like, to be loved like that. Jana cleared her throat. "Something tells me I should apologize for going along with the whole mermaid story."

"Not at all." He waved away her concern. "The idea was already in her head. Even if you hadn't played along she'd have stuck to it. She has a tendency to do that. To focus on things very intently. Pretending along with her kept a smile on her face."

She was happy to hear that. "Sometimes parents don't want their kids falling into fantasy."

"I don't like her to live there," Silas said. "But I also want her to be a child as long as she possibly can. That said, we'll keep the idea of mermaids in Nalani. Just to avoid any confusion once we're home."

She laughed. "Not a lot of mermaid activity in San Francisco?"

"Water's too cold. Or maybe you can tell me I'm wrong."

His smile warmed every corner of her heart. Her gaze skittered to the dessert table and found Sydney, Tehani and Daphne huddled into a group, watching them. The second they were spotted, they bashed into one another and nearly toppled like dominoes in their rush to disperse.

"I'm suddenly beginning to understand what it's like to have younger sisters," Silas muttered.

Jana grinned. "Would you like to take a walk?"

Relief swamped her and she stood up immediately. "Yes!" She'd agreed before her brain had kicked in to talk herself out of it. "A walk would be nice."

"Great." He pushed to his feet. "Let me just let Freya—"

Jana followed Silas's line of sight where she saw Freya and Cammie doing a kind of hula in their seats, laughing so loudly they could be heard over the music.

Jana touched a hand to Silas's arm as he looked shell-shocked.

"I guess maybe she doesn't need me."

"Oh, I think she always will," Jana assured him. "But we don't have to go far. We can stay

122 THE SINGLE DAD'S PROMISE

within sight of her." She just wanted to be closer to the water and hopefully drown out a bit of the crowd noise.

Jana pushed her bag onto her shoulder, walking beside Silas away from the party and toward the soothing tide. As the sounds faded, her mind cleared and she felt as if she could breathe easier. It occurred to her, as they made their way through the sand, that she didn't particularly feel the need to talk. As tingly as the thought of speaking to Silas had made her, there was a calm about being with him that eased her anxiety.

"So how long are you here for?" Silas's question broke the silence she was beginning to appreciate.

"I haven't decided." She shrugged off the idea of a time frame. "I recently took a leave of absence from work. I needed to," she added. "For... health reasons."

"Burnout?"

Jana tried to focus on the water but found the truth hovering behind her lips. "Recovery, actually." She stopped walking, pushed her bare feet deeper into the sand. Part of her just wanted to get it out in the open. "I finished radiation treatment for cancer earlier this year." She touched a nervous hand to her cropped hair.

She waited, expecting the usual *I'm so sorry* or other platitudes that always seemed to ring hollow. The things people said when they weren't sure what to say. It still surprised her, despite the number of folks who dealt with the illness, how difficult it was for most people to talk about.

"That must have been rough."

"It was." It took her a moment to realize he'd defied her expectations. "But I survived and I'm so thankful for that. I think things are finally getting back to normal for me." As normal as things were going to get. It felt cathartic, talking about it. Other than her doctors and nurses, there really hadn't been someone for her to confide in. She'd always regretted not being better at making friends, but she hadn't realized how much she wanted and needed them until she'd gotten sick. "While I was going through treatment, I told myself when I got on the other side, I was going to approach life differently. Get a little excitement going. Stop focusing so much on things that don't matter like routines and schedules and go on some adventures instead. See what the world has to offer." She waved a hand at the ocean. "Turns out Nalani landed at the top of my list."

"It's a good place to heal and start over," Silas said. "Are you okay now? So your treatment worked?"

"Mmm." She nodded, then followed his lead as he sat down on the sand, his back to the crowd. She stretched out her legs, leaned back on her hands. "I had my first six-month checkup right before I got on the plane. I practically drove from the lab right to the airport."

"Sounds like a good way to approach things. What about your family? Were they able to help—?"

"It's just me." Again, she expected the frown of sympathy, and this time received one. "My parents passed shortly after I graduated from college. I was a very-late-in-life baby, completely unexpected. But I'm glad I got those nineteen years with them." Sometimes the ten years that had since passed felt as if it had been no more than a few moments. Other times...

Other times it felt as if they'd been gone forever. That she'd been alone forever.

"Nineteen?" Silas inclined his head, and she could see him doing the math in his head. "You graduated from college at nineteen?"

"Eighteen, actually. But that was just for my BA."

"Just your...BA."

She could practically see the gears turning in his head as he did the math. "I didn't get my master's until I was twenty. In engineering," she added, when his confusion didn't seem to be clearing. "Then, of course, I got my PhD at twenty-three."

"Oh, right." He nodded despite the befuddlement on his face. "Sure. Okay. A PhD before most students even graduate college. And in engineering. Isn't that like...math?"

"In a way." She laughed, loving the turn the conversation had taken. He'd moved on from her illness reveal easily, as if he understood it was only a part of who she was. What a marvelous quality in a man. She curled her legs under her and faced him, finding herself quite intrigued.

"I failed algebra," he admitted. "Seriously, my high school advisors recommended I take intro to accounting to fulfill my math requirements, and so I could avoid geometry." He looked as if he were expecting her to argue. "I hope you don't find that strange or bad."

"Not at all." Her response triggered another one of those smiles of his. She really liked it when he smiled. "Math is a language of its own. It's like music in that way. It comes easier for some than others. I earned extra money in college tutoring students like you. So, thanks for that." She grinned.

"My parents would have gone bankrupt paying you to tutor me."

"We all have our strengths. Yours is helping people through difficult situations as a police officer. That comes easy for you whereas I'm much more comfortable away from the crowd." She glanced over her shoulder to the party that had far more people dancing, now that additional musicians had joined the ukulele players. But it

126 THE SINGLE DAD'S PROMISE

was Freya, Noah and Cammie who had taken center stage by creating their own hula line near their table. "It looks like Freya is coming out of her shell."

"She never ceases to impress or surprise me." Even as he spoke, Freya stopped and turned in circles, clearly looking for him. Cammie pointed toward them and Freya immediately waved, jumping up and down.

They waved back. Jana half expected Freya to come running down to join them, but instead she returned to her dancing.

"So what is it you do in the tech world with this engineering degree of yours?" Silas asked.

"Originally I was a consultant for companies who wanted to find the flaws in their products or programs." Or, put more simply, "My job was to try to break things and find weaknesses."

"Okay, now, that is a cool job."

"It was. For a while. Then I got bored and went out on my own to focus on my own ideas and inventions."

"Any success?"

"A few." She pursed her lips, considered. "I invented this thing called the WonderBubble."

"The—" His eyes went wide.

"Yeah, the WonderBubble." She held her hands out, indicating a sphere about the size of a soccer ball. "It's a portable projection device that incorporates personalized sounds, movement and light—"

"Oh, I am well acquainted with the Wonder-Bubble," he cut her off, the amazement on his face bolstering her confidence. "The original model came out about the time I brought Freya home from the hospital. The head of the NICU recommended it. I just bought the upgraded version a few months ago. It's my go-to when she can't sleep." He gaped at her. "You invented that?"

"I invented that." She sat up a bit straighter. "When I was still in school, I came across this article discussing the possible positive effects of light and sound on childhood anxiety. As someone who dealt with that myself I couldn't stop thinking about it. Eventually I focused on the beneficial effects of slow-moving patterns in soothing colors combined with stress-free acoustics. After a few years of working on a prototype, I filed for the patent and..." She shrugged. "That was that."

"So you aren't just an engineer, you're a genius."

"Luck played a part." She wasn't so confident as to not recognize that. "I came up with the right idea at the right time."

"And found a way to assist sensory-sensitive children," Silas said. "That's amazing. Didn't I recently read a number of states are acquiring specifically programmed ones for their elementary schools?"

"There's been talk." More than talk, actually. In a few weeks she'd have a new contract to sign.

"So, now you what, get to just sit around and think new things up?"

"I guess." The WonderBubble, and all the work that had gone into it, had blown all her creative currency. Her bank account and investment portfolio might be flush, but her inspiration trove was hovering around empty. Or, it had been until today. "I invested part of my proceeds into a tech startup a few years ago called HyperNova. They're doing a lot with medical devices and environmental applications." She could count on one hand the number of people she'd talked to about all this. "I guess I could have retired, but it felt wrong to walk away from something I'm good at, especially if I could come up with more things to help people. I just want to do the work, not run the place. Being a partner means I pick and choose what looks interesting to work on." Most of which were solitary projects. She didn't do very well with teams. She got lost too easily within herself to communicate well.

"And where does the art come in?" His narrowed eyes conveyed interest.

"The art?" It took her a moment to realize what he was talking about. "You mean the painting of Keane? That's just a way for me to relax. Gives one part of my brain a rest." While the other, more artistic side of her took over.

"Daddy!" Freya's call had them both turning. "Daddy, Mr. Mano needs to talk to you!" Freya raced toward them, her bag bouncing hard against her hip, sand flying up against her legs.

"Okay." Silas caught her as she dove into him. "Ugh." He pivoted her and dragged her into his lap, hugged his arms around her. "You're getting too big for this."

"No, I'm not." Freya beamed up at Jana, then looked out at the water. "Are you going to go swimming?"

Jana leaned in and whispered, "Not around this many people."

Freya giggled.

"Looks like I'm being summoned." Silas gestured to where Mano Iokepa and Sydney's husband, Theo, stood near the table where Freya and the other kids had been sitting. "Don't go anywhere, okay?" He didn't move at first. "I'll be back."

"Sure." She nodded. "Freya, would you like to keep me company?"

"Really?" The little girl looked as if she'd just been offered the crown to an underwater kingdom. "Can I, Daddy?"

"Sure. You stay with Miss Jana, though. No wandering off," Silas warned his daughter.

"I won't. Wanna see what's in my treasure bag?" Freya dropped into Silas's abandoned spot and dragged her bag in front of her. She

130   THE SINGLE DAD'S PROMISE

stopped and frowned up at her father. "It's a secret, Daddy."

"Right. Secret. Sorry." Silas shot Jana a grateful smile before he headed up the beach.

Jana watched him walk away. Her heart felt lighter than it had been in ages. But she didn't have time to dwell on it as Freya placed a plastic one-eyed chicken in her hands.

CHAPTER SIX

"GOOD TO FINALLY meet you in person." After detouring to grab another beer, Silas greeted Theo Fairfax with a hearty handshake. The birthday party was still going strong, if not getting stronger. People appeared to be having a fun time. "Nice shirt."

Mano ducked his chin to cover his amusement. The resort co-owner and hands-on manager was clearly in relaxed mode this evening, having ditched his usual dark suit for blue board shorts and a tattoo-exposing tank. The way he'd literally let his hair down put Mano Iokepa firmly in the arena of island royalty it was rumored he was descended from.

"I'm developing a style," Theo replied with a good-natured smile as he plucked the shirt with the pineapple frolicking with flamingos away from his chest. "Sydney said I'm starting to look like Benji's golf cart. Only thing that's missing is blinking lights."

"Bet you add some of those come Christmas," Mano teased.

Silas found himself looking for hints of the fish out of water Theo purported to be, but it was evident Mano had been right the other day. Theo, a good head shorter than Mano—but then, who wasn't?—was indeed in the midst of transforming into a local, right down to the easygoing expression on his lightly tanned face. His laid-back attitude pretty much fulfilled Silas's initial read of the man during their online meeting.

He felt a bit torn, however. He was here to help Mano out of a potential jam. But instead, all Silas could think was that he wished he was at the beach with Freya and Jana. Jana, he thought, as an unfamiliar bubble of anticipation lodged in his chest, who fascinated and intrigued and...appealed to him in more ways than he could count.

"Tehani emailed this to me before she headed over here." Mano pulled a folded-up piece of paper out of his shorts pocket. "Don Martin booked his excursions and tours through our concierge desk this afternoon as soon as he checked into his room."

"He hit the ground running," Theo commented. "He's probably evaluating how easily the two businesses work together."

"Probably." Silas scanned the list. Many of the activities were ones Silas would have considered had he been on a solo trip. "We've got the volcano and waterfall tour with Daphne…a helicopter trip with Sydney, dolphin watch and snorkel excursion with Keane on the *Nani Nalu*." Silas looked up at the other two men. "He's booked something with each person who works for Ohana. Scoping everyone out maybe?"

"That's how we see it," Theo confirmed. "Add to that he's got a hot stone massage scheduled at the spa." Mano glanced at his watch. "He should be there right now as a matter of fact. Then he's reserved a table for dinner at Southern Seas."

"So, covering all his bases. Nice job if you can get it." Silas could only imagine being paid to travel around, testing out potential investment properties for a company as big as GVI. "Looks like he's got something going each day of his stay."

"Now that isn't unusual," Mano said. "I just wish we knew what he was looking for."

"Weaknesses," Theo said before Silas could. "It's how they've taken over companies in the past. Find a soft spot to exploit and use it as leverage to gain the upper hand in negotiating. Unethical, perhaps, but not illegal."

"Theo's right on that," Silas agreed. "And they've stopped hiding their intentions. That said, you were right about their sneaky tactics and strategies, Theo." He'd spent a couple of his lunch hours at the coffee shop near GVI's office building "overhearing" employee conversations.

"We can make sneaky work for us," Mano said.

134   THE SINGLE DAD'S PROMISE

"What about Don Martin himself? What do we know about him?"

"Married." Silas had this bit memorized. "Two kids, both girls about ready to go to college. He's been with GVI for more than twenty years. He's vested for sure. And from all accounts, loyal."

"What do you remember about him, Theo?" Mano asked.

"Not a lot." Theo shrugged. "I wasn't exactly the social butterfly I am now." His cheeky grin had both men chuckling. "I spoke with Don a few times at the company holiday parties. He's a devoted family man. Adores his girls. Brags about them every chance he gets. Nice guy in that way." He paused, tilted his head. "Family's important to him."

"Good to know." Mano nodded. "He'd recognize you, you think? Even in costume?"

Theo knocked a gentle fist into Mano's shoulder. "Absolutely. Everyone at GVI knows I quit my job to move here. It would be impossible for him not to expect to run into me." He stopped, considered. "I wouldn't be surprised if a lot of people at GVI hold me responsible for the buyout deal falling through. Could be one reason they chose Martin to do recon. He's not in a position to be tempted away."

"Is that what Sydney did?" Mano asked innocently.

"Yup." And Theo didn't look bothered by the

ANNA J. STEWART 135

idea at all. "If anything, like you told Mano, he has a vested interest in keeping GVI afloat. Huh." Theo's brow furrowed.

"Careful," Mano warned Silas. "That's his thinking face."

"It is indeed." Theo appeared to be puzzling things out. "I think there's a way to use me to our advantage. Plant me directly in his path while he's here. Make it seem as though I'm keeping an eye on him while in actuality—"

"Silas can slide in and do the keeping an eye on." Mano grinned. "Sneaky. Smart. I like it."

"So do I," Silas agreed. "Just remember, I'm not in any legal capacity here. He crosses a line, it's not up to me to step in."

"No, it's the police chief's." Mano gestured to a dark-haired, island-tanned man sitting at a table nearby, his arm slipped around the woman beside him.

The relaxed expression on his face seemed to be aimed directly at his companion, a woman wearing a turquoise bikini top and long blond braids all the way down her back. There was a soft-sided beach-style bag tucked under one arm that appeared to be... Silas blinked. "Is that a cat?" A black cat with bright, lively eyes.

"What?" Mano glanced over. "Oh, yeah, that's Namaka. He goes everywhere with Jordan. Became a sort of office mascot over at Ohana."

Nothing would surprise Silas anymore. "This

136 THE SINGLE DAD'S PROMISE

might be a good time to introduce yourself to Chief Malloy," Mano suggested.

"Ah, I think I'll wait a bit." No way was he going to interrupt what looked like an enjoyable moment for the couple. And their companion.

"Jordan won't mind. Neither will Alec," Mano assured him.

"I take it Tehani has added me to the tours Martin's booked on?" Silas asked.

"She has. The volcano and waterfall tour is up first. Early start, though. Eight a.m. tomorrow. And it's pretty much all day."

"That means I need to make a decision about what to do with Freya. Speaking of…" Silas turned and located Freya and Jana near the shore.

Something inside of him shifted at the sight of them, sitting together, meticulously going through all the treasures Freya had collected over the years. He was also baffled. Freya had never attached herself to someone so easily and eagerly. Maybe it was the fantastical idea of Jana's imaginary mermaid identity, or maybe…maybe Freya had begun her own transformation since they'd arrived in Nalani.

A high-pitched horn blared from beyond the trees behind them. It sounded almost like someone was blowing on an out-of-tune conch shell. A few moments later, a golf cart whizzed into sight, screeching to a halt right at the end of the beach path.

The cart's green canopy had been turned into what looked like a nightclub ceiling, with blinking lights and a collection of miniature, sparkling disco ball ornaments above the driver's head.

"Tell me he's not wearing a white leisure suit," Mano deadpanned despite the wide smile curving his mouth.

"Wouldn't put it past him," Theo countered as Benji Tatupu climbed out from behind the wheel and helped his passenger out of her seat. "The last of the entertainment has arrived."

There was no leisure suit. Only very knobby knees on display, Silas noticed. The celebratory mood only grew more festive as the two were welcomed with cheers and laughter.

"You were right," Silas said as the seniors maneuvered through the crowd like royalty being welcomed at court. "Benji looks exactly how I remember him."

The spry woman on his arm wore a neon pink velour tracksuit that only made the white of her coiffed hair that much brighter. She, like her escort, was on the short side. She carried a boxy wicker bag tucked into the crook of her arm. But it was the smile on her face and the kick in her step that had Silas smiling along with everyone else. "Pippy, I presume?"

"Couldn't be anyone else," Theo confirmed as Marella and Keane weaved among their guests to greet Marella's grandmother and her island boyfriend, Benji. "Buckle up. Since they chose to make an entrance, something's about to go down."

Benji could have stepped right out of Silas's memories. On the lean and stooped side, with thinning gray hair and bowlegs, he wore clothes that hung a bit large, but the life inside of them had its own energy about it. The years might have slowed the man down, but they certainly hadn't diminished his excitement for living—or his penchant for making an entrance.

"We didn't think you were coming until the weekend." Marella's voice carried over the softened volume of the music as she hugged her grandmother. "Why didn't you tell us? We would have picked you up at the airport."

"Didn't want to spoil the surprise." Pippy held both hands out for Keane's, and she pulled him down for a kiss and hug. "Happy birthday!"

Silas might have been standing a few feet away, but it was impossible to miss the affection on Keane's face. "Thank you, Pippy. Best present I could have gotten."

"Not done yet," Pippy announced, beaming, so that even Silas was bracing for the unexpected. "Benji and I are having a promise ceremony!" She turned her hand over and showed off a sparkler of a ring glinting against the light from the torches. "Surprise!"

"What?" Marella's gasp of shock was swallowed up by the cries and cheers of the crowd.

"What's a…" She turned confused eyes on Keane. "Do you know what she's talking about?"

"It's something us old folks are doing these days," Pippy said, as if she'd been expecting this question. "It's a commitment ceremony without all the legalities. Don't want to be giving up those benefits I get from your grandfather," she said in a serious tone. "He worked a lot of years for his retirement. This way I get to be with Benji in the lifestyle we are accustomed to."

"And…you're okay with this?" Marella asked a proud-looking Benji as he slipped an arm around Pippy's shoulders.

"Whatever she wants, whatever makes her happy, I'm all for." He squeezed her tight and Silas heard Pippy giggle. "Plus, it means she's moving here permanently!"

"Oh, boy." Mano ducked his head and laughed, heading back to their table and away from the congratulatory swarm. "Alert the National Weather Service. Pippy Benoit is coming to town, permanently." He glanced at Theo. "You knew, didn't you?"

Silas had to admit, he didn't see a hint of surprise on the other man's face.

"I suspected," Theo confessed as they took a seat.

Everyone else was caught up in the party and the added reason to celebrate. When Silas looked back to Jana and Freya, it was obvious the new noise had captured their attention, but neither seemed interested in returning to the fray.

"I spotted Benji in Sky & Earth the other day," Theo said. "When I was picking up a birthday present for my sister. He was examining every ring on display. I guess you're never too old to find your perfect fit."

"Says the man who married his perfect fit on New Year's," Mano reminded him. "Flaunting wedded bliss doesn't suit you, Theo."

"Get used to it." Theo leaned his arms on the table and continued watching Pippy and Benji. "You don't ever think about getting married again?"

"As I informed Silas when he asked me the same question," Mano said, using a voice that had Silas wishing he was anywhere else. "I do not. I think we can all agree I am not marriage material."

Theo switched his attention to Silas, who held up both hands. "I'm on the shelf. Only good thing to come out of my marriage is sitting right over there." He pointed to Freya, who was on her feet showing off what could only be described as a very awkward hula. "I don't need anything or anyone else."

But even as he said it, Jana turned her head and his gaze met hers. She smiled and waved before focusing again on an insistent Freya. That bubble that had been bouncing in his chest burst and filled him with a kind of wonder he hadn't thought he was capable of feeling.

Silas couldn't reason it. Couldn't rationalize the odd, unfamiliar thoughts that shot through his mind, the tingles that sparked through his system whenever he looked at her. Love at first sight wasn't a thing; even entertaining the notion seemed to fly in the face of reason. Was it possible...

No. It wasn't.

But his baseless determination to cling to that certainty did leave him wondering if maybe, just maybe, he was wrong.

"AND THIS I FOUND at the playground in Golden Gate Park." Freya dropped back to her knees and dug out a ragged feather from her bag and placed it on the sand beside her other "treasures." "I'm keeping it in case a bird needs one."

Elbow resting on her bent knee, Jana leaned her chin into her hand, unable to keep the smile off her face. She had never been so utterly entertained in her life. The unfiltered innocence of the little girl in front of her was just...well, it was absolute perfection.

"That's a very good idea. And very nice of you, Freya."

"Thank you." Freya didn't look away from her bag. Already she'd pulled out a miniature snow globe featuring a teeny-tiny castle surrounded

142 THE SINGLE DAD'S PROMISE

with glitter, two worn postcards showing images of cable cars, a puka shell necklace that she must have acquired here, a number of buttons Freya declared had been left behind by fairies, a small compass that didn't work, and an eraser in the shape of a butterfly. "Winnie keeps an eye on all of this in the bag."

Jana blinked down at the plastic chicken in her lap. "Does she? Well." She picked it up again. "It seems she's doing a good job."

"She's one of my best friends," Freya declared. "I couldn't bring Roscoe because he didn't fit in our suitcase. He's a moose."

Of course he was. "I'm sure Roscoe is having a good time while you're on your trip."

"I hope so." Freya sighed as only a five-year-old could. "I'm running out of room in my bag." She pulled it up, peered inside, which wasn't difficult considering the worn state of it.

"You've had it quite a while, haven't you?" The frayed strap and straining fabric, once again, had Jana wishing she had a quick fix.

"I've had it forever," Freya said seriously as she carefully replaced every item back inside. "I take it everywhere."

"Even to school?"

Freya shrugged. "When I go." Something in her voice had Jana paying close attention.

"You don't like school?"

"No. The other kids are mean." She dug her fingers into the sand. "They don't like me."

Hence Freya's dismay at having made a friend in Cammie Townsend.

"Maybe they just don't know you yet," Jana suggested.

"They called me names." Freya's face scrunched and Jana's heart seized. "I heard one of them say I was weird."

No wonder she felt such an instant connection to Freya. Jana had been called that and far worse her entire life. She'd been an anomaly since birth. Completely unexpected, a genuine surprise baby, then by registering off the charts with her thinking and reasoning abilities. Being in a classroom with kids who were four, sometimes five years older than she was had tagged as gifted by her teachers and, well, weird by her classmates. These days she supposed she'd be considered neurodivergent. She suspected Freya was as well, given what Jana was seeing. They, and so many others just saw—and experienced—the world a bit differently from others.

"Daddy wouldn't tell me what that means." The hope in her eyes showed she expected Jana to do so. "But it sounds bad."

Putting aside any concern she might have about overstepping, Jana looked down at Winnie. "Weird just means you're different from everyone else. But you know what? Weird is okay, Freya. I promise it isn't a bad thing at all."

Freya's eyes narrowed. "They why did they call me that?"

"Because sometimes kids don't know how to deal with something or someone, so they say whatever they think will hurt." Kids teasing each another was one of the world's greatest mysteries. It didn't matter how far humanity had evolved, it was one of those constants most children had to struggle through. "You know what I think weird means?"

Freya shook her head.

"To me, it's a compliment. It means you stand out. That you don't fall in with the crowd. That you are uniquely you. Trust me, Freya." It felt good to be able to share this with someone who needed to hear it. "I was called weird all the time when I was growing up."

"You were?" The awe on her face was something Jana would never forget.

"I was. I went to school with kids who were a lot older than I was and I knew a lot of answers to questions none of them did. Because I lived in here a lot." She tapped a finger against her temple. "It's scary, being around a bunch of new people who aren't like you, and I never felt like I fit in. So, yeah." She really hoped she was getting through. "I was definitely called weird. But you know what my dad gave me one day?" She unzipped her bag to dig out her wallet, then pulled the cloth Scout-like badge from where she kept it safe. "He gave me this."

"What is it?"

Jana placed the fabric in Freya's cupped hands. "That is my Bee Brave badge. He drew it up and my mother sewed it." It was a little messy—her mother wasn't a stellar seamstress and there were loose threads and overrun stitching, but it was the closest thing she had to a treasure. "My dad drew this silly little bee over the word brave. And here, he added, *Always Unique. Always Loved.*" Even as she said the words, her throat tightened with emotion. She could recall so easily the day her parents had presented this to her, with a pseudo ceremony and everything. She'd always known how much they loved her, but that was the first time she remembered *feeling* it. "My dad always said I should wear being weird as a badge of honor, but I needed a reminder that I could be brave. That I should be brave. So, I carry this with me. And I have, every single day since."

"It's very pretty." The faded, gold-and-yellow fabric was thinning and aged. But to Jana it was as bright and shiny as the day her parents had given it to her. Freya handed it back so Jana could put it away again.

"You shouldn't try to run away from being different, Freya," Jana said as gently as she could. "You should only be utterly and completely you."

"Who else would I be?"

Jana laughed, falling a little bit in love. "Who indeed?" She reached out, touched the girl's braid that had fallen over one shoulder. "The world needs a lot more Freyas if you ask me."

"And more Janas, too," a male voice said.

Jana startled, not used to being snuck up on. Between the ocean and Freya, she'd forgotten everything and everyone else existed. Silas was standing there, balancing three small paper plates.

"Sorry to interrupt." He tried to lift his hands. "I bring cake."

"Oh." Just like that Jana's appetite returned. She accepted one of the plates with a smile. "That was nice of you."

"I'm a nice guy. Freya."

"Thank you, Daddy." Freya sat back down in the sand and Silas joined them. "I like cake and chocolate is my favorite," she told Jana.

"Mine, too," Jana agreed as she forked up a bite. She closed her eyes as the smooth, sweet chocolate entered her system. "I'm beginning to think everything tastes better in Nalani." Must be something about the salt air and warm breezes that accentuated every single flavor.

"You're not wrong." Silas kept an eye on Freya as she shoved a large chunk into her mouth. "Careful, Freya." He reached over and wiped a smudge of chocolate off her face as she grinned up at him.

"What was all the commotion about earlier?" Jana asked as she ate, resisting the urge to scarf the entire piece in a two bites.

"Benji and Pippy arrived and announced their... well, I guess it was kind of an engagement." He shook his head. "Have you ever heard of a promise ceremony?"

"No."

"According to them, it's something a lot of the older folks are doing. It's not a wedding, per se, but a public commitment thing. Emotional, not legal." He chuckled. "On the bright side, Benji was so distracted he forgot to call me Shark Boy."

"Other people called you Shark Boy, Daddy. I heard them."

"Yes, they did." That blush on his cheeks returned full force.

"I'm done." Freya shoved her half-finished cake at her father. "I want to go look for sea treasures."

"Okay. Just stay where I can see you, please."

"Will you watch my treasure bag?" she asked Jana and earned a look of surprise from her father.

"I'd be happy to." Jana pulled the bag—along with Winnie the chicken—closer.

Freya bounced away, not stopping until her sandaled feet splashed in the frothy tide.

"Thank you."

Silas's voice, the words he spoke, floated over Jana like a warm breeze as she ate her dessert. "For what?"

148   THE SINGLE DAD'S PROMISE

"For making her feel not so alone."

"She's not alone." She'd never spoken truer words. "She has you."

"Yes, she does. But that doesn't mean I always understand where she's coming from. I try to." He finished Freya's cake and set the empty plate on top of his own. "There are times when the fear I felt when she was born comes back. I felt so helpless watching her fight to live. I just want to make things easier for her. Fix things for her."

"You sound like my dad." Jana resisted the impulse to touch his hand. "But he eventually figured out he could do one thing well—be there for me. Just like you are for Freya. Don't worry." She looked over to where Freya was digging into the sand. "She'll find her way. Might be a bit bumpy sometimes, but she'll get there."

"She's already come through so much. Sometimes it's like those weeks she was in the NICU were the easy days."

During her research stage for the Wonder-Bubble, Jana had learned enough to remember there were a plethora of issues preemies faced long after they were discharged from the hospital. Not only physical, but emotional and psychological as well. "She's just her own person, separate from you and how you think," she said, trying to find some words of reassurance. "She sees things differently, experiences them differently. None of it's wrong. It's just...her."

"Something else your dad told you?" Silas asked.

"Pretty much." She shrugged. "Both my parents had to adjust to who I was. On top of being a complete surprise, they didn't expect me to be reading at two years old." She smiled, recalling photographs from those years. "I skipped over so much of the predictable development stages. My first day of school was third grade. I was about the age Freya is now."

"I can't even imagine." It was clear by his expression he was being truthful.

"But my parents also had each other, so they could tag-team me. Another person gives you other perspectives, more options. It's a lot more difficult when you're on your own."

"Tell me about it." He shook his head, following her gaze to the water. "I'm just never sure if I'm making the right choices for her."

Well, she was in this deep. She might as well take the plunge into something that was none of her business. "She's old enough to participate in those choices. And smart enough, from what I've seen."

"You think?"

"I know. Having some control helps build confidence and can reduce her fear responses. If she has a part in deciding, then she learns to process the experience another way."

"So, for instance…" He shifted his legs, seem-

150 THE SINGLE DAD'S PROMISE

ingly taking in every word she was saying. "I've got to take one of those Ohana tours tomorrow morning."

"Oh?" Jana's breath caught in her chest. "Which one?"

"The volcano and waterfall guided tour with Daphne. That's what I was talking to Mano and Theo about earlier."

"Let me guess." She nodded. "Surveillance duty?"

"Yeah. I mean, it's not going to be like the guy from GVI is doing anything bad, but we want to know what he's looking for while he's here."

"I envision him scribbling down notes in a little black book." Jana laughed and Silas joined in.

"Wouldn't be surprised. But the tour isn't suitable for Freya, which means I need to put her some place safe." Clearly, the idea wasn't sitting very well with him.

"So give her some options." The solution seemed simple to Jana. "You have them, share them with her."

"But what if she—?"

"Makes a mistake?" Jana shrugged. "Then she'll factor that in the next time she makes a choice. Don't underestimate her, Silas. She's far more capable than you probably realize."

"I know she's smart." There was a hint of defense in his voice.

"All kids are smart," Jana countered. "Each has

their own strengths. In their own way. Trust me. Trust her." She inclined her chin toward Freya. "Give it a try."

He didn't look convinced.

"I'm not a parent," she said even as that pang of longing hit low in her stomach. "But I've been where Freya is. I've been different in a world that doesn't quite see you for who and what you are. The worst thing that happens is she makes the wrong choice and she doesn't make it again. You'll be there to catch her. That's what really matters."

"You should have gone into teaching," Silas said. "Or child therapy. That's a lovely sentiment and observation."

"It's the scientist in me," she said, trying to keep the conversation light.

"Well, let's give it a shot." He turned that amazing smile of his toward her again, and this time it was on full, heart-stopping wattage. "While I've got good backup."

Panic almost seized her. "Oh, I—"

"Freya!" Silas waved an irritated Freya over.

"I didn't mean—"

"I know," Silas said softly. "But I need to do this before I chicken out."

"Daddy." Freya slogged her way through the sand, the annoyed look on her face reminding Jana all over again how much she admired the

152 THE SINGLE DAD'S PROMISE

determined girl. "I'm digging for seashells for my treasure bag."

"You can get back to that in a second. I need to make some…" He broke off when Jana cleared her throat. "Ah, right. Tomorrow, I have to work, so I need you to decide where you would like to spend the day."

She dropped to her knees, a frown marring her forehead. "Can't I go with you?"

"Not this time, sweetheart. But Mr. Mano has given us some options." He glanced at Jana, who nodded in encouragement. "You could go to the pre-K class at the same school where Cammie and Noah go."

"Would I be in their class?" The hope in Freya's eyes dimmed when Silas shook his head.

"I'm afraid not. But they'd be nearby."

Freya wrinkled her nose.

"I have a list of babysitters I could call," Silas suggested. "You could stay at the cottage while I'm working."

Freya caught her lower lip in her teeth. Nothing had hit yet.

"Or…" He shifted his tone, an indication that he was about to offer his preferred option. "There's a daycare facility at the resort." He'd made a quick stop after their trip to Luanda's to touch base with the two retired teachers who oversaw the children. "They'd have fun craft activities and even a visit to the kiddie pool. It's pretty new and Mr.

Mano would probably really like to know what you think about it."

"Could I stay with you?" Freya turned those pleading eyes on Jana. "I can be really quiet. I won't bother you."

Jana tilted her head, unexpected affection cocooning her. The very idea Freya felt safe with her was like a kind of dream come true. How tempting the idea was to simply say yes. "I'm not sure what I have going on tomorrow. And you know what? You have a couple of really good options to choose from." She could already feel the connection strengthening between them. Getting caught up too deeply with this man and his awesome little girl would only bring her heartbreak, and she'd had plenty of that already.

"Oh." Freya sighed. "I thought you liked me."

"Freya." Silas shook his head. "You know better than that."

"I do like you, Freya," Jana insisted, honestly. "But this is something I think I need to do. You see I'm working on healing my heart." How to put this so a five-year old could understand, especially when Jana still had difficulty with it herself. "It's been a very sad time lately and while I would love to be with you tomorrow, it just isn't possible. I've made a promise to myself that I just can't break"

"How did your heart get hurt?" Freya looked shocked.

154 THE SINGLE DAD'S PROMISE

Silas seemed about to suggest his daughter not ask, but he looked to Jana, as if acknowledging the decision was in her hands.

"I've been sick and that made my heart hurt. But getting better is why I came to Nalani," Jana told her. "So I could learn how to be happy again. And you know what? Meeting you and your daddy and all these people in Nalani, that's really helped."

"It has?" Freya's expression of doubt matched that of her father's from earlier.

"Yes, absolutely," Jana insisted. "But it sounds to me like you have to make a decision about where you want to spend tomorrow."

Freya ducked her head, stuck her finger in the sand and began drawing circles. "I don't want to go to a new school again."

"Okay," Silas agreed. "That leaves you with the day care center or a babysitter."

Apparently, this decision was a whopper to make because Freya remained silent for several minutes. "Mr. Mano made the day care center?"

"He...did."

Jana understood Silas's confused confirmation. It was as good a way to explain it as any, she supposed.

"I guess I'll go there, then." Freya heaved a heavy sigh. "When will you be back?"

"Before dinnertime," Silas said. "And they will have my phone number if you really need to talk to me. Thank you, Freya. For making this decision."

Freya still didn't look particularly pleased. "You won't forget about me, will you, Daddy? You won't leave me there and go away?"

Jana's heart skidded to a stop. *Why on earth...?*

"No, baby girl." Silas reached out and drew her into his arms, leading Jana to believe this wasn't the first time she'd made a comment like that. "I will never, ever leave you." He pressed a kiss against Freya's temple, his gaze meeting Jana's suddenly tear-filled one. "That is a promise. Now why don't you go find a treasure or two? It's almost bedtime."

CHAPTER SEVEN

"YOU DIDN'T HAVE TO leave the party with us," Silas told Jana a short while later as they strolled down the beach toward her cottage—and his. "I didn't really want to leave myself, but I need to keep Freya to a pretty steady sleep schedule." He tossed one of his cheeky grins in Jana's direction. "Her WonderBubble didn't fit in the suitcase." The shy smile he received in response sent a bit of a jolt of anticipation and attraction zinging through him.

"You're a good dad."

"Thanks. Some days it's harder than others."

Freya ran ahead of them, treasure bag held securely at her side as she darted in and out of the lapping waves, keeping her eyes open for those all-important shells. Selfishly, he was happy to saunter along the sand, stretching out the time he had with Jana. To say she intrigued him was an understatement. She was beautiful and funny and quiet and spirited and...

Try as he might, he couldn't recall the last time he'd been so enamored and had to hold himself back from thinking anything might come of that zinging. Maybe he was into the comfort of having a non-work-related adult conversation with someone new for a change. Or maybe...

Maybe, mermaid or not, there was a touch of emotional magic where Jana Powell was concerned. He just felt...better and happier around her.

"Thanks for your suggestion about Freya making some decisions for herself. She isn't the only one who needs to be pushed out of their comfort zone."

"In that, I'm becoming an expert." He could hear the laugh in her voice.

"It's a challenge not to just give in, to just take over and do things myself when something is difficult for her, or when she's struggling."

"Well, like I said before, I'm not a parent," Jana said easily, kicking playfully at the sand. "But in my experience when I was a child, how you deal with those situations makes all the difference. If you don't mind me saying?" She glanced at him, uncertainty shining in those silver-blue eyes of hers. "You didn't seem surprised when she asked if you were going to leave her behind."

"I wasn't." A wave of anger and resentment surged inside of him. "Some of the kids at her pre-K overheard the teachers talking about Freya's mom not being in the picture. They'd already decided that Freya was—"

"Weird?" Jana frowned.

"Yeah." He hated that word. "And you know how mean kids can be. Anything that isn't within their experience either scares them or turns them into terrors." It was the kindest way he could think to convey his feelings about that particularly nasty day. "One of the kids went so far as to tell Freya it was her fault her mother left. As you saw, I still haven't quite managed to convince her he was wrong."

"But he was wrong." Jana stopped walking, caught his arm and brought him to a stop beside her. "Your wife deciding to leave is on her, Silas. It's not on anyone else. You have nothing to feel guilty about."

"Don't I?" He was the one who had encouraged them to have kids. He was the one who wanted the full picture of a happy family. He was the one who hadn't seen what was truly going on in his own marriage.

"You do not." Her grip tightened, as if pushing him to not only hear her, but understand and accept what she was saying. "Blaming yourself for her leaving doesn't do you or Freya any good. Trust me. It's your ex-wife's loss not being a part of your life. Not being a mother to your beautiful little girl." There was a hint of sadness in her tone now, a longing he couldn't help but pick up on. "So many people would give everything to have something so incredible. But it was her decision to go."

He looked down to where her touch warmed him, seeped through him, along with her words of comfort and support. Seeing her, looking at her as the last of the sun's rays disappeared behind the shimmering ocean, he found himself entranced by her. "You're very good at cutting to the heart of the matter."

"My mother called it being filterless." She rolled her eyes and laughed, pulling her hand free and leaving him feeling slightly diminished. When she tucked her hair behind her ear, he realized it was a nervous habit she had. Had he done that? If so, it sure bolstered his confidence.

"You say that like it's a bad thing," he countered.

"Oh, trust me." Jana nodded. "It certainly can be. Personally, I just don't like wasting time on beating around the bush. At some point you're going to tell the truth, so just get it out. Only way to move on."

It wasn't the first time he'd heard the scientist in her: the practical application of societal interaction. And he liked it. A lot. Jana leaned into logic and practicality without the pretense of platitudes. And that, he realized, was incredibly attractive.

"Would you maybe like to have dinner with me sometime this week?" The question popped out of his mouth before his brain had a chance to fully develop the idea.

She shrugged and chuckled a little, even as her

cheeks went pink against the sunset. "I'd like very much to have dinner with you and Freya."

Freya. Right. "Or possibly just me? If I can find someone to watch her, of course."

"Oh." She blinked as if surprised. He'd hoped she wouldn't have been shocked to find out that he wanted to spend more time with her. Or maybe her scientist brain was only tuned to being a scientist and there was no room for anything else. "I, um, well, sure." There was that chuckle again, one tinged with uncertainty, a little embarrassment, and, if he wasn't reading too much into it, excitement. "That sounds nice."

Even as she flinched at her own response, Silas's heart inflated to the point of nearly lifting out of his chest.

"Okay, then." They started walking again, but Silas slowed the pace to delay their arrival at her cottage until the absolute last second. "I just need a day or so to figure out this whole surveillance gig I've got going for Mano."

"What is there to figure out exactly?"

"I don't want to stand out, being this single guy on a tour that's probably filled with honeymooners and families."

"But…" Her brow furrowed when she glanced at him. "Isn't the guy you're watching on his own?"

"Exactly. And he's there to investigate in some way, hence an ulterior motive. I don't want him thinking I have one as well."

"Oh. Huh." She nodded, as if processing the information. "Did you learn that working undercover?"

"I never made it to undercover." It was still a sore spot for him. He hadn't become a cop to work behind a desk all day, but how could he complain when he had the child he'd always hoped for? "But it is something they train you for. Depending on the situation, you go in with a partner, someone who has your back. But it's not like this guy is dangerous. The only weapon he's probably carrying is a tablet computer and mean typing skills."

Jana's cottage came into view as they rounded the wide corner on the beach and Silas silently bid farewell to this private time with Jana.

"Freya!" She'd fallen a short distance behind, caught up playing in the foamy surf as the tide answered the rising moon's call. "Come say goodnight to Miss Jana, please." The fact he could see his daughter's face fall, even from a distance, told Silas that Jana had had the same effect on Freya as she'd had on him. Well, maybe he'd been affected a bit differently.

Freya met them as they reached the neat white porch steps, then quickly jumped behind her father and peeked around him as she pointed. "What's that?"

"What's what?" Silas reached back to touch his daughter's shoulder and followed her line of sight. "Oh. Well. Looks like you have company, Jana."

Jana went to the porch railing and stroked a gentle finger down the head and back of a bright blue-and-green lizard. "This is my roommate, Noodles. It's okay," she assured a still uncertain Freya. "He's very friendly. He's lived here a long time, from what Sydney told me."

"You aren't scared?" Freya sounded as if she couldn't quite believe this was true. "But he's..."

"He's different," Jana said in a way that had Freya instantly relaxing. "He's nice company in the mornings but probably because he likes the bowl of fruit that I feed him. Supposedly, he has a girlfriend, but I haven't met her just yet." Jana looked over at Freya. "She's a lot more shy than Noodles."

Freya stepped around Silas, but still kept her distance, fist clenched in the hem of Silas's shirt.

"Do you want to come closer?" Jana held out her hand.

Noodles inclined his head, first in one direction, then the other, bulbous, bulging eyes blinking at Silas. He was kind of cute in a reptilian way, Silas supposed. And he certainly wasn't very big, measuring maybe six or eight inches in length. His pop of color against the white and yellow of the cottage was no doubt what made him stand out to Freya.

Freya released her hold on Silas's shirt but

pulled him along with her as she took a step forward, then another. And another. Noodles watched every move Freya made and even cast a confirming look at Jana before he bowed his head toward Freya's trembling fingers.

"Just be gentle," Jana suggested. "Nice and easy."

Freya touched her index finger to Noodles's head, an uneasy smile spreading across her face as she stroked his scales.

"He feels funny. Oh!" She jumped back when Noodles scampered away, peering at all of them from his new perch on the side of a post. "I didn't mean to scare him."

"It's okay," Jana told her. "You're new to him, too. You were very nice, though. He'll remember you next time." Jana pointed to her screen door. "Well, I guess this is me."

"I guess so." Silas wasn't in any hurry to leave, but Freya was rubbing her eyes, a sure sign she was starting to crash, and a tired Freya was not a happy Freya. "I'll be in touch? About dinner?" The more he thought about it, the more excited he became about making it happen.

Jana nodded. The smile was back on her face as she said, "Yes, please. Good night, Freya."

Silas exhaled the breath he'd been holding.

"Night!" Freya waved and tucked her hand in Silas's. Together, they swung their arms and laughed about the best parts of their day until they got to their own cabin nearby.

JANA HADN'T SLEPT IN since she'd come to Nalani. Not even on the days when she didn't have something booked early with Ohana Odysseys. Today she found herself blinking awake at dawn, feeling unexpectedly excited. Every night she was here she slept better than the night before.

She stretched, dislodging the lightweight blanket as she scooted up against the carved wooden headboard. The two windows of her bedroom faced the sparkling ocean, the sun's rays kissing the waves as they tumbled in and over the shore.

Kissing. She covered her mouth to stop the giggle from escaping. It had been the only thing missing from her walk home with Silas, although she had the distinct impression that had Freya not been with them, he would have kissed her. And she wanted him to. Her skin tingled at the thought.

"I could wake up to this every single day," she whispered to the universe and closed her eyes for a moment of silence and gratitude. It was a habit she'd developed during her treatment. Coming face-to-face with her own mortality had changed things for the better. The small stuff didn't stress her out the way it used to. Filtering what was important to her had become easier and what she appreciated and longed for...

She swallowed hard. Some thoughts needed to be stopped before they took her where she didn't want to go. It had been hard, accepting the idea of never having the kind of family she'd always thought she'd have one day. She'd just assumed she'd have...time.

It turned out she didn't. And now there was no going back. That wasn't possible.

"What you do have is your life," she reminded herself as the melancholy threatened to descend. "Not to mention a date in the near future." At least, she thought it was a date. She sat up, ran her hand up and down her suddenly chilly arms. She was shivering from the anticipation, she told herself as she shoved out of bed and headed into the shower. Soon she was lathering up with the locally made soap from Fresh Mojo that smelled like an island summer—crisp and fresh and intoxicating.

Once upon a time, the shower had been her coping mechanism when the creative spark went dormant, or, in her most recent case, had burned out. She relaxed so quickly just letting the water sluice over her. Lately, she'd become used to her mind being blank. In recent months, she'd resisted her desire for a recharge. It was why it took her more than a moment to recognize that her brain was beginning to fire.

She quickly ducked her head under the spray to finish, slammed off the water. She stood there for a second, gripping the faucet handle, find-

166   THE SINGLE DAD'S PROMISE

ing it hard to catch her breath. Thoughts spun at an impossible rate, at a speed that had her both smiling and sobbing as she struggled to keep up.

Jana grabbed a towel, dried her hair fast before she draped it around herself and scooted out of the shower. She couldn't get to her notebook fast enough. The notebook that, until yesterday, had remained as blank as her mind for the past six months. Pen in hand, she scribbled down ideas, including a sketch with arrows and notations and...

She had to blink away the tears of happiness as her hand flew over the page. It was only after she felt satisfied she'd purged all the ideas onto the paper that she grabbed her phone, snapped a picture, then emailed it to her assistant. Stepping back from the counter, she hugged her arms around herself, felt the water dripping down her legs onto the bare floor.

It took five minutes for her phone to ring and she answered the call instantly.

"Connie?"

"What kind of sabbatical are you on that you've come up with this?" Connie Fabray's voice sounded familiar and comforting. And, if Jana wasn't mistaken, more than a little relieved.

"Inspiration struck. What do you think?"

"What do I think?"

Jana rolled her eyes. Most times Connie's

sense of humor flummoxed Jana. Sometimes to the point of frustration. But they worked well together. Connie had earned her degree in engineering just two years ago, but it had been her organizational talents that had Jana signing her up. Connie kept a good work-life balance, something Jana wanted to try now that so much in her life had changed. A benefit of being one of the bosses. Jana had the freedom to hire whomever she wanted for whatever she needed.

"Well?" Jana prodded when Connie didn't continue. She knew it was a good idea, but her confidence had taken a major hit when it came to believing in herself. This one, though...

"I think whatever you're doing in Hawai'i you should keep doing. Why didn't we think of a travel-size WonderBubble before?"

"Because kids don't travel." Jana had already asked and answered that question and dozens of others. "Until they do." Somehow Silas's comment about not being able to pack Freya's home unit had snuck into her subconscious. "We need to get the team started on this now. A reduction in size by at least seventy-five percent. That's the goal."

"Yeah, I saw that. Ambitious."

"You bet. And I want a travel case designed specifically for it. Along with charging cords and

168   THE SINGLE DAD'S PROMISE

a long battery life." Her mind raced. "Eight hours minimum."

"Oookay." Connie hedged.

"I want a prototype in two months. Max."

"Two…okay, now I really need to know what's in the water over there. Two months?"

"Two months. Tell Clark I want to pull people for this. We need to be up and ready for production by the holidays. Halloween. So it's ready to go for Black Friday and the shopping rush."

"All right. I'll go talk to him as soon as I hang up. Does this mean…" Connie trailed off. "Does this mean you're coming back to work soon?"

"I don't know." And she didn't. But what she did know was that the fog in her brain was finally clearing and her mind was back to firing if not on all cylinders, then certainly, on most. "Maybe. We'll see what happens down the road."

"You didn't make any note of a name. We're going to have to start differentiating each model from one another."

"I don't care what we call the original," Jana said as inspiration struck again. "But the travel model is going to be called Freya." Who else could it be named after than the little girl who had inspired the idea in the first place?

"Interesting. Okay, making a note. Anything else?"

"Yes, but I'll follow through on that with an email. Let me know when Clark is on board. Oh, tell him I want Hannah and Emma on the team for sure. Anyone else is fine, but I want them on lead."

"Understood. You've been having too much Kona coffee, haven't you?"

"Not a drop." She'd found something far better. "But don't worry. I'll bring you back a lifetime supply. Talk soon." She hung up, clapped her hands and did a little hop and whoop of excitement. This was what she'd been missing. The jolt of inspiration and creativity that long ago had her mind inventing the WonderBubble.

Still wearing her towel, she dug her laptop out from under the bed where she'd stashed it upon her arrival. Ten minutes later, she'd fired off an email not only to Connie but also to her attorney and the last to her partners suggesting they turn all their production attention to the new model. It wasn't the profit margin that had her excited— although that was a definite bonus. It was the idea of making a smaller and more affordable model for kids to have and even those adults in need of this type of sensory overload assistance.

By the time she closed her computer, the sun was coming up and her stomach was rumbling. She spotted Noodles through the window, sitting on the other side of the glass. If it were possible for a gecko to look irritated, then he was succeeding. She grabbed mango out of the fridge and left it on the table for him before rushing to get dressed so she could implement her second plan of the morning.

This next one, however, could prove trickier to pull off.

CHAPTER EIGHT

As AGREEABLE AS Freya had been last night about going to the Hibiscus Bay Resort day care center, Silas was sad to say she'd since had a change of heart. It hadn't mattered that Silas assured her his evaluation of the facility meant she'd be in good hands and that the people there were looking forward to meeting her. Freya had been impossible to rouse after burying herself all the way to the foot of her bed, then screamed and wailed when Silas had asked her to get dressed.

It had taken a half hour for her to stop crying, but he'd stood his ground. There were important things he needed to do today and he wasn't going to backslide on his responsibilities, not when he knew his child was going to be well cared for. On the bright side, they didn't have a building full of neighbors to worry about, although he did wonder if Jana could hear them. There might be a good amount of distance between their cottages, but Freya's unhappiness could definitely break the sound barrier. He didn't know whether to be re-

172 THE SINGLE DAD'S PROMISE

lieved or lament the fact Jana didn't come knocking on their door. Probably a good thing. Jana had been so good with his daughter, he wasn't ready for her to experience Freya's sometimes uneven and unpredictable temperament.

He waited another ten minutes after the crying subsided before he knocked gently on Freya's bedroom door. "You dressed?"

"Yes." Freya sat on the edge of her wrinkled but made bed, arms folded across her chest, a pout firmly etched on her face. She'd chosen a pair of denim shorts and a bright yellow T-shirt sporting a rainbow. Her green eyes were sparking like emeralds caught in a volcano. She'd attempted to tame her hair, but the brush had gotten caught in the curls and tangles. The brush handle stuck out from the side of her head. "I don't want to go."

"Sometimes we have to do things we don't want to do." Like dealing with a cranky, stubborn five-year-old. "Stand up, please. We need to fix your hair."

"It's fine."

"It's not." He did his best to gently remove the brush from her hair. She didn't wince or cry out or complain as he tugged and pulled, a sure sign she was nursing one serious mad. "Mr. Mano and his friends were nice enough to bring us out here, Freya. I need to help them in exchange for that. You understand?"

"I want to go with you."

"Well, you can't." Not only because she was in a mood, but also because he couldn't be certain she wouldn't try to hula dance around the edge of the volcano.

"Then I want to stay with Jana."

"That's not an option." Silas had to bite his tongue. Freya wasn't the only one who wanted to see Jana again. He'd spent a good portion of his sleepless night trying to think of excuses to see her. There was so much more he wanted—needed—to know about her. He liked talking with her, loved looking at her and when she touched him...

"Ow!" Freya's hand flew up to grab his—he'd finally tugged the brush free. "Daddy, that hurt!"

"I'm sorry." It took him a good few minutes to get rid of all the tangles. "Okay. Braid or pigtails or loose?"

"Braid."

"Braid what?"

"I would like a braid." He could feel her struggling not to finish the sentence. "Please."

"Thank you. Go choose an elastic, please." He checked his watch. He had an hour before he needed to be at Ohana Odysseys for the tour check-in. That left him a short amount of time to feed them both and get Freya to the day care center.

"This one." She shoved a bright pink band into

his hand and resumed her position in front of him. "When are you coming to get me?"

Silas almost exhaled in relief. She'd come to terms with going. "I should be back around four."

"But that's forever from now!"

He could hear the tears coming back into her voice.

"It's not forever and when I pick you up, we'll have dinner together in town. Maybe at that chicken place you saw. The one with the funny dancing bird." If memory served, Hula Chicken was family-friendly both in their outdoor, barbecue atmosphere and in the food they offered. "Does that sound okay?"

"I guess."

"Okay, then." He made quick work of her braid—giving silent thanks to the countless YouTube videos he'd watched over the years. "Let's get something to eat—"

"I'm not hungry."

"Okay. Then we'll stop on the way so I can get some coffee." A quadruple shot of the largest size they had if he had a choice. "Get your bag, please, and meet me at the door."

It dawned on him as they walked down the hill to Vibe, the town's most popular coffee shop, that he much preferred the screaming compared to the silent treatment. What was up with that?

As they waited for his coffee, he handed Freya a banana, which she ate without protest, then they headed down Pulelehua Road leading toward the Hibiscus Bay Resort. He could feel his own anxiety climbing the closer they got, and he began to doubt his decision to drop her off. If she was in this frame of mind with him, he could only imagine how she was going to be with a room full of strangers.

"Daddy, who's that?" Freya pointed across the street to the wooden stall occupied by two local women. One was quite old and sat in a beautifully painted throne-like rocking chair and the other, younger woman stood behind the countertop loaded with stacks of pink bakery boxes.

"That's Maru's malasada cart you heard about. The doughnuts, remember?" He checked his watch again. "Would you like to stop?"

She nodded and tugged at his hand to pull him across the street.

"Aloha, Maru." Silas kept Freya in front of him as he greeted the grandmotherly woman. "I'm not sure you remember me—"

Her dark eyes sharpened and she nodded as if his question had been silly. "You're one of Remy's friends. Silas." She grinned and cackled. "Shark Boy."

"She knows you, Daddy," Freya whispered. Silas groaned.

"Everyone knows your daddy." Maru leaned forward in her chair. "And who might you be?"

"Freya." The confidence with which she announced her name had Silas straightening with pride. "I'm five."

"Aloha, Freya." Maru inclined her head as if looking deeper into Freya's eyes. "You're sad about something."

Freya glanced up at Silas.

"She's spending the day at the day care at the resort," Silas told the older woman. "She's not happy about it."

"I see." Maru suddenly turned serious. "It can be hard doing things we need to do instead of what we want to do."

"I want to stay with Jana."

"Jana." Maru tested the name out. "The pretty one with blond hair and lost eyes."

Silas had to admit, it was an apt description. "We'll see Jana another time, Freya."

"Waiting will make your reunion all the better," Maru told Freya. "Come, Freya." She extended a gnarled hand. For the first time, Freya accepted without hesitation and found herself tucked up close to Maru. "Nalani is the most beautiful place in the world, Freya. Do you know why?"

"No." Freya touched the bold flower pattern on Maru's muumuu.

"Because we're all Ohana here. Because we look after each other and help each other. And if there are those who come to hurt us, they will be stopped. By good people, like your daddy."

Silas remained silent. Maru was like Nalani

information central. It would have surprised him if the town's matriarch didn't know about GVI and their hopes to set up business in what was her home.

"I think you're going to have a very good time at the day care," Maru whispered, then motioned to the other woman. "Lani, give me a bag of our new mini malasadas."

"Sure, Tutu." The young woman offered Silas a warm smile and put half a dozen doughnut holes into a paper bag. "Here you go, Freya."

"Thank you." Freya looked inside. "They smell good."

"I learned to make these when I was your age," Maru said and gave Freya a quick hug. "You share these with your new friends. You have nothing to be scared about, *keiki*. You go and have a good day and your daddy will do his job."

Freya sighed. "Okay."

"Mahalo, Maru," Silas said, taking Freya's free hand.

"A 'ole pilikia." No problem. "Come back tomorrow for some real-size ones." She waved them off as if dismissing them from her royal court.

"She was nice, Daddy." Freya began to skip beside him. "Can I eat one now?"

"Go ahead." They stopped long enough for her to pluck a small round malasada out of the bag. She'd barely gotten her first nibble when her face lit up and she took a bigger bite.

"These are yummy!"

"Glad you like them. Careful with...never mind." He didn't care if she got covered with sugar. Not if she'd started smiling again.

The Hibiscus Bay Resort welcomed them with its abundant vines of hibiscus twining around the entirety of the entrance. The glass doors, including the rotating one, were offset by koa wood frames carved with representations of island life, from symbols to creatures, to the floral landscape. Inside, the breeze rustled the giant palm leaves of the trees in oversize planters. The air was filled with jasmine and the ocean, the combination creating an invigorating energy that was no doubt partially responsible for the smiles on the guests' faces.

"Daddy, look! It's Mr. Mano!" Freya's squeal of happiness had Mano turning away from the conversation he'd been having with one of the registration clerks. Freya waved and pulled a wide smile out of the very businesslike-looking Mano. Gone were the board shorts and tank, replaced by another dark suit like the one he'd worn to the airport.

"Aloha, Freya. Silas." Mano approached and his gaze fell instantly on the paper bag in Freya's hand. "Ah, you've met Maru, I see."

"She gave us these." Freya held the bag up. "Want one?"

"Mahalo." He took one out and popped it into

his mouth. "I've been eating these since before I was your age." He crouched down. "Are you ready for your stay at the center?"

She stepped back to Silas. "I don't know."

Silas shot his friend a frustrated look.

"I had a feeling you might be a little anxious. That's why I'm here. I would be pleased to take you to it, so your daddy can go to work. May I? That way he'll be back sooner."

It was a lie, Silas thought, but a harmless one he was okay with.

When Freya still didn't look sold, Mano rested his arm on his knee. "I've been hoping someone would be able to tell me what they like and don't like about the day care. It's really new, Freya. You'd be one of the first ones there. Do you think you could help me?" He stood and held out a hand.

Freya shrugged. "I guess. You'll be back, won't you, Daddy?"

The fear in Freya's voice didn't escape Mano's notice, but he didn't say anything, simply turned his concerned eyes to Silas's daughter.

"As soon as I can, I promise." Silas watched his friend lead his daughter away. It was another step. For both of them. "Be a good girl, please."

"I will." Freya held up the bag for Mano to take another malasada, an action that had Silas feeling somewhat more at ease as he left the resort.

His cover story of being here because of a bad

breakup, if it turned out to be necessary to share, was simple and straightforward. Nothing he'd have trouble remembering. No reason to use a different name. As far as Don Martin knew, Silas had no connection to Ohana or the resort, so any suspicion should be negligible. Still, he liked to be prepared.

That constant bit of worry that lived inside of him these days eased back a bit. Reassured that Freya was being looked after, Silas found his pace slowing as he drank his coffee. He did a little window-shopping along Pulelehua Road, beginning with the new arrivals on display in Luanda's. The Blue Moon Bar and Grill's employees were wiping down chairs and tables on the back porch, which overlooked the ocean and gave customers a stunning view during breakfast. Bicyclists zoomed past, handlebar bells ringing, people calling out good morning and waving as if Silas was more than just a visitor in town.

He made a mental note to return to the corner art gallery across from the police station to purchase a gift for the neighbor who frequently babysat Freya. Passing by Vibe, he was grateful he'd come by sooner, since the line for an early morning hit of caffeine was now out the door.

There was something special about Nalani as it awoke, he thought, continuing on his way. He could feel the energy building with more and more people venturing onto the street and stores beginning to open. It was just so easy here, so relaxed and serene. It was a difficult place to leave. He'd learned that on his first and only visit. Maybe that was a reason he hadn't come back; he knew that once he did, it would be even harder to return home again.

Silas finished the last of his coffee and approached the sturdy, bamboo-accented structure that housed the Ohana Odysseys Travel and Excursion Tours office. There was a group of people milling about at the foot of the stairs, many of whom were drinking coffee made available at a kiosk nearby. It hadn't dawned on him that he could have gotten his morning jolt right at the start of the tour.

"Morning." Champion surfer in training Jordan Adair said, her long, sun-kissed blond braids whipping around her shoulders when she waved to him.

Silas had made it a point, before leaving the party last night, to introduce himself not only to Jordan, but like Mano had suggested, to Police Chief Alec Aheona Malloy. Silas had liked the man instantly and agreed with Mano's comment that the police chief was indeed pretty laid-back, but not when it came to his duty.

Alec and Jordan's affection for one another was obvious. Much like with the rest of his friends who had paired off, there was a coziness about their relationship that left Silas feeling slightly

182 THE SINGLE DAD'S PROMISE

envious. Strange. Even now he frowned at that notion. He didn't recall feeling like that with his paired-off friends back on the mainland.

"Good morning." He circled the edge of a group of women checking in with Daphne, who would be heading the tour. "Looks like a good turnout for today."

"This tour always sells out," Jordan told him. "You want a refill?" She motioned to the cup in his hand. "Help yourself."

"Ah, no, thanks." He was already buzzing from his triple shot. He scanned the crowd, looking for Don Martin. "Do I just get in line to check in with Daphne?"

"Yep." Jordan reached around him to hand off a cup to a woman who had joined them. "Good morning!"

"Hi." The woman turned a million-watt smile on Silas, her light brown eyes dancing. She wore trendy cutoffs and a bright pink tank top that had him hoping she'd brought lots of sun block. "I'm Tildy." She winked and fluttered her fingers at him. "My friends and I are here on a girlfriends' getaway." She pointed to the group of women nearby who showed no qualms about watching their interaction. Two of them even waved.

"Uh, Silas." Panicking, he shot a look at Jordan, who offered both an apologetic smile and shrug. His cover story dropped straight out of his head. The last thing he wanted to do was tell

ANNA J. STEWART

this woman he was trying to heal a broken heart. "Nice to meet you, Tildy."

"All on your own, Silas?"

It wasn't Tildy's question so much as the hopeful tone in her voice that had Silas scrambling to rethink his plan.

"Ah—"

"There you are."

Silas gave himself credit for not jumping when Jana came up alongside him and tucked herself in under his arm. She turned her face up to his, smiled into his eyes in a way that had every thought draining out of his head. "I was afraid you were going to be late." She slid an arm around his waist and squeezed. "Who's your new friend, honey?"

"This is, um, Tildy." Torn between amusement and shock, he almost laughed at the abject disappointment on the other woman's face. "Tildy, this is—"

"His girlfriend, Jana. Hi." She tilted her head, held out her hand. "Nice to meet you, Tildy."

"Yeah, hi." Tildy's smile vanished in the blink of an eye. "My mistake. I guess we'll see you on the bus." She returned to her friends, who immediately stuck their heads together and moved as a pack toward the bus.

Silas couldn't help but laugh now. "I would ask where you appeared from, but it honestly doesn't matter." He surprised them both by pull-

184 THE SINGLE DAD'S PROMISE

ing her in close and dropping a kiss on her lips. He breathed deep, drawing in the scent of her. The action should have satisfied the part of him that had been dying to kiss her. Instead, it only intensified the desire exponentially. "I think it's safe to say you just saved me."

"Oh, you'd have found a way to escape," Jana said, laughing. Her nervous gaze had shifted away. Her cheeks went pink and sent a wave of pleasure coursing through him. "It might have meant jumping into a volcano, though."

It wasn't relief he was feeling, he realized. It was pure, unadulterated joy. He knew he'd been missing her, but he hadn't understood how much. "What are you doing here?" By all rights he should have released her, but having her in his arms felt so utterly perfect he wasn't willing to relinquish the privilege just yet.

"Well. Thanks, Jordan." Jana accepted a coffee from their very amused barista. "I got to thinking about it last night. You talked about how undercover officers often work with partners. Four eyes are better than two, so I changed my plans for today." She shrugged. "I texted Tehani to see if she could squeeze me in on the tour." She stepped back and they turned around. "Besides, now you don't have to lie about why you're here. Not really, anyway. You just have to play along."

She sipped her coffee as Silas's gaze landed on Daphne and the man she was speaking to. A little on the short and squat side, Don Martin was doing his best to blend in with the island feel. Silas recognized the green, leaf-patterned shirt from the sale rack at Luanda's while the cargo shorts he'd chosen exposed his very pale, very mainland legs.

"I'd ask if that was him," Jana said quietly. "But he's kind of giving himself away. Poor guy looks as if he hasn't seen the sun in years. Shall we?"

"Sure."

She released him, but slipped her hand down to capture his. Never in his life had an action felt so utterly and completely natural. Whatever else he'd thought about Jana Powell up until now, impulsivity hadn't even made the list. He couldn't wait to see what happened next with her by his side.

"Morning, Daphne." Jana jumped right in as Daphne marked Don Martin's name off the list on her tablet computer. "Sorry we're late." She tugged Silas forward.

Daphne's gaze shifted to their linked hands, back up to Jana's bright face. She seemed to be purposely avoiding Silas as her lips curved in a slow, knowing smile. "Good morning, Jana. And Silas. Glad to have you on board with us today. This is Mr. Martin."

"Don, please." Don Martin said instantly. "Nice to meet you. You two here on your honeymoon?"

Silas's face went volcanic rock hot.

"Not yet," Jana said easily. "He hasn't gotten up the nerve yet to propose. But hopefully soon."

186 THE SINGLE DAD'S PROMISE

She turned those high beam eyes on him again. "Right, honey?"

"We'll see how this trip goes." Playing along with Jana was going to keep him on his toes. "First vacation together."

Don removed his glasses and smiled at them. "Smart move. My wife and I did the same thing. If you can't travel together, you can't live together."

Jana gaped and nodded. "That is exactly what I told him. It's lovely to meet you, Don. Is this your first tour with Ohana?" She effortlessly guided the three of them toward the bus, away from Daphne so she could finish checking in the rest of the guests.

"It is, actually. I'm staying at the Hibiscus Bay."

"We had dinner there a couple of nights ago," Jana lied. "It was absolutely lovely. We decided to rent a beach cottage for our stay since we have Silas's little girl with us. I'm kind of regretting the cottage now, though. The resort looks like the perfect home away from home."

"It's impressive," Don agreed. His attention shifted to Silas. "How old is your daughter?"

It was as if Jana had led him exactly where Silas and Mano had intended to take the corporate scout. "She's just turned five," Silas said. "She's trying out the day care at the resort today while we take the tour."

"Five's a great age," Don said with a genuine

smile on his round face. "They're testing everything around then. Themselves and our patience."

"Couldn't have said it better myself," Silas agreed.

"Okay, everyone!" Daphne called above the din of conversation. "Everyone is here and we've got a two-hour drive ahead of us, so let's get this baby loaded up and ready to move out!" She waved her tablet toward the door that opened with a gentle hiss. "Our usual driver is sick today, so we have a special guest on board. Be sure you say hi to Keane Harper as you climb on!"

"Guess we'll see you on board," Jana said, before nudging Silas forward. "Shall we?"

Amused, entertained, and more than a little enthralled, Silas nodded. "After you."

JANA COULDN'T BELIEVE how much fun it was to pretend. Especially when she'd gotten the kiss she'd been thinking about earlier that morning. When the thought of joining Silas on the tour first occurred to her, she had no idea how it might play out. The plan had been to pull him aside and give him a quick rundown of her notion. But as she saw him standing at the coffee bar with that woman, something had come over Jana.

Jana had been all about new experiences and adventures on her recovery trip, but the last thing she expected to feel was jealousy! She'd almost checked her arms to see if she'd been turning green. It was only when she noticed that Silas looked almost panic-stricken that she figured she had an advantage.

The next thing she'd known, she was sliding into a parallel universe where she apparently had no inhibitions or concerns and was more than willing to stake her claim on one Silas Garwood.

Ninety minutes or so later, the bus continued to bump along on the road to Mauna Loa, one of the two active volcanoes on the Big Island. The transport bus maxed out at eighteen passengers, but this particular tour had fifteen locked in, with the back aisle used to stash two large coolers and the boxes containing their lunches and various snacks for the day.

Tehani had been more than amenable to putting Jana on the tour, especially once Jana told her she was willing to help keep GVI's hands off Ohana Odysseys, the resort and Nalani in general. Jana had already taken the tour two days after she'd gotten here, but that gave her the freedom to tune that out and focus on what Don Martin might be doing. And, if she was lucky, perhaps even what he was thinking.

She'd chosen the pair of seats behind Don Martin and had, more than once, scooched forward slightly when he was typing on his phone.

While Daphne regaled the passengers with one of the island myths, Silas leaned over and whispered, "I can hear the wheels turning in your head."

"Sorry." She should have known she'd think too loudly. "Feeling a little amped up."

It had to be the adrenaline rush from her impulsive decision-making and surely didn't have anything to do with the man sitting beside her. She squeezed his hand and couldn't help but smile. Being with him, just having him near, made all that white noise of life fade into the distance. She'd never met anyone who made her feel this way, as if she was right where she was supposed to be. The improbability factor was no doubt in the quadrillions that they'd come to Nalani at the same time, yet...

Yet here they were.

The bus bounced and shook as they exited onto a turnoff that led them into what looked like one of Hawai'i's many forested areas.

"I want to thank each of you for reading your tour instructions." Daphne's voice came through load and clear through the speakers. "I did a quick check as we climbed on board and I'm glad to see everyone wearing sturdy walking shoes. Rest assured we do carry some spare hiking and rain boots on the bus just in case. But it looks like we're in good shape today. Everyone wearing sunblock?" She bent down to peer out the window, her long red braid falling over her shoulder. "We've got gorgeous weather, but that means no cloud cover, so please be proactive in protecting yourself."

Jana dug into the backpack she'd loaded with essentials and pulled out the foldable straw hat she'd bought her first day in Nalani. Her smile at Silas's assessing gaze was sheepish. "I know it's…" She plunked it on her head and drew the drawstring under her chin. "I can sunburn in a snowstorm." It didn't matter she had slathered on half a tube of sunblock before leaving the cottage.

"Gotta protect this."

He touched a finger to her nose so softly she shouldn't have felt a thing. But she definitely felt something and that something shot straight to her toes and set them to tingling. He reached into his back pocket for his phone.

"Everything okay?" She glanced at his screen.

"Apparently. No messages about Freya."

She tightened her fingers around his. She could feel the tension in his muscles. "I'm sure she's fine." It was on the tip of her tongue to remind him that Mano was there if Freya needed anything, but she didn't want to volunteer any information that Don Martin might take to connect the two of them to the resort's owner.

"Just feels strange not having her with me." His voice was low, as if he, too, didn't want to be overheard.

Jana couldn't argue. Even she had to admit she thought of the two of them as a pair. But maybe

ANNA J. STEWART 191

this was going to be a good day, a good break, for both of them.

When the bus finally stopped, Jana looked out at the parking area. It was filled with multiple vehicles and numerous tours. Jana had a long drink of water from the bottle she'd brought. The walk to the volcano last time had taken a lot out of her—she was still building up her stamina. But they were earlier today, and it wasn't supposed to be as hot. She was hoping that meant the hike would be easier.

"You okay?" Silas asked as passengers began to file out. "You're practically cracking my knuckles."

"Oh." She immediately let go of his hand. "Sorry. Don't know why I'm anxious."

"It's an active volcano," Silas teased her. "I'm anxious myself." They stood together when Don Martin slipped out of his seat and headed to the door.

They were the last ones leaving the bus. Keane watched the two of them as they approached, and that familiar grin they'd seen on Daphne's face earlier was on full display. "You two having fun?"

"Yes," Jana didn't hesitate to answer. "I'm undercover," she told their driver and her new friend. "We're playing make-believe."

"Uh-huh." Keane nodded and pulled the key out of the ignition. "Very convincing, from my point of view. In case you were wondering."

"We weren't," Silas said in a tone that left Jana wondering if he was joking or not.

They joined the rest of the tour outside where Daphne was giving her instructions about staying together, looking for the red flag she carried so they could keep her in sight, and to not go off the trail.

"Keep in mind, your cell service might be sketchy for the next few hours," Daphne said, continuing her spiel. "But that's a good thing in my opinion. I recommend you take the time on this tour to observe with your eyes." She pinned her gaze on Tildy's group, currently taking a series of selfies with their phones. "And not with a lens."

Jana ducked her head to avoid being seen laughing after spotting Daphne rolling her eyes.

"Okay, everyone!" Daphne held up her flag. "With me, please!"

"You doing okay there, Don?" Silas asked when the older man didn't seem in a rush to follow.

"Fine." Don's smile was quick, but cursory. "How long did she say this hike was?"

"About an hour," Jana told him.

"Then an hour back. Right."

"I don't move super fast," Jana told him. "I can hang back with you if you need to go more slowly."

Don's lips twitched. "I think I can keep up."

"Give a holler if you change your mind," Jana

said. She turned to Silas. "Shall we?" Daphne and the rest of the group were already ahead. "I hear the view is spectacular. A real opportunity for the island to do some showing off."

"The island shows off?" Don asked as if he didn't quite understand.

"Every single day," Silas said and squeezed Jana's hand. "Let's do this."

IT HAD BEEN easy for Silas to speak of the performance the islands put on every minute of the day. One of his constant memories of Nalani—of the Big Island, in particular—had been the perfect beauty that only got stronger with the passage of time.

The ups and downs of the path they took as they trailed behind Daphne and their fellow tourists was the latest creation the island had built for itself. The dark, hard rock beneath their feet was only a hint of what was to come. With each step they took, he could feel the volcanic heat rise. Combined with the sun beating down on them and, as Daphne had warned, the lack of any cloud cover, the temperature was clearly climbing.

Jana had released his hand a while ago. He'd noticed, of course, and he'd noticed he was moving at a faster clip than Jana was comfortable with apparently. He'd thought her comment to Don had simply been to placate him, but now Silas wasn't so sure.

194 THE SINGLE DAD'S PROMISE

He turned around and spotted Jana sitting on a high rock, digging into her bag for her water bottle and a plastic container.

"She okay?" Don asked as he huffed, coming up to Silas.

"I'm sure she is. I'll stay with her. Go on." He nodded to the group that was moving out of sight. "You don't want to miss this."

Don managed a weak smile and continued on.

He double-timed it back to Jana. "I'd ask if you're okay, but I think I see my answer." He crouched in front of her, reached to tilt her pink hat back. "What's going on?"

"I'm fine." She tapped out a pill from the container and glugged it down with more water. "I just need a few minutes."

He shifted around to sit next to her.

"You should go," Jana told him, that playful, amused tone she'd had on the bus long gone. "It's something you need to see."

"I've seen it before." Any longing he'd felt to see the volcano again vanished. He didn't want to hover, but he also wasn't about to leave her alone. "You're pale."

"I bet I am." She bent put her hands on her forehead. "It'll pass. It always does. Just need to give the pill a chance to kick in." She seemed to fight to take a deep breath. "So stupid. It's been a while since I've felt this way. I'd forgotten." The tightness in her voice told him she'd hoped never to feel this way again.

"This is because you were sick, isn't it?"

"Mmm-hmm." Nodding, she closed her eyes as if she were trying to center herself. "I didn't have this problem on this hike the last time. It never occurred to me I'd have one now." She pressed a hand against her chest. "Sometimes the mind forgets but the body never does."

He'd debated before about asking, but the opportunity had never felt right. Now? He didn't see a way not to. "Can I ask what you had?"

He watched for her reaction, needed to know what his question might trigger. He thought maybe she'd push back, not want to talk about it, or even just dismiss his concern and interest. But when she shifted to rest her cheek in her hand, her eyes were filled with a stark reality.

"About a year ago I was diagnosed with stage two endometrial cancer."

"Okay." He knew enough that it wasn't an easy diagnosis, either to hear about or treat. So many things went through his mind, not the least of which was a big wave of fear. He took hold of her hand again, slipped his fingers through hers and held on tight. "I'm sorry."

She stared down at their hands. "Yeah. Me, too."

He wanted to find the words, needed to figure out something to say that didn't offend or trivialize or… "So, what you're feeling now is a side effect of your treatment?"

Another nod. "I had six months of intense radiation. Along with—" She stopped, looked away before she straightened and took a deep breath. "Along with a complete hysterectomy. I now know precisely how a battery feels when it's completely drained of a charge. There were days I didn't have the energy to get out of bed and other days when I felt perfectly fine." She shook her head, as if trying to dislodge the past. "I avoided chemo, so there was that. Not that it helped this." She touched a hand to her hat-covered head. "Still lost my hair. But I'm still here, so yay? I guess?"

"Don't guess." His grip on her hand tightened. He'd never felt so helpless yet so impressed at the same time. "I'm sorry you had to go through all that alone."

Another shrug, which told him she'd been working overtime to try to diminish the fight she'd found herself in. "I guess the universe wanted to remind me I'm not completely on the other side yet, but I'll get there." She freed her hand, picked her water back up and drank. "Please don't feel sorry for me." The sass in her voice had his lips twitching. "I'm far more fortunate than a lot of other women in my position have been. At least I'll get to see my thirtieth birthday."

"None of that takes away from what you've been through." He was acquainted with enough people who had fought cancer to have a sense of the toll it took, both emotionally and physically. "You've been through something difficult. It's a trauma. You have to give yourself grace to grieve and recover. And for the record, this isn't pity I'm feeling."

"No?"

"No. It's..."

Her gaze sharpened, as if challenging him to find the perfect words. Something he'd never been particularly good at.

"It's admiration. And gratitude," he finally said. "You're still here. You're still you and the you I'm coming to know is amazing and strong, not to mention incredibly generous with my daughter." A daughter, he now realized, that could be a reminder of what she'd never have herself. "Nothing you've told me changes how I see you except to prove you're an even more incredible woman than I originally thought."

"How are you real?" Tears filled her eyes and she wiped them away with a ferocity that surprised him. "This is crazy. You aren't supposed to exist. Men like you..." She let out a tiny sob as a solitary tear escaped her reach. "Men like you aren't supposed to exist."

"I exist. And I'm here." He wrapped an arm around her shoulders and drew her against him, feeling an odd sense of pride when she gave in, clung to him and cried. "I'm not going anywhere."

He pressed his lips against her hair, rocked her gently. He hadn't lied. Not about any of it. Not about her or what she'd been through or…

Or what he thought of her. He smiled, shocked and stunned to admit he was doing the one thing he never expected to do again.

He was falling in love.

CHAPTER NINE

JANA WOULD PROBABLY never be sure if it was taking a break, drinking water, or spending time in Silas's arms that finally gave her the energy to make it back to the bus and continue on with the tour. Given those choices, despite never considering herself a romantic, and maybe it was just the sun and heat, she was leaning toward it being Silas.

From the moment she'd met him she'd known he was special; felt an unexpected pull toward him. She'd given up on feeling this strongly about anyone, ages ago—one of the consequences of being "different" that she'd alluded to with Freya. But now, with Silas? She glowed on the inside in anticipation.

Maybe the universe had put him in her path for her to find.

Was this…was this what it felt like to fall in love?

The fact he now knew the truth about her situation and didn't turn and walk away but instead embraced her to the point that she never wanted to leave his arms? That seemed like a very distinct and unexpected fork in her road.

Holding his hand again, now that they were back on the bus and headed for what Daphne billed as a surprise location for their lunch, felt less like an act and far more…natural. It hadn't escaped anyone on the tour's notice that neither of them had made it to the volcano, but thankfully, no one had been pushy enough to question what had happened, only if everything was all right. Thankfully, by the time Keane put the bus into gear, her anti-nausea medication had kicked in and she was feeling if not completely up to snuff, certainly less green.

Given how Daphne's gaze kept shifting to Jana while she continued with her information deluge about this area of the Big Island, however, Jana had no doubt she was in for a conversation once they disembarked.

Sure enough, after waiting for everyone else to get off the bus, she and Silas found Daphne and Keane standing at the foot of the steps while the others strolled through the secluded picnic area overlooking a stunning cavern of island flora. This time the warm sun took the AC chill off her arms and had her feeling less shaky.

"What's going on?" Daphne reached out for Jana as she stepped down. "Are you okay?"

"I'm fine. Really." The last thing she wanted

was for people to make a huge fuss. "Just too much fun and a little too much caffeine, I think."

Daphne looked at Silas, then to Keane, then back to Silas. Jana's stomach tightened as she prepared herself for Silas reciting what she'd told him, but all he did was move closer to her.

"I'm sure once she gets something to eat she'll be back to normal," Silas said.

Jana's stomach turned at the idea of food, even as she admitted he was probably right. "I'm okay, Daphne. I promise. Don't let me ruin this for anyone, please." She certainly didn't want to be a distraction or a hiccup on a tour that was being monitored by someone who could very well damage Nalani's two biggest businesses.

"Okay." Daphne still didn't look convinced. "Well, go grab yourself a seat. Silas and Keane can help me lug out the lunches and drinks. Please." She motioned to one of the picnic tables beneath an arch of pretty palm leaves. "For my own peace of mind. Just go relax. I want you to be able to see the falls. They're my favorite part of the tour."

Jana smiled, nodded and stepped out from Silas's protective watch. She pressed a hand against her rumbling stomach. She started toward one of the empty tables, then detoured when she saw Don Martin tapping out something on his phone.

"Mind if I join you?" Grateful to have something to focus on other than still feeling a bit icky, she gestured to the bench across from him.

Don glanced up, a concerned look on his face as he nodded. "Of course. Are you feeling better?" he asked when she settled in.

"I am, thanks." She flashed him what she hoped was a bright smile. "Just overdid it this morning. I have…" How to phrase this? "I've been recovering from an illness and my energy levels like to surprise me at times."

Don put his phone to the side, leaned his arms on the table. His expression wasn't entirely readable, but she definitely saw recognition in his eyes. "My wife battled stage three breast cancer six years ago."

"I'm…sorry." It was an automatic response and suddenly she understood why it tended to be the first words out of someone's mouth. "How is she now?"

"Thriving." The pride and love in his eyes made Jana wonder how he could do the job he did given he had such an open heart. "It was rough for a couple of years. The ups and downs are sometimes worse than the illness itself. It's hard, standing by when someone you love is going through that." His gaze flickered over Jana's shoulder. She turned enough to be able to see Silas lugging one of the giant coolers off the bus and set it heavily on the ground. "How much did you tell him?"

"Most of it, actually." All of what he needed

to know anyway. She didn't want to burden Silas with the details of what her treatment had consisted of. Especially not when he'd gotten a glimpse of the toll it had taken. "We're still... learning about each other. He didn't balk."

"Then he's a good one." Don's smile was kind. "One thing my wife was determined to do was to not let her illness define her. She listened to her body, most of the time, and has lived every single day as fully as possible since her diagnosis. She taught me and our girls so much and in the end..." He shrugged, seeming a bit embarrassed now. "In the end I fell in love with her all over again."

Jana couldn't help it. She reached over, covered his restless hand with hers. "Sounds like she's lucky to have you."

"I'm the lucky one. And I think, maybe, Silas is lucky, too."

Jana's face went hot, but not in that "I'm going to pitch over and faint" kind of way this time. "Sometimes it feels as if we're just getting started." It was true. Sort of.

"You're serious enough to come out to Nalani together. With his daughter."

"Mmm." It surprised her that she didn't like lying to him. "Nalani's a pretty special town. With very special people. It was the perfect place to come and..." And what? "Start over."

His brow furrowed, his eyes darkening a bit before he nodded. "I imagine it could be."

204 THE SINGLE DAD'S PROMISE

Their attention was pulled to the far tables where the rest of the tour group had gathered to take a picture with the mountainous, foliage-covered caverns behind them. "I'll go over and help them out, stop them from making it a selfie." Don got to his feet. "Be back in a minute."

"Okay." She watched him walk away, then take one cell phone after another and start snapping pictures. But whatever entertainment value the sight offered, she found herself instead watching Silas interacting with his friends. His laughter caught on the breeze, filling her heart so fully she realized she'd never felt like that before. The good-natured teasing among them, the easy way they worked together as Keane stacked thin cardboard boxes under his chin and headed for the tables, had her appreciating the smaller moments like this. When life just...went on. As it should.

With the photos done and the lunches distributed, Jana was feeling as close to normal as she had when she'd first climbed onto the bus. So much so that when Silas brought her and Don their lunches and Daphne followed up with frosty bottles of water, she realized that while she'd lied to Don about a number of things, she'd been right about Nalani.

It was indeed a perfect place to start over.

SILAS SPENT THE better part of the afternoon tour watching Jana come back into her own. It was odd, seeing someone so vital all but collapse in on themselves, but then recover to the point of being an even stronger version of who they'd been before. That was who she struck him as. And no matter how hard he tried to compartmentalize his emotions and growing feelings for her, he couldn't help but see her in terms of the future. Of what might be, what he was beginning to hope might very well be possible.

Keane steered the bus toward their last stop and Silas checked his watch again.

Jana's hand covered his, letting him know she'd awoken from the doze she'd fallen into shortly after getting back aboard. She'd rested her head on his shoulder, an action that had triggered some intense emotions. Emotions he was having difficulty reconciling given they'd only known one another for such a short time. "I'm sure Freya's fine," Jana murmured.

Silas swallowed hard, touched that she understood what he was thinking. Shocked that she could pick up on it so easily. "If you want to call and check, Daphne told me there's a satellite phone up front for emergencies. She can call the resort if you're concerned."

He shook his head, took a deep breath. "No. I need to get used to her being away from me and she definitely needs to get used to being away from me at times." He turned his hand over, threaded his fingers through hers. An action, he thought, that had quickly become second nature. "You doing okay?"

"Okay enough that if you ask me again, I'm going to dump my bottle of water over your head." But there was humor in the warning. Another good sign she was feeling better.

"Understood." The bus lurched and bumped. Some of the passengers rose in their seats before bouncing back down. Nervous laughter echoed through the group.

"I promise this is all worth it," Daphne's voice crackled over the speaker. "Keane, if you could avoid some of those potholes, that'd be great. Just a few more minutes to go, folks."

Sure enough, Keane soon turned the bus toward a well-marked turnoff and came to a halt. As everyone filed out, Daphne signaled for him and Jana to hold back, while Keane went to wrangle the disembarked passengers.

"Something wrong?" Silas asked as Daphne came down the aisle.

"Not at all." She stopped in front of them. "It's quite a hike to the waterfall, remember. About a half hour in, then another half out."

"I'll be fine," Jana insisted. "Please, I want to—"

"I don't want you on that hike," Daphne said in a tone Silas had rarely heard her use. "There's a shorter, less steep path just steps from here. If you want to see the falls, that's the way you go."

Jana turned to rest a knee on her seat so she could see where Daphne was pointing. "That's the kiddie path."

"Yes, it is. This isn't about liability, Jana. This is about me, your friend, who's worried about you. Take that off my mind, please. And yes, while you will miss the comic antics of Tildy and her goofy friends, I promise, the second you see that waterfall again you won't care how you got there. There's more water in there." She gestured to the cooler. "Take what you can carry and go at a comfortable pace. We'll meet you back on the bus."

Jana gaped, dropped back in her seat and stared at Daphne's retreating back. "She's serious."

"Sounds like." Silas leaned over and grabbed two bottles out of the cooler, tucked them into her backpack, which he then took, prepared to carry it himself. "Ready?"

"Did you two plan this?" she demanded as she followed him off the bus.

"No, but I'm grateful she gave us the option." The accusation wasn't wholly unexpected. He had considered telling Daphne, if only so someone else was in the know in order to keep an eye on Jana, but he'd decided against it. It wasn't his story to tell and, truth be told, it wasn't his place. He wanted it to be, though.

"I'm not fragile." She dropped down behind him off the bus. "I don't need to be coddled."

"I think coddling is what would happen if

Daphne were told why you really weren't feeling well."

Jana's mouth twisted. She glared at him. Silas stood his ground.

"You can keep complaining about taking an easier path, or we can get back on the bus." He loosened the straps of her backpack before sliding his arms through. "Personally, I'd really like to see the falls. And—" He made certain to look into her eyes as he continued. "I only want to see them with you."

He hid his amusement when she flung her arms wide.

"Fine. But I'm only agreeing because I also really want to see the falls again." She stalked off ahead of him, turned around long enough to add, "With you, please."

Silas hitched the pack on his back and followed.

It didn't take him long to appreciate Daphne's insisting they take the easier path. The activity warning on the hike had been moderate, but this one wasn't exactly, well, a walk in the park. The rocky soil and sometimes slippery mud, not to mention a few trickling creeks to make their way through or over, meant it was slow going at times. Jana seemed determined to outpace him, but it wasn't long before they were walking pretty closely together.

He could hear her breathing, not struggling exactly, but she was having to work at it. He made certain to stop every five minutes or so and hand her one of the water bottles. On the third drink, she accepted it with a grateful smile and finally dropped the attitude.

She stopped short at one point, and because he'd been watching the ground, nearly bashed into her.

"What's wrong?"

"Nothing," she whispered. "I can hear it." She looked at him, eyes wide with wonder. "Can you?"

It took him a moment to block out the noise in his head, to focus on the breeze rustling through the trees and listen beyond the distant sounds that had nothing to do with water. Sure enough, the sound of the gentle roar reached him.

She reached back for his hand and pulled him beside her.

Breaking through the end of the path was like stepping through a portal into another world. The mud and rocks transformed into lush greenery beneath their feet, arching and rounding out over the jagged landscape that allowed for a view of the eighty-foot falls tumbling into the pool below.

Jana's hand tightened around his and he inched closer, blinking in awe at the sight. That roar they'd heard from a distance had grown louder. Overhead and all around them, the treetops bent and swayed. It was like a moving picture frame with the spectacular sight of nature's continued prowess as the image.

She stepped forward, nearly to the edge, and peered down, straining over the security railing.

"Don't even think about it," he warned with what he hoped was a lighthearted chuckle. "You heard what Daphne said. No diving or jumping or swimming."

"I know." But he could feel the struggle to resist temptation as she clung to him. "But wouldn't that be amazing?"

"For a moment," he agreed. "Then it would be painful."

"But what a moment that would be."

The awe reflected on her face when she looked at him left Silas humbled at how she saw the world. Humbled at being anywhere in her vicinity. Every time he focused on her, he noted something new, something even more wonderful to behold.

"It's even more beautiful the second time," she said. He moved in behind her, so he could rest his hands on her shoulders. "It's like we're the only two people to ever see it. And it's…perfect." She lifted her chin and, like him, caught the gentle spray of mist against her face. "I don't care how we got here." She turned and smiled. "I'll just always be grateful that we did."

In that moment, Silas wanted nothing more than to…

His eyes caught her gaze, a gaze that widened

with surprise then desire as he dipped his head, brushed his mouth against hers. A featherlight touch that felt almost imagined until the spark of longing ignited inside of him and he kissed her. His hand stroked the side of her neck, cupped her face as he angled the kiss, and surrendered to what he'd been thinking about, dreaming about, since the moment he'd first seen her swimming in the ocean.

He recognized her hesitancy, felt her uncertainty break as the hand that had been relaxed against his chest tugged him closer, and he burned this moment, the feel of her, the taste of her, into his mind.

Voices echoed in the distance, loud enough to break through the haze in his brain. He released her, pulled back only far enough so they could both breathe. When he opened his eyes again, he saw her touch her tongue to her lips, as if trying to taste him again.

"Wow." She blinked up at him, confusion and amusement mingling in eyes that no longer carried that hint of concern. "That was..." Her joyful laugh brought a smile out of him. "That was just wow. And even better than the first."

He pressed his forehead against hers. Resisted everything inside of him screaming to kiss her again. "*That* was perfect."

"Can we do it again?"

The innocent question nearly destroyed what-

THE SINGLE DAD'S PROMISE

ever control he was holding on to. "Not here." He inclined his head, indicating their fellow tour members coming through the clearing on their own path. "But later." He gently pressed his lips to her forehead before he stepped back. "Definitely later."

THE TELLTALE SIGN that they had returned to town came in the form of dozens of notifications from cell phones reconnecting at the same time. Ringtones sounded, alerts chimed, and vibrations nearly set the bus to rocking as just about everyone on the tour got out their devices.

Silas couldn't help but watch a frustrated Daphne shoot Keane an irritated look before she shut off her microphone and dropped into her seat, defeated by the lure of technology.

"Daphne is kind of right," Jana murmured. "It's sad that after the day we've had, we're all sucked so easily back into this world." She leaned forward, unabashedly looking over Don Martin's shoulders. "Are those your daughters?"

Don grinned back at her, held up his phone to show off the image on the screen. "They sure are. That's Adriana, my youngest." He pointed to the dark-haired young woman on the left. "And this is Diana. She's graduating college next fall."

"They're beautiful," Jana said. "You should bring them and your wife out here the next time you visit. It's the perfect secluded spot no one knows about. It's all about the personal touch, right?"

Silas looked out the opposite window to hide a smile. Jana was nothing if not subtle.

"Yes." Don nodded and glanced away. "I've noticed."

Silas was one of the last to fall prey to the incessant chiming of his cell. One voice mail. One text message. All from...

His stomach dropped all the way to his toes.

"What's wrong?" Jana leaned back, touched his hand.

"Mano called." He scanned the text. "Freya had a meltdown. His word." Which told Silas it had probably been a pretty big one. Mano wasn't a man prone to exaggeration. His stomach twisted into an anxious knot.

"Call him," Jana urged, once again picking up on his panic. "It'll be quicker." She pulled out her phone as he hit the call back number, lifted the cell to his ear.

"She's fine." Mano's somewhat amused tone eased a bit of the stress building inside of Silas. "We had a small issue for a while, but she's okay now. Just took her a moment to get there."

Silas blew out a relieved breath. "What happened?"

"The strap on her treasure bag broke."

Silas tilted his head back, closed his eyes. He looked to Jana. "Her purse broke."

Jana's silent "Oh" said everything he was thinking.

"That was enough apparently," Mano said. "I'd like to say she dealt with it beautifully, but…"

"GPS says we're about a half hour away." Jana held up her phone with the map app open.

"If we don't hit any traffic." He craned his neck to check the road. "I should be there in about an hour."

"She's fine now, aren't you, Freya?" Mano's question had Silas sitting straight up.

"She's with you? You're in the day care center?"

"She's with me in my office. Hang on. Freya, it's your dad."

Silas heard shuffling and rustling before a very quiet, "Daddy? Are you coming to get me?"

"I'm on my way, sweetie." He grabbed hold of Jana's hand. "Are you doing okay?"

"I'm okay." She didn't sound exactly so to Silas's ears. "Mr. Mano came down and took care of me. Daddy, my treasure bag broke. Everything fell out. I almost lost Winnie and my snow globe broke."

"I'm so sorry." Silas was doing his best to keep calm. The last thing he wanted to do was stress her out further. "We'll get you a new bag, I promise."

"Mr. Mano gave me one from the hotel. It's yellow and everything."

"I hope you thanked him for it."

"Uh-huh."

"I'm going to be there soon. Just be a good girl for a bit longer, okay?"

"Okay. Mr. Mano got me a book so I could color. And he told me all about Haki and the menehunes and Hawai'i has mermaids just like—" She broke off. "Mermaids are called *Na-ma-ka*. Isn't that so cool, Daddy?"

"That is very cool." Silas had a hard time wrapping his mind around the idea of Mano reciting fairy tales or finding a coloring book and crayons. "I'm glad you're having a good time."

"Uh-huh. I am. Can we see Jana when you come get me, Daddy? I really want to see the mer— I really want to see Jana again."

Silas turned his head and looked into Jana's concerned gaze. "I'll bring Jana with me when I come get you, how does that sound?"

"Yay! Thank you, Daddy. Here's Mr. Mano again."

"Silas."

"I don't know how I'll ever make this up to you," Silas couldn't quite find the words to both apologize and thank his friend.

"Friends don't need to *make things up* to one another," Mano said. "It's been a learning experience for both of us. Maybe one day I'll thank you for it." His laugh stated otherwise. "We'll see you soon, yeah?"

216   THE SINGLE DAD'S PROMISE

"Very soon. Thanks, brah."

"Brah?" Jana nudged him with her shoulder. "Careful. You're sounding like a local. She okay?"

The all too familiar guilt beat down on him. "I should have been there."

"You can't be with her twenty-four seven, Silas. Not anymore." There was sympathy but also determination in her tone. "She needs to learn how to navigate the world on her own."

"She's only five."

"When I was five I—"

"Freya isn't you." He hadn't meant it to come out so sharply, but his frustration and anxiety were mingling in an unsettling way. "I know you're trying to help." He forced himself to look at her, to meet her gaze. "But she's not your daughter, she's mine. And I have to raise her the way I think is best. I shouldn't have left her with strangers this long."

He saw the hurt flash in her eyes. "Of course." Her lips quirked into an uncertain smile. "You're absolutely right. This is none of my business."

"I didn't say that." Except he had and he felt absolutely crummy for having done so. "It's just—"

"You can't keep her in a bubble her entire life. As much as you want to." There was a distance now, a detachment he'd never heard in her voice before. "She's with Mano. She's safe. It might be difficult to see at this moment but what happened today will help her better navigate moving forward. Don't blame yourself because life happened." She sat back in her seat and stared out her window. "Trust me, that's a dead-end road."

CHAPTER TEN

"IT'S PROBABLY BEST if I head back to my place." Jana had waited until they were in Nalani, off the bus and mingling with the other tour members saying their goodbyes before she said anything to Silas. Attempting to keep up at least some pretense of their "date," where Don Martin was concerned, she touched a gentle hand to Silas's arm. "Thanks for a nice day."

He caught her hand before she could walk away, the apology shining in his eyes even before the words came out of his mouth. "I'm sorry, Jana. I didn't mean to—"

"It's okay." She offered an understanding smile, wished she couldn't recall what their last kiss had felt like, what being in his arms had felt like. She couldn't let herself consider, even for a second, that there was anything for them beyond the boundaries of Nalani. The sooner she distanced herself, the better. "Really. You were totally right. I shouldn't be telling you how to raise your daughter. So go. Get to Freya."

"But I told her you were coming with me."

It wasn't exactly the plea she'd hoped to hear. "You'll figure something out." She wasn't being mean or calculating. The truth was she needed a serious reset to pull herself out of the fantasy she'd let herself fall into. She wanted to chalk it up to her playing a role, but the truth was, she had feelings for Silas. Feelings that were clearly only going to get her into trouble. "I think we both got a little carried away with things. Go. Freya needs you."

Doubt and regret shone on his handsome face and she almost changed her mind.

"Come with us tomorrow evening. We're booked on the dinner cruise."

Jana shook her head, pulled her hand free. It was all she could do not to jump on board with that idea. "I've already been on one. You and Freya should enjoy it together. Oh, one thing." She began to walk backward slowly. "If you stop in at The Hawaiian Snuggler, Shani showed me some amazing new hand-quilted bags she got in. One of those would work well as a new treasure bag for Freya."

"Jana—"

She turned away before she changed her mind. Making her way through the crowd, she spotted Daphne bidding farewell to Tildy and her group and happily accepting their envelopes filled with tips. Jana held hers out to add to the collection.

"Thanks for understanding about...things," she said as Daphne took the blue envelope. "All in all it was a great day."

"Agreed." Daphne's generous smile dimmed as she glanced around. "Where's Silas?"

"He's heading to the resort." She gestured nervously in that direction. "Freya had some issues while he was gone and he wanted to get to her."

"Oh." Daphne frowned. "And you aren't going with him? I thought—"

"None of our business, Daph," Keane singsonged as he hauled one of the empty coolers behind them.

"It's just, I thought..." The disappointment on Daphne's face mirrored what Jana was feeling. "Seeing the two of you up at the falls I thought maybe something was happening."

"Something did happen and it was lovely." Kissing Silas was something she was never going to forget. What she needed to focus on now was the reality of her situation. Nalani made everything feel surreal, like a fantasy. Whatever social interactions she'd had with men previously had been disappointing and in some cases disastrous. An island romance or any kind of happily-ever-after simply was not on the cards for her. "I'm just going to relax for the rest of the evening, maybe take a swim."

"Sydney, Tehani and I are going to grab dinner

at the Blue Moon around seven," Daphne said. "Why don't you join us?"

"Oh, I don't…" Something Sydney said the other day sprang up in the back of her mind. She didn't want to intrude, but the invitation inherently implied she wouldn't be doing that. "You know what?" She was so tired of not doing what she wanted to because she was afraid. "Thank you. I'd love to come."

"Great." Daphne brightened. "I'll let them know. See you there."

Jana scooted around the bus and found Don Martin typing away on his phone. "It was nice to meet you," she called to him as she passed.

Don glanced up with what she could only describe as a guilty expression on his face. "Nice to meet you, too." He held up his phone. "I was just texting my wife to tell her about my day."

Curious, Jana walked over. "How come she didn't come with you?"

"Oh, well." Don pushed his sunglasses higher up on his nose. "This is partially a business trip. I'm a… I guess you could say I'm sort of a reviewer."

"For an online blog?" Jana feigned surprise. "Are you like an influencer? Can I follow you?"

"Nothing like that." Don chuckled. "I just evaluate potential investment properties. Are you okay?"

She nodded. "I'm fine. But I'm guessing you probably heard all that on the bus."

"I did." His nod was sympathetic. "He's scared. Being responsible for another life, especially on his own." He shook his head. "I couldn't imagine having to raise my girls by myself. Give him time. He'll come around and realize you're right."

"He's right, too." She appreciated his support. "Freya is his daughter. I don't have any claim to tell him anything."

He put his phone away, pushed his hat back on his head. "It's not a matter of whether you have a claim. It's a different perspective and those can be difficult to hear. One thing I learned early on, soon after Diana was born, was that my wife and I had different views of how to deal with parenthood. It takes time to come to a mutual understanding of how things should be done. I remember her telling me that we aren't raising children to be children. We're raising them to be adults." He reached out, grabbed her hand and squeezed. "He'll come around."

If only Don knew the truth. That the only reason she and Silas had been on the tour to begin with had been to keep an eye on him. They must have been successful if he was trying to patch up what he saw as a potential breakup.

"Thank you, Don. I hope I'll see you again before either of us leaves." She realized that she meant it, despite feeling guilty about deceiving him. Playing undercover observer was all well and good until your subject became a person that you felt a kinship with.

"Ohana's got me booked just about every hour I'm here, so I'm sure you will." He gave her a quick wave before he walked off into town.

The weight that had been pressing down on Jana lifted as she walked in the opposite direction toward her cottage. She had a few hours before she needed to come back for dinner. Just enough time to lose herself in the ocean and, hopefully, wash away the last of the bitterness that clung. Not toward Silas. But toward herself. She should have remembered that putting yourself out there often meant getting pushed away. It was a risk, one she thought had been worth taking.

She wouldn't regret those moments she'd had with Silas at the waterfall, but couldn't allow herself to dwell on them, either. Kissing Silas had been everything she'd ever thought a kiss should be. Everything she had never thought she would experience. But it was more than evident now that the moment was all she was going to get.

It was just going to have to be enough.

As ANXIOUS AS Silas was to get to the resort and Freya, he couldn't ignore the idea that despite his verbal missteps and her hurt feelings, Jana had still suggested where he could find a replacement treasure bag for Freya. It solved a problem and left him feeling even more miserable than before.

He'd only met her, what, two days ago? His shutting her down shouldn't be a big deal and yet the idea he'd hurt her... He wasn't certain he'd ever forgive himself.

He rubbed a hand against the unfamiliar ache in his chest.

He'd brought Jana into their lives, pulled her in, really. He'd made it a point to include her and make her feel wanted. But when she offered what was probably invaluable information that he should take to heart, he'd balked. Worse than balked.

He'd blocked her attempt to connect further.

That shock, that flash of pain in her eyes was something he never wanted to see again. Gazing in the window of The Hawaiian Snuggler, he was amazed at the incredible selection of hand-stitched, island-themed fabric items of every kind, in varying colors and sizes.

The store was small and currently filled with a quartet of customers. But he could see the display of bags that had probably caught Jana's attention. Hands shoved in his pockets, he waited rather impatiently for some space to clear before he headed inside. He needed to get to Freya, but he also wanted to bring her something that would ease the memory of how her day had gone.

"Aloha." The dark-haired, artistically tattooed woman behind the counter greeted him when he finally entered. She pinned her dark eyes on him.

"You seem like you know what you're looking for."

"A friend of mine told me about these bags." He beelined for the soft-sided messenger style that was similar to the one Freya had just lost. The bright yellow flowers embroidered on some were a definite plus. "My daughter's favorite bag broke. She calls it her treasure bag."

"How lovely of your friend to recommend my store. I'm Shani." She walked around the counter. "What do you think about these? How old is your daughter?"

"She's five. She takes her bag everywhere and she's not always gentle with it. That said…" Most of what he was seeing, however, had a white background. The intricately stitched floral designs were beautiful and a number of them were in variations of yellow. He sighed. But knowing Freya, if he got her one of these, it wouldn't stay white for long. "She does love yellow."

"Does she?" Shani's warm smile was so friendly. "If it's for treasures, then you're correct. She's going to need something strong and secure." She tapped a finger against her lips. The island-inspired tattoos on her arm flexed. "Give me just a moment, would you? I have something in the back that might work."

Silas continued looking, picking up a bag that seemed wide enough to hold Winnie the one-eyed chicken. It could do if it weren't quite so…

226 THE SINGLE DAD'S PROMISE

"One of my local quilters has begun to make these." Shani returned with a selection of three quilted bags, each with a sliding strap. She motioned him over to the counter where she set them out. "I wasn't certain they'd be a good fit for the store, but I said I'd give them a test run. They call them back bags. They're supposed to be more gentle on the shoulders for people with back issues. There are some pockets on the outside." Each of the zippers had a silver charm that she pulled on to show him. "One for a cell phone, which of course she doesn't need yet. The inside is fully lined and there are more pockets. The strap can be adjusted here." She shortened it, then lengthened it again. "It can grow with her and the best thing is they're machine washable. Nice and solid stitching." She tugged on the main zipper. "And the fabric is extremely durable."

Silas picked up the middle bag, one that was a mishmash of yellow patterns and fabrics, but with a subtle background color of the ocean. It struck him as a bit chaotic, but it also came across as very, very Freya. He checked the zippers, the charms...

He smiled. The tiny metal mermaid dangling from the main zipper was the deciding factor. "I'll take this one."

"Yeah?" Shani looked pleased. "Your little girl likes mermaids, does she?"

"Yes, she does," Silas murmured, thinking of Jana. "We both do."

With thoughts of one particular mermaid swimming through his head, Silas made the purchase and headed straight for the Hibiscus Bay. After asking where to find Mano's office, he made his way inside the resort. He had to admit, taking in the spectacular, nature-forward designed space was enough to take the edge off his nerves.

Maybe it was the relaxing aroma of jasmine? It could be the plethora of miniature palm and twisty banyan trees planted in strategic, sun-catching positions.

Or maybe it was simply that he was close to retrieving Freya. His footsteps echoed against the shiny tiled floor as he rounded the corner and knocked gently on the arched doorframe leading into the waiting area of Mano's official space.

The woman sitting behind a desk situated in a rather lush and tropically decorated office stopped typing on her laptop and glanced at him. Her island skin all but glowed, and her jet-black hair was worn in a long, intricate braid down her back. Before he could even open his mouth, she stood.

"You must be Mr. Garwood," she said as Silas approached.

"Silas, please."

"Pleasure to meet you, Silas." Her smile was warm and welcoming, similar to so many he'd encountered in Nalani. "I'm Alaua, Mano's assistant."

Beyond the hand-carved, wooden, double doors, Silas heard the distinctive, soul-soothing sound of Freya's laughter. The last knot of unease untangled inside of him as he offered what he hoped was a relaxed smile.

"I hope Freya hasn't been too much trouble."

Alaua dismissed his concerned with a wave of her hand. "Children are always on learning curves, aren't they?" There wasn't a hint of disapproval or stress in her voice. "If anything, she's helped break up the usual tedium of the day. Please." She gestured to the doors. "Mano said you should go right in."

"Thank you."

Upon entering, Silas wondered if he'd somehow stepped into another dimension. A dimension where a suit-clad Mano sat in his high-back, leather-upholstered, executive chair with Freya curled into the crook of his arm. Silas's daughter clung to one side of a very thick hardcover book, while Mano held up the other side.

Freya's eyes snapped up from the pages. "Daddy!" She shoved the book at Mano before scrambling off his lap. She raced around the massive desk and latched onto Silas like a barnacle. "You're here!"

"I'm here." He bent down and scooped her up, brushing an errant curl off her forehead. He didn't

ANNA J. STEWART

see any trace of sadness or fear, and if there had been tears, they'd dried long ago.

"Have you been good for Mr. Mano?"

"She's been very good," Mano answered before Freya could. "We've been reading about Hawaiian mythology."

"There are so many stories, Daddy! About *namakas*, that's mermaids, remember, and did you know they have little tricky creatures called—" she paused, her lips pinching "—menehunes. That's what they're called?" she asked Mano.

"Perfect." He shrugged. "It's only a matter of time before you two run into Haki. She's our resident menehune expert."

"I can't wait to meet her," Freya announced. "Mano said if anyone's ever seen a *namaka*, it's her."

"Then we should definitely keep our eyes out for her," Silas agreed. "I'm sorry I'm a bit later than planned. I stopped to get you a present, Freya."

"You did?" She leaned back, nearly tumbled out of his hold as she looked at the door. "Where's Jana? You said Jana was coming."

"Jana couldn't make it. She said to tell you she's sorry and that she'll see you soon." Whether Jana wanted to see Silas again could depend on whether he could extricate his massive foot from his mouth. Despite his best attempt to assure her, he could feel Freya deflate in his arms. "But the

230 THE SINGLE DAD'S PROMISE

present was her idea. Would you like to see what it is?"

He set her down before she could answer, led her over to the small sofa situated beneath one of the two windows in the office. While Freya accepted and dug into the beautifully presented gift bag Shani had put together for him, Silas backed away toward Mano.

"Do I want to know the details?" Silas's question was quiet in the hopes Freya wouldn't hear him asking. "It must have been bad if the day care called you in."

"She was scared. Losing something that was very important to her while she was in a strange place caused a meltdown. But she's okay now. Not to mention, I think she reads at a higher level than I do." Mano bent down to pick up the brown and yellow tote bag Silas recognized as one of the reusable ones from Luanda's. "In related news, I don't think you will ever have to worry about Freya being afraid to express her true emotions in any situation. She can get her point across when she wants to."

Silas grimaced. "I'm so sorry for the ruckus."

"You don't owe anyone an apology, Silas. We all have to figure our way through new situations," Mano said simply. "You and Freya included. How was the tour?"

"Great." Didn't that sound completely underwhelming. "Jana came along and made friends with Don Martin. You aren't surprised," he added at Mano's amused smile.

"I am not." Mano eyed Silas. "I only met Jana once before Keane's party and while she struck me as rather shy, I could tell she was working on coming out of her shell."

Silas had to agree, although to his mind, Jana hadn't just come out of her shell, she'd leaped out carrying sparklers and spinning a baton.

"Yeah, well, she was more on target than I was where Don was concerned." Truth be told, he'd been so distracted by Jana's turn he'd all but forgotten why they were really on the tour to begin with. But Jana had gotten what they'd needed. Don Martin was the kind of man Silas's research had suggested: a family man who didn't look like he was particularly happy with or convinced about the assignment he'd been given.

"Oh, Daddy!" Freya pulled the purse out of the gift bag, her eyes wide with wonder. "It's so pretty! And it's yellow! Look!" She tugged on one of the charms. "Mermaids!"

"It's your new treasure bag." Silas picked up her old, torn bag and brought it over to her. "Why don't you see how things fit? There are lots of pockets and zippers. Test them all out. It's made of a tapestry-type fabric," he told Mano when he rejoined him. "That bag will probably outlast all of us."

232 THE SINGLE DAD'S PROMISE

"Shani knows her quality," Mano agreed. "So, Don Martin. Potential friend or absolute foe?"

"Somewhere in the middle is my guess," Silas said. "Jana definitely tapped into the family angle with him."

"Good," Mano said. "Well, what's your gut telling you? Did he find any weaknesses he can tell GVI about?"

"Not that I could see." Evaluating the man had been the point of Silas going on the tour, despite the distraction of having Jana by his side. "At least not as far as Daphne and Keane are considered. Anything unexpected that came up, they pivoted perfectly and were prepared for. She kept control of the entire party, made adjustments when she needed to." He paused. "Gently yet firmly warned others when necessary."

"Warned who about what?"

Freya was singing softly to herself as she plucked out each of her treasures and settled them in their new, pocketed home.

"Selfie sticks should be illegal." Silas couldn't ignore Mano's curious expression. "I didn't see it myself, but a woman named Tildy nearly toppled off the edge where she was standing at Mauna Loa." Silas shook his head. "I'm surprised Daphne didn't break that stupid selfie stick in two and throw it into the fire. She was ticked, but maintained her cool."

"Takes a lot to rile Daphne," Mano said. "How come you didn't see it?"

"I didn't make it up that far." Silas shifted on his feet. "Jana wasn't feeling well, so I stayed back with her." It wasn't his place to tell Mano or anyone else about Jana's illness or her recovery. "We did make it to the waterfall, though." Happiness radiated through him as he recalled kissing Jana. Thought about kissing her again.

"I'd ask about the story behind that smile, but something tells me it's not for young ears." Mano returned to his desk, picked up the book Freya had been reading from, along with a handful of children's books sitting on the edge. "Alaua ran down to Honu Haven to pick some books out for Freya. We thought she might enjoy some island-based stories and fairy tales." He handed them to Silas. "A child can never have too many books, correct?"

"That's always been my theory. Thank you."

"Hmm." Mano seemed to be considering something. "You should know, I've found a new project to work on. Not sure how you'll feel about it, but I decided to let inspiration take the lead."

"Sounds ominous." But Silas's curiosity was piqued. "Lay it on me."

"To start, would you consider asking Freya to check out the elementary school tomorrow morning? Nothing official," he said quickly when Silas frowned. "I'd like her to see it and I'd like you to speak with the principal about options."

Silas frowned. "I don't think—"

"I know you're hesitant after her initial experience at pre-K," Mano admitted. "But I'm betting you'll find the structure at Kamea more in line with what Freya may need. You didn't mention how well she reads. I'm not talking about her story books." He gestured to the mythology text she'd been reading from before pulling a thin workbook out of the stacks. He handed it to Silas. "She also knows her numbers. And her math skills? I still count on my fingers sometimes."

If Mano was trying to make a joke, it wasn't working. Silas knew he was serious.

Silas flipped through the pages. He blinked, surprised to see the entire book had been completed in Freya's shaky yet readable writing. Addition, subtraction, even some word problems and basic division. "She did all this?" He looked at his friend, skeptical. "Just this afternoon? You didn't help her?" So many of his conversations with Freya's teacher had revolved around her lack of socializing ability, and while he knew Freya was smart, her teacher certainly hadn't accentuated that point.

"If I did, it wasn't much." Mano sat on the edge of his desk. "I'm not an expert in child-rearing or education, obviously. But what I do know is Kamea Elementary was recently named the best elementary school in the islands. We worked hard to achieve that status. The entirety of Nalani has been part of it."

A new knot of anticipation tightened in Silas's chest.

"We're a small town," Mano went on. "So it's a small school. There's a fabulous staff and the principal is a good friend of mine. I want you to talk to her."

"About what exactly?"

Mano's gaze drifted to Freya. "Freya's not a normal five-year-old, Silas."

Silas bristled. "What's normal?"

"Okay." Mao winced. "Poor choice of words. But you know what I mean. Her mind works differently than yours or mine. She's…smarter. Hungrier to learn things. All kids are sponges, but she's on another level. If I can see this after a few days, surely you know this."

Silas nodded. "I asked the school back home about that and while they agreed she tested above average, there weren't a lot of options for specialized education that didn't cost a fortune. I asked if extra time with her teacher was possible, but…" He trailed off. Teachers had enough on their plates with their set schedules. Asking for more wasn't fair. So he'd done what he could on his own, but like Mano, he wasn't exactly an education expert.

"Kamea Elementary offers that specialized education," Mano said. "For free. We do a lot of fundraisers to keep the programs going and to keep our teachers in the pay range they deserve. Happy teachers, happier students. You said you were worried there wasn't a place for Freya back home. Maybe her place is here. Maybe yours is, too."

It took Silas an extra beat to catch on. "This isn't just about Freya. You're trying to get me to move out here." His mind spun with the complications.

Mano shrugged. "I think it's taken you so long to come back because you know, deep down, that this is where you belong. It's where you've always belonged."

Silas disagreed, tamping down the excitement the very idea triggered. "It's not practical, Mano. It's not…logical."

"Not everything is." Mano heaved a sigh and returned to his chair.

"But…" Silas gaped. "But I've got my job. My pension. Health care—"

"Start with the school," Mano cut him off. "Go with an open mind. If you don't think it's right for her or if Freya doesn't like it, then you have your answer."

"And you'll back off this idea?"

"Of course. If you want me to, yes," Mano assured him with that grin of his that had concluded countless, successful business deals. "Doesn't mean the others will, though."

CHAPTER ELEVEN

"YOU LOOK LIKE you're feeling better." Daphne rose from the table by the window at the Blue Moon Bar and Grill to welcome Jana with a quick, friendly hug. She motioned for her to sit at one of the four empty spaces.

"I took a swim." Jana chose the seat closest to the window that overlooked the ocean. An ocean she had become addicted to. She kept waiting for the peace she'd found in Nalani to fade, but instead the sensation only grew stronger. "That always makes me feel better."

"I'll take your word for it." Daphne sat and ran a hand down the length of her red hair. She wore a bright green sundress with thin straps and carried that relaxed, hang-loose aura. "Give me the forest over the ocean any day. Sydney got caught up at work and Tehani's running behind because of Kai. Marella's joining us, too. I think she's looking for a break from Pippy. Or more likely Keane."

"From Keane?" Jana frowned. "Is everything okay?"

"Oh, those two are fine." Daphne waved away

238   THE SINGLE DAD'S PROMISE

her concern with an assuredness. "It's more that Keane is hovering and Marella, well, Marella isn't one who accepts help easily. Not that she needs it," Daphne added quickly, signaling to their server. "I'm about to start a betting pool on whether she stays still long enough to have the baby, or if she just moves on to the next task on her agenda."

"That's something." Jana laughed, then ordered the nonalcoholic mocktail of the day. A pineapple and mango concoction their server insisted was delicious. "It must be nice," she said after Daphne ordered a bottle of wine for the table. "Having so many good friends that you work and play with."

Daphne inclined her head. "You say that as if you don't have any friends."

"I don't, not really." Jana shrugged. She didn't feel particularly sad about it. It's simply what was. "I've gone out with coworkers on occasion. And I've dated off and on. I'm just not comfortable around people. Or I never used to be. It's different here. Everything is…" She flashed an uneasy smile. "Sorry. My filter doesn't always work. Never sure what I should say to…anyone." Except Silas. She'd never once hesitated when she was talking to Silas or Freya. Until she'd said the wrong thing. She pressed her hands against her cheeks. "That must sound so—"

"Hey." Daphne's hand shot across the table and touched her arm. "No apology needed. And it doesn't sound like anything bad. Personally, I'm glad you've decided to open yourself up to us. And if you're worried about fitting in, don't. We are happy to include you in our circle."

"So you didn't ask me to join you out of pity?" She'd meant it as a joke. Kind of.

"We don't do pity." Daphne waved to signal their location in the glassed-in room of the restaurant. "We only do Ohana. There you guys are."

"Sorry we're late." Sydney slid into the seat across from Jana. "I'm so glad you could join us. I heard you had a bit of a spell today up at Mauna Loa. You doing okay?"

"I'm fine, thanks. Oh." She shifted as Tehani sat in the seat beside her and set Kai down in his carrier on the floor between them.

"I know," Tehani said as she reached down to unbuckle his safety harness. "Wyatt was supposed to watch him tonight, but Pua's garbage disposal broke down and he's replacing it for her. He'll come get Kai if he gets done soon."

"I told her its fine," Sydney said as Jana and Daphne's drinks were delivered. "Kai is the only exception to no males at girls' nights. I just need a glass for that." She pointed to the bottle of white wine.

"Same," Tehani added, shifting around to get comfortable. "I won't have to feed Kai again for a good few hours."

Jana couldn't pull her attention away from the

240 THE SINGLE DAD'S PROMISE

eight-month old baby. He was so beautiful with those big eyes and cap full of dark curly hair. All chubby arms and legs that were kicking and paddling as if he were swimming in the ocean. The gentle baby sounds—the gasps and squeals—had Jana's heart beating double time.

"Would you like to hold him?"

Tehani's question startled Jana out of her trance. Her initial instinct was to decline, but she was getting better at dealing with that uncertain part of herself. "May I?"

"Of course." Tehani leaned down to lift Kai out of his carrier. "Just be warned, he's heavier than he looks."

Kai let out a happy cry as Jana cradled him in her arms, his head resting against her shoulder. Kai blinked up at her, his mouth curving as he drooled. "You've done this before," Tehani teased.

"No, actually." Jana reached for her napkin to wipe his mouth. "I haven't." She rocked him gently and earned a wider grin. She smiled back. "He's beautiful."

"He's good to practice on," Sydney announced.

"Careful." Marella said as she arrived at the table. A loose-fitting, blue-and-white, tie-dyed maxi dress swirled around her ankles. She had her dark hair piled high on the top of her head and had that glow of "wow, it's hot this evening" about her. "That's what I said to Keane and look what happened." She eased herself into the chair at the end of the table, offered Jana a quick wave. "Good to see you, Jana."

"Hi." Whatever unease Jana felt about joining the friends had gone. She rested her palm flat against Kai's stomach, reveled in the warmth she felt.

"I think we've lost her," Tehani joked. "My son's first conquered heart."

"Please." Sydney rolled her eyes. "More like hundredth."

"He looks quite content," Daphne said. "You're good with him."

"Probably because I'm just sitting here," Jana responded.

"Still." Sydney paused. "You know, Silas has a knack with kids. I bet he's aces with babies, too."

"Proving yet again that subtlety is not your strong suit." Daphne shot Jana an apologetic look. "We have a tendency to stick our nose into other people's relationships. Feel free to ignore us, Jana." She leaned back as their server brought waters for the table before pouring wine for Sydney, Tehani and Daphne. "Or at least ignore Sydney."

"You were the one who told me what you saw by the waterfall," Sydney accused on a laugh.

Jana's face went sun-flare hot.

"You've completely forgotten what secret means, haven't you?" Daphne grumbled.

"The waterfall?" Marella leaned her chin in her hand. "This sounds juicy. So you and Silas—"

242 THE SINGLE DAD'S PROMISE

"Leave it be, Marella," Tehani said.

"Don't scare her away," Daphne said. "We like you, Jana. And we like Silas. We all think it would be amazing if the two of you..." She motioned to Kai and filled Jana's head with all sorts of impossible dreams. "You know. Dum dum, da-dum."

Sydney rolled her eyes. "That is the worst impression of the wedding march I've ever heard."

Wedding...? Surprise overrode whatever panic Jana might have felt at the idea. "We've only known each other a couple of days." She brushed a finger across Kai's round cheek. "No one falls in love that fast. And no one gets married that fast." Even as she said it, there was a strange doubt circling in the back of her mind.

"Funny." Marella pulled the bread basket closer to her and broke off a sweet roll. "I recall thinking something similar after meeting Keane," Marella mused.

"Which totally makes sense seeing as you kissed Keane before you even knew his name," Tehani teased. "Walked right up to him and planted one on him. Never laid eyes on him before."

"Seriously?" Jana blinked in surprise. How does someone, anyone, do something like that?

"Extenuating circumstances," Marella defended herself easily. "I'd just discovered my then boyfriend making out with one of my sister's bridesmaids."

Jana blinked. "And kissing Keane was…retribution?"

Marella grinned. "Best impulse move I've ever made in my life. It can work out, Jana. If it's meant to be, it can be. You just have to let it happen."

There was no denying she found the idea tempting but also confusing and…daunting. From an early age, she'd done her best to bury the loneliness she always felt but that didn't stop the longing to find someone to share her life with. It wasn't until her diagnosis that she realized she may very well be out of time, which stifled that dream more completely. But now, in this place, with these people, the dream had been rekindled. The fact she'd finally opened herself up to friendship— with Sydney and Marella and Tehani and all the rest—may very well have been the preparation she'd needed for when Silas arrived in Nalani.

It took her a moment to find the right words without blurting out everything she'd been thinking. "I appreciate what you all are attempting to do." Fantasies were all well and good, but she lived in the real world. The world where hours ago she'd probably brought an end to whatever had been building between her and Silas. "But I accepted a long time ago I won't have what the rest of you do. Marriage, a husband. Children."

244   THE SINGLE DAD'S PROMISE

She shook her head, dropped her gaze back to the baby in her arms. "They aren't for me."

"Pffffth." Daphne took a drink of her wine. "It's the twenty-first century. Like Marella just said, you can have anything you want. You just have to—"

"No. I mean, they truly aren't for me." She paused, took a bracing breath. "I can't have children."

The silence was expected and when she glanced up, she found the four women exchanging uncertain expressions.

Strange. Jana felt oddly relieved. She'd kept this to herself for the better part of a year and now, in one day, she'd said it out loud not only once, but twice. It was almost therapeutic, being able to share.

Daphne cleared her throat. "I'm not really used to being the verbal gaffe person. Syd, can you give me some help here?"

Sydney knocked her shoulder against Daphne's and forced a weak smile.

"Please don't let me bring the mood down." The last thing Jana wanted was to cast a depressing pall over the group. "Believe me, I'm very grateful for what I have. My cancer was found in time. My treatment went as well as could be expected. I still have my life and that's amazing."

"But—" Daphne tried again.

"There are plenty of people who live complete

and full lives without having children," Jana went on. "Or without getting pregnant. Me not having a family didn't come completely out of left field. I mean, here I am, a grown adult turning thirty next week and I've never had a serious relationship. Heck, I've never even had a second date." The self-deprecating humor was a protective shield she'd learned to use long ago. "It's this." She tapped a finger against her temple. "My head gets in the way. All the time. With a pad and pencil, with a computer, with machinery, I'm stellar. I can do anything. But with people?"

"You're perfectly fine with people," Sydney assured her.

"Here in Nalani, maybe." It was nice to pretend that was the case. "But this isn't real life. For me, anyway. I know it is for you. It's funny." She waited for the sadness to strike, but when it did, it didn't hit with the ferocity she'd acclimated to. Maybe it was being able to talk about this with other women, with…friends. Or maybe it was the baby in her arms that both restarted that longing and also healed her a bit. "I didn't even really think I wanted to have a baby until I knew I couldn't." She swallowed hard as Kai reached out and grabbed her finger. "Now it's just been a matter of coming to terms with it. And I have. Truly."

"Do you mind me asking, I mean." Tehani seemed to be struggling. "Are you sure? Maybe the doctors—"

"I'm very sure." Jana nodded. "The treatment I needed last year was…extensive. And complete."

"Oh, Jana." Daphne's sympathy was clear.

"That's why I came to Nalani. To recover. To heal." She lifted Kai up so she could press her lips to his temple and inhale that baby smell she'd heard so much about. The softness of that scent had her closing her eyes as she smiled. "And you all have been a big part of that. So please, don't feel sorry for me. That's the last thing I want. And as far as Silas goes." Even saying his name had her heart skipping a beat, which made absolutely no sense to her logic-leaning mind. "It's lovely you all think I'm deserving of someone like him, but the reality is Nalani is a fantasy. And maybe Silas is, too."

"He doesn't have to be," Sydney said.

Jana shook her head. "From the moment I arrived in Nalani, you all have included me, even when I didn't want you to." She turned gently accusing eyes on Sydney, who chuckled. "For the first time in my life, I have friends. When all is said and done, I can't think of anything better than that. That's a gift I'll treasure for the rest of my life."

"Well, shoot." Marella wiped the tears off her cheeks. "We absolutely need to get a toast going here." She raised her water glass and the others followed suit. "To new friends."

"No," Sydney corrected her. "To Ohana."

ANNA J. STEWART 247

Their glasses clinked, and Jana smiled, memories of Silas and Freya swimming through her thoughts. "To Ohana."

"How come we're going all the way down here, Daddy?" The day care incident of earlier in the day seemingly forgotten, Freya skipped beside Silas on the beach, kicking up sand as she clung to the shortened strap of her new bag. It had been the hit Jana had suggested it would be. It made Silas all the more determined to put things right with her.

"I thought maybe you'd like to show Jana your new treasure bag."

"I would like to do that." She beamed up at him. "But does that mean we can't go swimming?"

"We can do that, too." He'd stuffed Freya's floaties into her bag. "But there's also something I would like to talk to you about." He tugged her toward Jana's porch and, after knocking and realizing she wasn't home, decided they could wait a bit. He sat on the top step, pulled Freya close. "We need to decide what to do about school, Freya."

She pouted. "I don't like school."

"I know, and I understand why."

"They were mean to me. Now they don't talk to me. And I can't read my books."

Silas sat up straighter. "What do you mean?" He hadn't heard this part before.

248 THE SINGLE DAD'S PROMISE

"I wanted to read some of the books in the big library, but the teacher wouldn't let me. She said I wasn't old enough to read on my own, but I can, Daddy. I do it all the time."

"Yes, you do." He smoothed her hair back. "I'm sorry that happened." Suddenly her difficulties in adjusting began to make more sense. Not to mention he wasn't getting the full story from her school.

"I like my books at home. They're bigger. So can't I just read at home instead of going to school?"

Clearly, she'd given this idea some thought. "There are other things you need to learn apart from reading, Freya."

"You can teach me."

Silas was a man who knew his limitations and he knew for a fact he wasn't equipped for home-schooling.

"It wouldn't be hard. Mr. Mano said I'm very smart."

And there, Silas realized, was his way in. "You like Mr. Mano a lot, don't you?"

"Uh-huh. He's nice. And he helped me not be upset when my bag broke. He gave me ice cream and didn't mind all my questions!"

Something else Silas hadn't heard. "Mr. Mano told me about the school they have here. He thinks you'd like it."

Freya didn't look confused or as put off by the

suggestion as Silas expected. Instead, he could only describe her expression as intrigued. "Is it where Cammie and Noah go?"

"It is." He chose his words carefully. "What do you think about maybe going over there tomorrow morning and looking around? Seeing what it's all about? Maybe meet some of the teachers?"

Freya kicked off her sandals. "Would Cammie be there?"

Silas nodded. "It's a school day, so I'm betting she will be."

"Could we see Maru first and get doughnuts?"

"We could do that. Is that a yes?"

"Yes. Can we go swimming now?" She jumped up, not a hint of the trepidation he was certain she'd express over the idea of school. "Please, please, please?"

"Sounds like that better be a yes." Jana's voice had Silas turning. She'd snuck up on them, approached from the side and rounded the corner of her cottage as stealthily as her house gecko. "Hi."

"Hi." Silas searched for a hint of the hurt he'd seen on her face earlier, waited for the tension he'd felt as she'd backed away from him. "Oh, Freya wanted to show you her new bag from Shani."

"It's so cool!" Freya leaped forward, grabbed Jana's hands and pulled her closer, then pushed her bag in front of her and did a dance. "It's yel-

250 THE SINGLE DAD'S PROMISE

low and blue and look!" She touched the charm. "It has mermaids on it!"

Jana bent down, took her time examining the bag, gave a firm nod of approval. "That is truly beautiful, Freya."

"Daddy said you found it." She threw her arms around Jana's neck and squeezed. "Thank you."

Silas watched Jana's eyes mist as she returned the embrace.

"Guess what?" Freya said when she stepped back. "I'm going to school tomorrow! Mr. Mano said it's good."

"Mr. Mano did, huh?" Jana smiled gently. "Sounds like an amazing idea."

"We're going to get doughnuts on the way. Can you come with us?"

"Jana might have other plans, Freya."

"I don't," Jana said, then added, "But I don't want to intrude. A first day of school is a very special thing. I think it should probably stay between father and daughter."

"But I want you to come," Freya said. "Daddy! Please tell Jana to come with us."

"You wouldn't be intruding," Silas told Jana firmly. "And I'm sorry if I ever made you feel as if you were. It would be nice having someone to share this with." Someone who understood how difficult this might be for himself and Freya.

Jana looked between the two of them, then nodded. "All right. I would love to come with you."

"Yay!" Freya jumped up and down. "Okay, now I want to swim, please, Daddy."

"Go on, you two," Jana said when Silas glanced at her. "I've already had my swim for the evening, so I'll just sit here and watch."

"We'll come pick you up in the morning? Around seven?"

She nodded and took his seat when he stood. "I'll be ready."

CHAPTER TWELVE

An odd, faint knocking sounded as Jana turned off the water for her early morning shower. She grabbed a towel and wrapped it around her when the knock sounded again. Stronger this time. Shoving her dripping hair back from her face, she stepped out, tucked the knot tighter under her arm and made her way toward the front of the cottage. The clock showed it was just past six.

She waited. Nothing. Jana shook her head. Her mind was playing tricks on her. The insomnia had come back last night, leaving her feeling sluggish and frustrated but at least she'd had a lovely ocean view and the last of her paint supplies to keep herself occupied. Staring up at the ceiling fan, waiting for sleep to claim her, had been a lesson in futility.

She spun on her heel, nearly slipped in the puddle she'd left in the kitchen.

Jana heard it again.

"Noodles."

It had to be that silly gecko. Must have gotten

into something that required noise to set himself free. Curious, she hurried to the door, pulled it open and...

"Freya." She blinked, half-certain she was imagining things.

"Hi." Freya's hands twisted together, a sure sign, at least to Jana, that something was up. She had her bag slung across her body, but it looked suspiciously more full than it had last night.

"Where's your dad?" Jana leaned out the door, looked in both directions, but didn't see any sign of Silas. "Freya?" She leaned back, grabbed hold of her towel with one hand and guided the little girl inside.

"He's sleeping. I snuck out. But I left the door open."

She'd left the door...

Unlike Jana, Freya was already dressed. Her summer yellow sundress left Jana blinking against the brightness. Her braids were crooked and uneven, obviously a self-attempt. Jana steered Freya to the sofa, then retrieved her cell phone only to remember she didn't have Silas's number. She joined Freya and sat on the edge of the sofa beside her. "What's wrong?"

Freya ducked her head. "I'm scared."

"Of what?" Had something happened to Silas? Or was this about...? An odd relief sank through her, but her tension didn't abate completely. "This is about school, isn't it?"

"I don't want to go," Freya said. "And I can't tell Daddy because he says I have to go and I don't want to be teased or yelled at again." She lifted tearstained cheeks to Jana. "Can I live with you? I'll be good. I brought some clothes with me, too. I won't make any noise and I..."

"Freya." Jana nearly choked on her name. She drew the child close, wrapped her tight so she could feel the comfort Jana offered. "Freya, I'm sorry, but you can't live with me."

Freya sagged in her arms.

"You are your daddy's little girl," Jana murmured. "You're the most important thing in his life. What would he do without you?"

"I don't know." Freya frowned. "I just don't want to go. I tried to be brave. I got dressed and everything." She plucked at the fabric of her dress. "Please don't make me go."

Jana understood, but she couldn't look at this through only her own childhood experience. As Silas had pointed out yesterday, Freya wasn't hers. That said, Jana was the one facing the situation at the moment.

"It's no fun doing things we don't want to do, is it?" Her mind raced for a logical explanation Freya would understand.

"No."

"You know, a little while ago, I had to do something that scared me. Scared me a lot. I wanted to run away, too."

"You did?" Freya asked, her tone curious. "But you're a grown-up."

"We don't stop being scared because we grow up." Far from it. "In fact, sometimes you get scared even more. Like I did. But it was something I had to do if I wanted to…" *Live.* "It was just something I needed to do. And it was hard. Really hard. But you know what?"

"What?"

"I'm so glad I did it. If I didn't, I wouldn't be here today." It was so strange, talking about the cancer treatment that had all but paralyzed her with fear, with a five-year-old. "I wouldn't have visited Nalani. I wouldn't have met Mr. Mano or Noodles, and I wouldn't have met you and your dad." Tears pricked the backs of her eyes as she felt a tiny part of herself begin to heal. "That makes what I had to do worth it, Freya. You know, there's a saying a lot of grown-ups use and maybe it can help you."

"What is it?"

"Feel the fear and do it anyway."

Freya's mouth scrunched. "But I don't want to do it."

Jana winced. So much for her first shot at parenting. "Okay, I want you to sit right here for a few minutes. I need to get dressed. Then we'll go back home and talk to your dad."

"But…" Freya's eyes filled and her lips trembled. "He's going to be mad at me."

256 THE SINGLE DAD'S PROMISE

If Jana was quick enough they might get back to the other cottage before Silas realized Freya was gone.

"But we don't want him worried, do we? Stay right here, all right?" She pressed a quick kiss to the top of Freya's head before she scurried back to her bedroom.

She'd never dressed so quickly in her life, jumping into her clothes after barely looking at them. She ran a comb through her still wet hair, tossed her towel over the top of the shower door, hurried back to the sitting room and jammed her feet into her sandals.

Part of her expected to find her own door open and Freya gone. Instead, Freya had shifted onto her knees and was currently in an in-depth conversation with Noodles, who had taken up a spot on the window ledge.

"Let's go, Freya." Jana grabbed her small purse and keys, held out her hand.

Freya heaved a sigh and slowly unfolded herself off the sofa. "Daddy's going to be mad." She slipped her hand into Jana's.

"He won't stay that way for long." After locking up, Jana did her best to maintain a pace slow enough for Freya to keep up. "You know leaving your house like this was wrong, don't you?"

"Yes." Freya's feet kicked up sand as they walked. "But—"

"There are no buts, Freya. It's not safe to go

wandering around by yourself." Especially so close to the water. Jana had seen enough last night to know that Freya was an okay swimmer, but that was only with floaties and Silas holding her. Not to mention the ocean was rarely forgiving or kind. "I want you to promise me you won't ever do something like this again."

"But I thought you were my friend."

Despite Silas's cabin being only yards away, Jana stopped walking, her legs having grown heavy plowing through the sand. She took a deep breath and tried to focus on curtailing the panic inside her. She stooped down, caught Freya's hands in hers and gently squeezed. "I am your friend, Freya. But friends don't let other friends make bad decisions. We hold them accountable..." She was slipping down a too-adult verbal road even for the very clever Freya to understand. "We look out for one another and we tell them when they've done something wrong. It's part of the job of being a friend."

"So you're doing your job taking me back to Daddy?"

"I am." She touched Freya's hair. "Because I lo—" Jana cleared her throat. Other than her parents, she'd never uttered those words to another person. But with Freya, the instinct was simply there. She did love her. More than she had any right to. "Because I care about you. Because I want the best for you and so does your daddy. I promise." She pulled her in, kissed her forehead. "Going to this school, I bet, will be good for you, and you know what?"

"What?" Freya mumbled.

"It could turn out to be okay. What if no one makes fun of you?"

The total disbelief on the child's face was almost comical.

"What if no one is mean?" Jana tried again. "What if you make friends? What if you like your teachers and learn stuff that's new? What if you can't wait to go back?"

She was getting through. Sort of. The doubt and, more importantly, a lot of the fear had begun to disappear from Freya's face.

"I think you going to school today could be a very good thing," Jana said with confidence. "But we won't know for sure until you give it a try." Inspiration struck. "Hang on." She opened her purse, pulled out her wallet, then the worn Bee Brave badge her father had made for her. Until now she couldn't have imagined parting with it, even for a short while. But right now? She couldn't imagine holding on to it. "Would you like to keep this in your pocket today?"

Freya's eyes went wide and she nodded. "Can I?"

Jana handed the badge to her. Freya tucked it into the front pocket of her sundress, patted it gently against her tummy. "It helped me feel better when I was scared. I think it can help you, too. Just keep it close."

"I will." Freya whispered. "Will you still come with me to school?"

"Yes." If Silas was still okay with that.

"Freya!"

Silas's shout and the sound of a screen door banging open had Jana shooting to her feet.

"I told you," Freya whispered. "He's mad."

"He's scared," Jana responded as they started walking again. "Just like you were a little while ago. Go on. Hurry up to him." She let go of Freya's hand and the little girl raced over to her father.

Jana had to stop at the sight of Silas dropping to his knees and catching her in a hard hug. The ferocity with which he held his child reminded her so much of her father. For a moment, she could almost feel her own father's embrace. She offered a weak smile as Silas's gaze met hers.

He squeezed his eyes shut for a second, then grabbed Freya's arms and held her away from him, stared directly into her eyes.

"What were you thinking?"

Jana resumed her path toward them.

"You scared me so much, do you know that?"

"I'm sorry," Freya apologized and rocked back on her heels. "Jana told me I did a bad thing. But I needed to talk to her, Daddy. I—" she looked up as Jana joined them "—I thought maybe I could

260 THE SINGLE DAD'S PROMISE

live with her and then I wouldn't have to go to school."

Silas sank back on his heels.

The defeat Jana saw on his face hurt her heart. She'd do anything to take away his pain. She could still see the panic, as well, and could only imagine what must have gone through his head when he'd found his daughter gone. His hair was mussed from sleep, the dark blue pajama bottoms stark against the barely-there tan. There was something oddly intimate about seeing him this way, but right now all she could do was try to ease him into normal dad mode.

"I brought her back as quickly as I could," Jana told him. "But we had a talk about how being scared is okay, and that sometimes we have to do things we don't want to do. Also, that running away is never the answer."

"Uh-huh. That." Freya nodded solemnly. "I'm sorry, Daddy. I won't ever run away again, I promise."

"Why don't you go inside and unpack your clothes and things, Freya?" Jana said with a warning look at Silas when he turned shocked eyes on her. "I'll make sure your dad isn't mad anymore, okay?"

"Okay." She walked to the porch, turned around. "Can we still go get doughnuts from Maru?"

"Doughnuts," Silas muttered under his breath.

"My heart forgot how to beat and she's thinking doughnuts."

"We'll see." Jana put a hand to his shoulder. "First time I've ever said those words," she admitted once Freya had disappeared inside.

Silas had no sooner got to his feet than he wrapped his arms around her in a hug as tight as she'd given Freya moments before.

"Thank you." His breath was warm against her ear as he clung to her. "When I woke up and she was gone—"

"I know." She held on to him, to reassure him, to reassure herself that everything was okay. His heart beat frantically against her cheek and she looked up, determined to say something profound that would ease his worry and…

That wasn't worry or fear she saw in his beautiful eyes. It was… She couldn't quite put it into words, but for the first time in her life she felt as if she were the only person in his universe.

She rose up on her toes, her own pulse jumping into an unsteady rhythm as she pressed her mouth to his. It was a kiss she'd thought about offering during those unending sleepless hours, the promise of which had probably attributed to her insomnia.

His hands slipped down to the base of her spine, pulled her closer as he kissed her back. It robbed her of breath. And, of doubt.

Her brain rarely stopped long enough for her

262 THE SINGLE DAD'S PROMISE

to catch a coherent thought, and yet, in Silas's arms, everything seemed to come to a glorious halt. It was, she realized as his lips caressed hers and left her grinning, the first time she'd felt utterly and completely happy.

"I tried to get her back here before you woke up," she murmured when he lifted his head.

He chuckled, nuzzling her cheek. "I'm going to have to put bells on all the doors."

"No you won't." The idea had her smiling, even as her heart continued to soar in her chest. This was what she'd always heard about. Read about. Refused to let herself dream about. Having a special someone. The someone. "Trust me, she won't do something like that again."

"I don't know what to do about her. About this school thing. What if she hates it? Or what if she loves it?" He stepped back, but didn't release his hold on Jana.

"Why don't you stop worrying about the what-ifs and wait until they're a reality." It was a lesson she'd had to learn during her treatments. Worrying about things that hadn't happened yet only fed the fear. "You do what you said you were going to do yesterday," she told him. "You're going to take her to school and see what happens. Nothing more."

He didn't look convinced. "Maybe she's right. Maybe I just—"

Jana placed a finger over his lips. Lips she

couldn't wait to kiss again. "Freya is right to feel what she feels. She's not going to break, Silas. You have to stop assuming she will. She's a tough little girl. She thought out every step of her plan this morning. She got up, got dressed for school, then panicked and packed her bag to leave. That's not a child who is going to be easily defeated."

"Right. You're right. Of course I'm just so grateful she came to you."

Jana smiled, bolstered by his confidence in her. "I'll understand if you'd rather I not come with you this morning. To take her to school," she added at his blank look.

"Are you kidding?" He leaned in and pressed his mouth to hers again. It was such a natural kiss, such a perfect moment, the touch of him emptied her mind of every other thought. It almost, *almost*, made the previous kiss pale by comparison. "She might not need the added support, but I do. But we won't be stopping for doughnuts." He grinned at Jana's pout. "She has to learn about consequences. But after school, maybe we can take her for shave ice."

Jana put her hands to his cheeks and brought his mouth down to hers for another kiss. Because she could. And because it felt right. "That's a great compromise."

DESPITE MORE THAN ten years as a cop, Silas honestly could not remember ever being more petrified than when he'd pushed open the door to Freya's room and realized she was missing.

Even now, almost two hours later, as he and Jana walked alongside Freya, each holding one of her swinging hands, he knew that moment would probably be the worst one in his life. The strap of her treasure bag slung across her chest, almost as if acting like a kind of shield.

The fact that Freya was skipping and not trying to hold back as they headed to Kamea Elementary kept him from surrendering to that panic he'd awoken to. Instead, he focused on the fact that Freya had felt safe going to Jana. Okay, maybe there was a little envy over that, but it was the first time Freya had ever looked to anyone other than Silas for anything. That was a good thing.

Wasn't it?

Instead of taking the very long route to the school, they turned off Pulelehua Road, passing by an old-style movie theater.

Silas stopped, shielded his eyes and looked up at the marquee for the Andrena Theater. "Well, that's a shame." Mahalo and aloha were spelled out in stark black letters. "This was a fun place to go to when I visited the first time." The retro theater had a classic, lush red velvet interior and sparkling brass accents. "They don't make movie theaters like this anymore."

"What's a theater?" Freya asked in a way that had Silas blinking, only to realize he never had taken his daughter to an actual theater. Streaming services and a large-screen TV had sufficed since she'd been born.

"It's where people go to watch movies on a giant screen," Jana told her. "You can eat popcorn and candy and sit in these big comfy chairs."

"That sounds like fun! Can we go to a theater, Daddy?"

"This one's closed, unfortunately." But to ease his daughter's disappointment added, "Maybe when we get home."

It was another two blocks to the school, which Freya spent chatting to him and Jana, the birds, a dog and anyone else she recognized. To be honest, Silas was overwhelmed by the idea of the three of them walking like this, as if they were a family.

He'd never had time to lament having lost a partner when Caroline left, but now he felt the void.

A void he began to believe could be filled by Jana.

The school itself wasn't very large, but it was more modern than he remembered. Single story, with large, wide windows. The play, eating and common areas were bountiful. Thick grass lined the spaces around the expansive jungle gym. There were two sand boxes, currently occupied by a group of kids, and everything from monkey bars, to dozens of swings, to hopscotch, four square and basketball. He saw various game ta-

266 THE SINGLE DAD'S PROMISE

bles, lockers and a huge collection of surfboards in various sizes resting against the side of the building. It felt warm and inviting, and that, he realized, was a step in the right direction.

The number of children wasn't overwhelming, but they did range in age. When he looked down at Freya, she stepped closer to him, eyeing the trio heading toward them. One was a very familiar, smiling face.

The tension in his stomach eased at the sight of Cammie Townsend.

"Hi, Freya!" Cammie had burst out of the pack, racing over to catch Freya in a big hug. Freya's hands slipped out of his and Jana's hold as Cammie swung her around. They wobbled, but both girls were giggling when they finally stopped spinning.

The two women with Cammie approached. One was older, taller and thinner, with big dark eyes and round cheeks. Her companion was probably his own age, blonde and blue-eyed. They both displayed wide, friendly smiles that helped put him at ease. "Do you have a welcoming committee like this for all potential students?"

"We try to. Aloha, Mr. Garwood. I'm Mahina Kaili. School principal." He'd guess the older woman was a lifelong Nalani resident. "I'm so pleased you've agreed to let Freya join us today, and that she's agreed to come. Mano spoke very highly of the two of you. We chatted just last night as a matter of fact."

And no doubt got an earful about Freya's day care center meltdown. "Freya." Silas called his daughter over, something he wasn't used to doing, seeing as how she was normally suction-cupped to him. "Come meet Ms. Kaili, please."

Freya quit chasing Cammie around one of the swing sets and raced over. "Hi." She tilted her head up and fell back against Silas.

Ms. Kaili crouched, her flower-patterned skirt tightening around her knees. "Aloha, Freya. I've heard a lot about you."

"You have?" She turned quizzical eyes up at Silas.

"She's a friend of Mr. Mano's," Silas told her.

"Mr. Mano's my friend." Freya reached up and grabbed Silas's hand. "I've never had friends before we came here and now I have a whole bunch!"

"We'll have to make sure you find more while you're here. I wonder if you could help me with something, Freya." Ms. Kaili accepted a puzzle block from the other woman. Ms. Kaili held it out to Freya. "Do you like puzzle games, Freya?"

"Oooh! Yes! I have this at home." She grabbed it and began twisting it around to match up the colors. Her hands moved so fast they were almost a blur. "Daddy mixes it up for me at night." Cammie moved in as Freya's twisting increased in speed. "He always tries to trick me, but I always solve it."

268 THE SINGLE DAD'S PROMISE

"It's our breakfast routine," Silas explained, glancing at Jana. Finding both approval and amusement on her face left him almost giddy.

More twisting on Freya's part. More turning. Her actions and chatter while she worked drew the attention of the other students. Pretty soon, she had a crowd. "I think I just…" Freya stuck her tongue out of the corner of her mouth. "Here." She held it out. "Finished."

Ms. Kaili accepted it, her mouth stretching into a wide smile. "Mahalo, Freya. I've been trying to solve it for days. You're very smart, aren't you?"

Freya beamed.

"That was awesome!" A boy of maybe eight or nine moved in. "So cool!"

Freya shrugged.

"Way cool," another one agreed. "I'm Ahe. This is Stanley." He pointed to the first boy. "We're playing Ping-Pong. Wanna come play?"

"I don't know how," Freya said.

"I do." Cammie grabbed her hand. "We can teach you. Come on!"

Silas was left feeling a bit abandoned as Freya raced off with Cammie and her new friends, her treasure bag bopping against her back. The rest of the students broke apart, but he couldn't see any sign of hostility or discomfort.

"This is Jessica Lono." Ms. Kaili stepped back and the other woman came forward. "She's one of our classroom assistants. I've asked her to be Freya's guide today."

"Did she pass?" Jana asked.

"I'm sorry?" Silas tried to pull his attention away from the sight of Cammie teaching Freya how to hold a Ping-Pong paddle. On her first attempt, his daughter whacked the table hard enough that he felt it in his own arm. But no one made fun of her. If anything, the two boys and Cammie all circled around to help her figure it out. "This is my friend Jana Powell."

"Pleasure, Ms. Powell," Ms. Kaili said. "And it wasn't really a pass/fail kind of test. I just like to see how certain students do with that particular toy."

"You were testing her spatial awareness and problem-solving skills."

Ms. Kaili nodded. "Yes."

"She's trying to determine the best grade to start Freya at," Jana told Silas before turning back to the educators. "You don't want her bored."

"Exactly," Jessica Lono said. "We want her challenged. What will keep her engaged and in a good mindset. We have a number of students in advanced placements. We don't generalize by age. Instead, we do our best to assess each student individually."

"Mano told us about her reading ability," Ms. Kaili said. "And while I think she might do well in third or even fourth level, I'm going to keep her in second. That way she can be with Cammie and she'll feel more comfortable." She looked to Silas. "I understand Freya has had difficulty in school back home?"

Silas gave a brief rundown. "It's left her leery of attending."

"Maybe not anymore," Jana added, chuckling and pointing to the kids concentrating on their game. Silas realized he was laughing, too, now.

"Well, if we do our jobs properly today, she won't be able to resist coming back. For as long as you're here," Ms. Kaili said quickly. "School lets out around two. Are there any food allergies we need to be aware of? Is she on any medications?"

"No to both allergies and medications," Silas said. "But she's a picky eater. Unless it's pineapple."

"Shouldn't be a problem," Jessica said. "We never run out of that. We have your cell number if we need it. And I'll be here when you come pick her up if you'd like a rundown of her day."

"That would be great, thanks."

"All right, then." Ms. Kaili checked her watch. "We've got about ten minutes before classes begin. We'll see you this afternoon."

"Thank you," Silas said as he and Jana headed inside. "Wow." He couldn't help but feel a bit shell-shocked. "Is this place for real?"

"Seems to be the norm for Nalani, doesn't it?" Jana moved closer. It struck him how utterly perfect it felt having her at his side. "I'd bet anything she's going to be fine."

"Freya! We're leaving!"

Freya spun around and got hit in the back of the head with a Ping-Pong ball. He froze, then forced himself to breathe when she and Cammie laughed. Freya waved at them, then immediately turned back around to her new friends.

"Yeah." Jana entwined his arm with hers, putting him at ease. "She's going to be just fine."

CHAPTER THIRTEEN

"GOT THE LAST TWO before Maru and Lani closed the stall."

Jana accepted the offered macadamia-nut-cream malasada and bit in before he had a chance to sit down beside her on the park bench.

"No reason for us to suffer just because Freya has to miss out."

"Not going to argue." Powdered sugar blasted out and around her mouth as she chewed. "Sorry. I'm starving!" she said, laughing. "Wasn't sure I'd ever feel like eating again."

Silas shook his head. "Thank you for taking care of her."

"Of course." She didn't want to prolong this conversation much further. The truth was still the truth. She wasn't Freya's mother. Though she was thrilled to be her friend. And Silas's. "Are you really going to keep doing that?" She pointed to the watch he was checking.

"What? Oh. That. Sorry." He took a small bite of his malasada. "I feel completely off-kilter."

"You are," Jana teased. "What can I do to distract you?"

"Just looking at you is distracting enough."

Her face warmed and she accepted the compliment without comment. Being around him really did leave her feeling a part of something. Something special. "Give it here." She held out her sugarcoated hand. "Seriously. Give me your watch." He sighed, took it off and handed it to her. "You can have it back when you pick up Freya."

"We. When we pick up Freya."

Her heart tipped over. "Yeah?"

He nodded. "Yeah."

"I'd like that." She nudged her shoulder against his. Sitting beside him on the bench across from Maru's stand, where she could hear the ocean rumbling behind her, Jana sighed in contentment. "Are we off Don Martin duty today?"

"You are," Silas said. "He's booked on the dinner cruise tonight on the *Nani Nalu*, so Tehani booked me two places. I told Freya we can watch for dolphins."

"While you spy on the spy," Jana teased. "Can you even see dolphins at night?"

"You tell me." He swiped a napkin down her nose. "You're supposed to be the mermaid. Maybe you can use your special underwater sonar powers to call some forth."

She grinned. "I'll do my best." Was this what happiness felt like? No worries. No real cares.

274 THE SINGLE DAD'S PROMISE

Just sitting on a bench beneath the Hawaiian sun, basking under the shade of swaying palm trees. "Anything in particular you'd like to do while we wait for two o'clock?"

"I'm up for anything." He polished off his malasada, catching up to her, then stood and held out his hand. "Shall we wander and see what we find?"

She beamed at him, determined to embrace this carefree feeling for as long as it lasted. After so much loneliness, she'd found everything she'd ever wanted in this tiny island town. How could she turn her back on it now? She slipped her hand into his and squeezed. "Let's do it."

THEY WALKED AND ate and shopped and laughed. From exploring every store to trying the freshly baked mango cookies with white chocolate from Little Owl Bakery, there wasn't an inch of Nalani's main street they didn't experience.

Up past the resort, toward the church, a series of white tents had gone up between the beginning of their sojourn and early afternoon. The crowds funneled in that direction and Silas offered no resistance when Jana turned bright and expectant eyes on him.

He couldn't help but think, as they walked up the gently sloping hill, how natural today felt. As if this was how he was meant to be living his life. In the sunshine and sea air, surrounded by a community that lifted him up and left him feeling as if anything and everything was possible.

And Jana.

If he was floating on air, she was what tethered him to the ground. To her. He never thought anything could bring him more joy than watching Freya conquer her own tiny part of the world, but watching Jana open herself up and blossom into this exuberant woman was yet another sign that Nalani had worked its very specific kind of magic on her. On them.

His original plan had been to use what vacation time he had stored up working at the department. Now he felt himself dreading the very idea of returning home. Especially if Freya's school experience—

"You're doing it again." Jana's hand tightened around his as she slowed down to stop among the throng of customers filling the aisles between the vendor tents. "We're living in the moment for a little while longer." She turned that brilliant, blazing smile on him and his entire world tipped onto its side.

"Hard habit to break." Impossible was more like it. He'd become so reliant on schedules and timetables for such a long time that he'd all but forgotten how to live outside of that. And yet Jana, with all she'd dealt with over the past year, was teaching him how to take a big step toward what might be a better way.

276 THE SINGLE DAD'S PROMISE

The air was filled with the aromatic scent of cooking sugar. They passed in front of a tent where a giant copper kettle filled with caramel was being stirred and topped off with freshly popped popcorn. His stomach rumbled.

"I heard that." Jana laughed, knocked her shoulder against his arm and then gasped, pointing a few tents ahead. "Peelin' Pine. Tehani told me about that place. It's all things pineapple. Come on."

Silas didn't have a choice since she tugged him along through the crowd for the tables filled with various jars of pineapple-infused goodness. From hot sauces to salad dressings to a salsa he couldn't resist trying. The sweet and slightly tangy taste did the hula on his tongue. "That's delicious."

"Yeah?" Janna dipped a chip into the sample bowl and closed her eyes when she tasted it. "Oh my gosh. I have to get this. Freya would like this, too."

It was that moment. That was the moment Silas knew he was done for. Despite her push for him to put his daughter out of his mind for a while, Freya had taken up residence in Jana's own thoughts. And the way Jana kept looking at him, almost as if she was afraid he might disappear on her, he suddenly had a new mission in life: to erase that expression from her face permanently.

He reached out his free hand, brushed a strand of hair behind her ear.

"What?" she asked without hesitation. "Do I have—"

"No," he murmured and gave in to the temptation to kiss her. "You overwhelm me sometimes."

"Is that good?" She didn't look sure.

"It's more than good." He waved over the vendor so they could buy the salsa. "It's everything."

They did considerable damage to their wallets and filled up not one but two purchased and recycled shopping bags with items such as local blossom honey and a hand-carved wooden bowl Jana couldn't resist, as well as an assortment of sea glass and shell keychains that would make wonderful holiday gifts. Either Jana was planning on staying long enough to give them out to her new friends or she was throwing caution to the wind and embracing the unexpected. Either way, he considered her shopping spree an experience he'd never forget.

They made their way back into the downtown area, as a countdown clock ticked louder in Silas's head.

Beep-beep!

"Shark Boy!"

Silas nearly tripped over his own slippahs.

Jana giggled as he caught himself in time for Benji to swing his disco-decorated golf cart to a stop beside them. Sitting on the passenger seat was a very large pig wearing a shirt that matched

Benji's neon pink one smattered with leaping, boggle-eyed cartoon sharks.

"Hey, Benji." Silas offered a quick wave and tried to contain his embarrassment. "Just you and Kahlua, huh? Pippy ditch you today?"

"She's shopping for a dress for our promise ceremony." Benji beamed, his wrinkled, tanned face glowing with pride. "I'm not allowed to see. You're a pretty one." Benji looked at Jana. "Saw you at the birthday party the other night." His eyes narrowed. "You're the painter. Keane showed off your work."

"Ah." Jana balked. "I just do that for fun and to relax. I'm actually a—"

Benji flipped off his engine, shifted in his seat. "I saw a video on that Tubey thing a while back. There're these people who set up and paint moments as they happen. Like during weddings and graduations and things."

Jana nodded. "I love those videos."

Silas bit the inside of his cheek. She really didn't see where this was going, did she?

"That picture you painted was wonderful," Benji said. "All those colors and… Would you come to the ceremony and do one for my Pippy?"

"I…" Jana blinked, her spine straightening. "I wouldn't know where to—"

"Ceremony won't be for a while yet," Benji continued. "Gives you plenty of time to figure it out."

"Um." Jana turned mildly panicked eyes on Silas, who shrugged.

"It's your fault you're talented. Plus, you said you didn't know how long you were staying." Even as he said it, Silas felt the pang of reality strike. Her stay might be open-ended, but his wasn't. In fact, he was fast running out of time where Nalani—and Jana—were concerned. Unless he acquiesced to Mano's suggestion that he make the move out here. He glanced at Jana, determined not to make her a factor in his decision. Even as he realized she was part of the equation. "There's no reason you can't stick around. Say yes. Take a chance." He tightened his arm around her shoulders. "That's what you came here to do, isn't it?"

She looked mildly irritated that he'd been listening to her so closely. But she looked back to Benji, no doubt finding that pleading expression on the old man's face too difficult to ignore. "Okay. If you trust me, I guess I'll give it a shot."

"Excellent!" Benji cheered. "Now I just have to keep this a secret. You tell me how much—"

"No charge." Jana held up her hand. "I mean it. It'll be my ceremony gift to you and Pippy. No arguments," she added at Benji's sudden look of doubt. "It might not be worth anything in the end. I can't charge you two to be my guinea pigs."

Kahlua oinked in response and stuck her snout in the air.

280 THE SINGLE DAD'S PROMISE

"No offense intended." Jana laughed. "I'll be seeing you around, Benji. We'll talk details of what you might want."

"Count on it. Bye, Shark Boy!" Benji started up his cart again and put-putted down the street.

"I'm going to be Shark Boy for the rest of my life, aren't I?"

"Sure looks like it," Jana said. "Guess what?" She reached into her pocket and pulled out his watch. "It's one forty-five. Time to find out how Freya's day went. You ready?"

Silas could tell by her tone she'd picked up on his nervousness. "I am."

As they walked, he thought about the future. A future for himself. A future for Freya. A future for them as a family. He drew Jana closer, enjoying the sensation of her leaning into him, tightening her hold on him.

There was no denying the connection between them. Every moment he spent with her felt, well, for want of a better term, magical. Something about Jana Powell made him truly believe anything—and everything—was possible.

"AND THEN, DO YOU know what happened next?" Freya was so busy recalling, in her words, the most awesomest day she'd ever had in her whole life, her shave ice was half melted before she paid it much attention.

"What happened next?" Jana licked up coconut and lime syrup pooling into the plastic lip around her own ice.

"We got to do math problems at the board! I got to write on the chalkboard! It was so cool! I never got picked to do that before. And I didn't get any wrong. My teacher Mrs. Malie said I did really well and Miss Jessica gave me a high five when I got back to my desk. And you know what else?"

Jana felt as if she were on a verbal tilt-a-whirl, but she had no desire to step off. The high-pitched excitement Freya was projecting felt as if she'd had the entire world opened up to her in a matter of hours, which, of course, she pretty much had. Silas had been so struck by his daughter's enthusiasm and happiness when they'd arrived at the school, Jana's suggestion they get a treat to celebrate had slipped by mostly unnoticed.

Seated at one of the small window tables at Seas & Breeze, Freya continued to share every detail of her day. Jana listened as best she could, but she was distracted by Silas standing out on the street.

"I heard someone had a very good day at school today."

Jana glanced up to find Daphne, bookended by Cammie on one side and Noah on the other.

"It was so much fun!" Freya confirmed and slurped up the side of her cone, dropped out of her seat and went to the counter with Cammie and Noah.

282 THE SINGLE DAD'S PROMISE

"That must be a relief for Silas." Daphne sat in one of the metal chairs. "Or, maybe not. Do you know why he's out there pacing and mumbling to himself?"

"He's reading the evaluation Freya's teacher gave him when we picked her up." He kept flipping pages, so Jana figured he was getting an eyeful.

"My guess is Mano's plan is working."

"What plan?" Jana frowned.

Daphne sat back, signaled to the woman behind the counter that she'd be up to pay for the kids' cones in a second. "The plan to get Silas to move to Nalani. He's picked up where Remy left off."

"Remy Calvert. Sydney's brother." Jana recalled.

"The man who built Ohana Odysseys from the ground up. With a lot of help from Tehani." Daphne flipped her braid over her shoulder. "Remy always hoped his college friends would buy into the business, move here and run it together. The whole work-to-live rather than live-to-work was pretty much his motto. Despite the amount of time he put into the business."

Anticipation danced in her belly. "Do you think Silas will do it? Move here?"

Daphne smiled. "If we have our way."

"Our?" Just how many people were behind this plot?

"Mano isn't the only one who would like Silas

to move here." Daphne shrugged. "He's pretty dug in about the mainland but maybe he'll find additional pros that'll outweigh the cons. I'm betting Freya's day today might end up pushing him in that direction."

Jana knew precisely what Daphne was thinking. When it came to Freya, Silas would do whatever it took to ensure stability and happiness. "It's hard," Jana said softly. "Leaving everything you know behind. All the things you're used to. Starting over."

"You're doing pretty well at it," Daphne said. "I admire you, Jana."

"You do? Why?"

"Because you chose to run toward something instead of away." Daphne's hands tightened into fists before she relaxed. "I went through some family...difficulties a while back. Nalani was the only place I could think to come." She paused. "To hide. But life has a way of finding you no matter where you are. You've faced everything that's been thrown at you head-on, so yeah." She smiled. "I definitely admire you."

Jana had no words, so she occupied herself finishing her cone while Silas walked back inside.

"Everything okay?" she asked.

"Apparently." He handed Jana the evaluation. "See for yourself. Hey, Daph."

"Been a bit of a roller coaster for you lately,

284   THE SINGLE DAD'S PROMISE

hasn't it?" She reached up, touched his arm. "You hanging in?"

"Do I have another option?" he admitted on a laugh. "I didn't get this complete a rundown from the educational therapist I took her to back in February."

Jana scanned the pages, not entirely surprised by what she read. Over the course of Freya's day, instructors had administered various tests in the guise of schoolwork. The results definitively placed Freya in the high-IQ range, especially in mathematics and reading comprehension. It was Freya's socialization skills that were on the low side, but again, not a surprise.

The last two pages spelled out a detailed plan of focus should Freya stay at Kamea Elementary, along with a recommendation on how to approach her education back home in the public schools or, if he had the financial capability, private ones.

Jana knew the education system pretty well. Her unique experiences as a student and then working with educators across the country while the deal to put the WonderBubble in classrooms gave her perspective from both sides. It was rare indeed to find a school dedicated to providing personal, student-by-student instruction. To Jana's mind, there wasn't a question as to whether Freya would completely thrive at this school.

Cammie raced over, a purple cone of soft shave ice clutched in her hand. "Mama D, can Freya sleep over tonight? We can go to school together tomorrow."

Freya was hot on her heels. "Can I, Daddy?" Her treat was just about soup, but she continued to cling to the soggy paper cone.

"A sleepover?" Silas blinked in surprise. "Are you sure? You've never been on one before."

Jana had to feel sorry for the guy. He was taking some serious dad punches today and this one looked as it if had landed hard in his solar plexus.

"Please, Daddy! I've never been invited to one and Cammie is my bestest friend ever! She has lots of toys and books. Please, please, please!" Freya grabbed his shirt with a sticky hand and jumped up and down. Jana quickly covered her mouth to hide her smile.

He'd wanted this trip to be good for his daughter. He should have been careful what he wished for.

"What about the dinner boat tonight?" Silas reminded her. "I thought you wanted to go look for dolphins."

For a moment, Freya looked torn.

"Keane has those dinner cruises all the time," Daphne said. "No reason you two couldn't do it together another time. Freya's welcome to stay overnight with us."

"Yay!" Cammie and Freya joined hands and jumped in a circle.

Silas's expression had turned sheepish. He

286   THE SINGLE DAD'S PROMISE

faced Jana. "You should probably come with me, actually."

"Oh?" Jana blinked at him. He was so cute when he was nervous. Was it the audience, she wondered, or was he worried she'd say no?

"Well, I mean, Don Martin's going to be there," Silas said. "He'd probably be suspicious, or at least curious if I showed up without you."

Jana nodded. "Probably."

"I'd want you to come with me anyway," he said quickly. "Sorry I'm making a mess of this."

"It's not a mess," Jana assured him. "It's cute and before you hurt something, I'd love to come."

"I need to pay for the cones," Daphne said. "Why don't you bring Freya by our house on your way to the marina. Freya, what do you like to eat for dinner?"

"She likes chicken," Silas said. "And French fries."

"Me, too!" Cammie announced. "With ranch dressing."

Freya wrinkled her nose. "Yuck. I like ketchup."

"Luckily we have both," Daphne assured them. "See you around six?" She headed off to the register, both girls trailing behind her.

"I've just been played, haven't I?"

"Must be those cop instincts," Jana teased. "Come on. Let's buy you a cone."

CHAPTER FOURTEEN

SILAS SPENT THE rest of the afternoon feeling as if he were walking across a swaying dock. Every time he started to get his footing, something new threw him off balance. This wasn't necessarily a bad thing. But as a man who had worked hard to keep his and his daughter's life on an even keel, it made him a bit uncertain about what the future might hold.

Freya's change in attitude and behavior—good and bad—made her seem like a different child. She was so open here, so engaged and interested in things. Never in his wildest dreams had he considered she'd want to go on a sleepover. But this was what he'd always wanted, wasn't it? Progress?

"Looks like I've got my work cut out for me tonight." Jana squeezed his hand.

After dropping Freya off, they made the short journey from Daphne and Griff's house down to the marina in relative silence. The evening had come in gently, easing the warmth of the day back. The ocean seemed calm. The air filled with the promise of well-made food and good conversation.

"Hey." She stepped in front of him, gave him one of those heart-stopping smiles he'd become so fond of. "You in there or did I leave you back with Freya?"

"Sorry." He shook his head and moved again to her side. The more time he spent with her, the more he wanted to. Everything about their connection felt right. Felt perfect. Fated almost. And wasn't that intimidating. "I'm a bit foggy, I guess."

"Then consider me your personal a defogger."

It wasn't just Freya who was undergoing a change. He was as well.

Jana looked stunning. She wore a gorgeous sky-blue sundress that had buttons from chest to toe. The delicate sandals on her feet exposed brightly painted toes.

"Guess we don't have any choice but to concentrate on the evening," Silas said. "Since Daphne made us promise to turn off our cell phones until we're back on dry land. Just another part of her plan."

"You mean her plan to play matchmaker?" Jana blinked overly wide eyes at him. "Not that she's needed to. Right?" Her smile turned to one of amusement. "You don't mind?"

"Being matched up with you?" She stepped in

front of him, rose up and kissed him. "Not in the least. Just be warned." Her eyes filled with uncertainty before he caught a flash of determination. "It's very possible I'm falling in love with you, Silas Garwood."

"Yeah?" He touched her face. "Well, the feeling's mutual." Maybe it was the island air, maybe it was fate. Or maybe he'd finally found himself in the right place at the right time. With the absolute right person.

He paused so she could go ahead of him when they reached the gangplank of the *Nani Nalu*. Their sandals slapped against the wooden planks.

Jana had clearly remembered her way to the boat, but even if she hadn't, he'd have found it easily.

The sixty-five-foot catamaran sparkled against the sun as it was beginning to set, with its brilliant white paint and blue trim. It was the boat of his memories but had been lovingly refurbished under Keane's careful watch. It looked as if it had just floated off the workshop floor.

Owning a boat like this, following in Polunu and Akahi's footsteps by showing off the Big Island's perfection to tourists, had been a secret dream Keane only voiced once that Silas could recall. During that one summer after college. But as with most dreams uttered while in Nalani, it had come true, even though it has been a difficult one.

290 THE SINGLE DAD'S PROMISE

"Correct me if I'm wrong," Silas said to Keane and Wyatt as they reached the catamaran. "But seeing as this is a dinner cruise, shouldn't you be loading food onto the boat instead of off it?"

Wyatt handed Keane a large, aluminum-wrapped tray that Keane placed into a large cart with wheels.

"At the last minute, we had a large group reschedule for next week." Keane accepted the last tray before Wyatt stepped aside. "That leaves just you two, Don Martin, and a newlywed couple who have apparently lost the ability to speak to anyone other than each other. I'd rather offload the extra food now rather than risk it spoiling later."

"What are you going to do with it?" Jana asked.

"A friend of ours runs a women's shelter in Hilo," Wyatt said. "Sydney and Theo have Kai for the night, so I'm picking up Tehani and together we'll drive it out there. Sorry to miss the onboard festivities, though." His grin had Silas wondering if there was more to Daphne's matchmaking for the evening than they realized. "You want us to come back for when you dock, Keane?"

"Nah." Keane checked his watch. "Mano should be here any time. He asked to pilot tonight. It helps clear his head," he told Silas. "Between him and Silas we're covered. Go have a fun, baby-free night."

"Now, that sounds like a plan. Aloha." He

threw Silas and Jana a wide grin as he wheeled the somewhat wobbly cart down the gangplank toward the marina entrance.

"Am I right in thinking Pippy and Benji are going to have their promise ceremony before Wyatt and Tehani finally make it official?" Silas asked.

"Looks like," Keane said. "Come on aboard. Jana, you know the routine. Ah. Here comes our straggler." He raised his arm over his head to signal their location. "Polunu's experimenting with some new drinks. Bar's open."

"Cool." Silas couldn't wait to get a beer. He'd more than earned it today.

"Mr. Martin." Keane stopped short when Don Martin approached. "Is something wrong?"

When Silas turned and looked to the GVI representative, he immediately understood the tension he'd heard in Keane's voice. While the man's appearance was in keeping with the dedicated island tourist, with his board shorts and multicolored flowered shirt, there were no sunglasses to hide the rather stern expression on his face.

Don Martin halted on the dock, hands planted on his hips. His gaze briefly shifted to Jana and Silas. "My assistant saw the pictures I posted on my social media account. She recognized you." He pointed at Silas. "She said you approached her on her lunch break a couple of weeks ago. You were asking questions about my company.

292   THE SINGLE DAD'S PROMISE

About me. You were passing yourself off as a police officer."

Silas nodded. "I am a police officer."

Don Martin had the look of a man on a mission and apparently Silas was it.

"You didn't make friends with me on accident," Don accused. "You targeted me. You pretended to like me so you could follow me around. Why?"

It was the flash of hurt in the man's eyes when Don looked at Jana that gave Silas some hope of salvaging the situation. Betrayal was a curious emotion. It didn't make you run. It made you…sad.

"I didn't pretend." Jana stepped around Silas to approach him, and was out of reach before Silas could stop her. "I do like you, Don. I like that you told me about your wife and your girls. I know I'm not great at it, but that honestly was me trying to make a new friend."

"But for a reason."

"Yes." That she didn't deny and it had Silas cringing and Keane looking a bit uneasy. "At first."

Behind Don, Mano made his way to the boat. He'd ditched his suit for the more relaxed shorts and tank top. His hair was down—he was definitely in island rather than work mode. That said, the second he spotted them, his dark eyes flashed. Intensity could have been Mano Iokepa's middle name. His stride slowed, his body tensed as he came closer.

Jana shifted again, keeping Don Martin's attention on her. "I wanted to help Silas and his friends stop your company from attempting a takeover," Jana said. "I wanted to help them keep this place as it is, without all the high commerce and impersonal ideas GVI will want to establish. But that doesn't mean I didn't like you. Because I do."

Don mumbled a few words and looked a bit lost for a moment. "How did you even find out about GVI's plans?"

"I told them."

Don jumped and nearly fell backward at Mano's voice.

"Apologies." Mano frowned, as if confused about the reaction. "I've been told I have a tendency to speak sharply sometimes. Why don't we take this conversation on the boat?"

"Please." Jana held out her hand to Don. "Let us explain."

"You're coming after our home," Keane said sharply. "We don't owe you an apology for it. Nalani is everything to us and we'll do whatever we need to in order to defend it."

"Or we could finish the conversation here," Mano said. "There was no cruelty intended, Mr. Martin. We put on a show, yes. We wanted to make certain you understood what makes Nalani special. We wanted, we hoped you'd see the importance of personal hospitality. Of welcome. Of Ohana."

294 THE SINGLE DAD'S PROMISE

"Yeah, well, it doesn't matter what I saw or the report I was going to make," Don said. "My assistant didn't just tell me my cover was blown. She told my bosses." He looked truly pained as he rubbed a hand across his forehead. "They've decided they don't want my evaluation any longer. And I'm due back in the office day after tomorrow."

Something in his voice, in the way his eyes kept darting to the side had Silas pushing. "There's more, isn't there?"

Don sighed, dropped his hand, a flash of desperation crossing his face. "I shouldn't be... I've got my entire life invested in GVI. My retirement, my family's health care, my kids' college expenses. I can't just walk away like Theo Fairfax did. I'm too old to start over. I have people who depend on me."

"Right now, Nalani is depending on you." Jana moved closer but stayed on the boat. "Please, Don. You've seen this place in person. You've been part of Nalani for days. You've gotten to know so many of the people who live here. You know how perfect it is. As it is. There are ways around your issues and we can help you find them. But if there's something they still need to know—" she gestured toward town "—you don't want to wake up in a few days and feel responsible for ruining a place that needs to exist."

Don looked at Jana, then at Silas. Then Keane

and Mano. Silas could all but see the wheels turning in his head. He sagged a bit, blew out a long breath. "It isn't that they don't want my evaluation anymore. They don't need me to find a way in."

"Why?" Mano asked.

"Because they've already found one. Through three of your shareholders," he finally said to Mano. "They've signed on to help GVI take over the Hibiscus Bay Resort. From there, it's only a matter of time before they gobble up Ohana Odysseys, too."

"WELL, THIS EVENING took an unexpected turn, didn't it?"

Standing at the bow of the *Nani Nalu*, Jana glanced over her shoulder as Silas draped one of Ohana Odysseys' complimentary shawls around her bare shoulders. She'd been shivering a bit. It was always colder out on the water, but the sensation of a warm sky and cool breezes felt glorious against her skin. Mano had taken the boat out, then anchored them just off the southern coast of the Big Island. In the distance, she could see the gently glowing Kumukahi Light at Kapoho, one of the oldest lighthouses in all of the islands.

"Thank you." He slipped an arm around her, brought her in close and rested his chin on the top of her head. "For convincing him to tell us about GVI."

296 THE SINGLE DAD'S PROMISE

Jana snuggled against him. "He wasn't wrong about me spying on him. But I'm not sorry about it."

"I was the spy," Silas said lightly. "You were the bridge. You helped him see Nalani for what it is."

"Ohana did that," Jana said. "What Remy built, what Sydney and the others continue with in his name allowed for Don and so many to see how special this place is. I nudged," she added. "And I was glad to help."

She'd never felt so useful before. To be part of something that was bigger than herself, not an invention that ended up in people's homes, but to have possibly helped to preserve Nalani. She couldn't imagine ever doing anything more important than that.

"You're an amazing woman, Jana Powell."

She tilted her head back, beamed up at him. The way he looked at her, the way he held her, she couldn't imagine life ever being the same after having met—and fallen in love with—Silas Garwood.

He brushed his mouth against hers. She turned into him, snuggling as close as she could. The ocean lapped against the gently bobbing boat.

"You said to let you know when dessert was served." The murmur against her lips had her smile widening. "Maru's granddaughter Lani is working in the galley tonight. Guess what she brought?"

ANNA J. STEWART 297

"Malasadas?" The very idea left her anxious to return to the table.

"Four different kinds. Feel like branching out?"

"You bet."

She kept the shawl tucked around her as they returned to the table. Keane had taken the initiative and settled the newlywed couple up in the bar where they could be alone. Personally, Jana didn't think they'd even noticed there were other people around. Plus, it had given the rest of them the privacy to talk.

"The power of malasadas." Silas pulled out her chair just as Lani brought out a tray of pillowy, soft, freshly fried doughnuts.

"Chocolate, passion fruit, pineapple and haupia. And there's more below if you run out," she shot a teasing look at Jana. "Enjoy."

"Mahalo, Lani." Mano glanced at his watch. "We've got time before we need to head back. Maybe enough time for Don to decide what he's going to do from here."

Don pondered the two fingers of Scotch that Polunu had poured for him at the bar. "I've destroyed thirty years of employment in one night." He toasted the night sky. "A beautiful evening to be sure." He set his glass on the table with a clunk. "But maybe it doesn't have to be a total loss."

"What are you thinking?" Silas asked.

Jana kept her attention on the pineapple malasada in her hands. She was really going to miss these when she went home. *If* she went home.

The image of her permanently in Nalani roared to life inside of her. Maybe…she glanced at Silas. Maybe it wasn't only Silas who was thinking about a change.

"I'm thinking that turnabout is fair play," Don said. "You were right, Jana. No one should even be considering turning Nalani into some kind of commercial wasteland. My first thought when I had arrived was to bring my family here. With GVI in charge, I'd want to stay as far away as possible." He eyed Mano. "Given what I've revealed to you, as soon as I get back, I'll resign. In fact, I'll retire." He cringed. "Beyond the fact it could be illegal, I don't want anything I do tipping them off that you're on to them. So I'm going to give them, give you, two, maybe three months."

"To do what, exactly?" Keane asked as he finished off one of the chocolate malasadas.

"I'm not sure. Probably not much. Maybe I can find out which shareholders have turned on you, Mano. And if I leave GVI free and clear to do so, I'll share what I know. GVI needs this deal to happen. They were circling the drain when Theo was still working there and things have only gotten worse. If they don't find a new investment property to take over and either make it a success or tank it for the tax write-off, they're done."

"If that happens, you risk losing your retirement," Mano said. "We'd understand if you don't want to take the chance—"

"No." He shook his head. "No. I helped create this mess. I'm not going to save myself when everything else is in jeopardy."

"What is it?" Silas nudged her arm.

"Huh?" Jana glanced at him.

"We can hear you thinking," Keane explained. "And that look on your face is strange."

"I always look this way." But now that they asked... "What exactly is your title with GVI, Don?"

"Special consultant for new projects. I'm a scout of sorts. I go where they send me, investigate new opportunities for investments. Failing companies that are desperate to sell. I evaluate and report back. It sounds horrid, I'm sure, but I like my job. I just don't like my employers."

"Special consultant for new projects." Jana mulled the title, took another bite of her dessert. "How do you feel about remote work?"

"Loved it when it was necessary," Don admitted.

"Have you heard of a company called Hyper-Nova?"

"The research and development think tank?" Don nodded. "Of course."

"Jana's an owner," Silas told the table.

"I'm thinking, when you're ready and in the clear..." Jana dropped her gaze to avoid the shocked expressions looking back at her. "HyperNova might be in a position to offer you a job. Full benefits, of course. We'll meet or better your current salary. Retirement, health care. And…" She held up a finger. "After six months, you're vested in our employee college scholarship program."

"You're kidding," Don balked. "She's kidding, right?" he asked Silas.

"I don't think she is," Mano mused.

"Unless you have a better idea?" Jana asked Mano. "I mean, if there's a place for him at the Hibiscus?"

"There might have been," Mano said. "If I hadn't already decided to hire on a security consultant. We're getting a lot of interest from some high-profile companies and individuals. I'm going to need someone to come on board and help me make a number of changes." His eyes shifted to Silas. "What do you think?"

Jana swallowed the sudden tears in her throat.

"I—what?" Silas shook his head as if he'd tuned out. "Are you offering me a job? Here, in Nalani?"

"You've read Freya's evaluation," Mano said. "There's no chance you'll pull her out of Kamea Elementary. Not with what they're offering."

Jana bit the inside of her cheek to stop from smiling. "Nalani should be like the new cozy mystery capital, with all this secret plotting you guys do."

"Remy wanted you here," Mano stated. "He wanted you part of Ohana Odysseys. Sydney does, too. Everyone does. Sell your place back in San Francisco. Put in your papers. You can stay in the cottage as long as you want, or until you find a place you like. And you move here, to Nalani. You and Freya. And, if you still need your cop fix, I bet Chief Malloy will be happy to keep you in mind for when he needs help."

Jana could hear Silas's breath catch in his chest.

"You've figured it all out for me, haven't you?" Silas accused his friend. For a second, Jana worried Mano had gone a step too far, taken the reins out of Silas's hands. She looked at him, but there was no tension. Only… "I'll agree on one condition."

"We can talk salary at another—"

"I'm not worried about the money," Silas cut him off. "This is about Ohana. Mine and Freya's. I want you to stand in for Remy, as Freya's godfather. Her uncle. And I want your promise that you will look after her if for some reason I can't."

Two tears escaped Jana's control.

"That's my condition, brah," Silas stated. "You get me, Freya gets you." Silas stood up, held out his hand. "Only way this works."

Keane, Don, and Jana watched as Mano set his drink aside, slowly stood. He clasped Silas's hand hard.

"You have a deal."

CHAPTER FIFTEEN

IT WAS CLOSE to midnight by the time Silas was walking Jana back to her cottage. There had been a lot more discussion, a lot more bonding, and a lot more coming to terms with how much Silas was about to change his and Freya's lives. But none of it made him uneasy or worried. Because he knew he had the best support system in place. There was a lot to do, and none of it would happen easily, but it was going to be worth it. He took a deep breath, looked over at Jana as they strode along the beach.

"I feel like I'm walking on air." Jana's comment reflected his own feelings. "It's nice when things can work out for the better. I'm so excited for you and Freya." She squeezed his arm. Those bright eyes of hers danced in the moonlight. "You both are going to thrive here."

"Hopefully." And hopefully Jana would be part of that thriving as well. That said, Nalani wasn't out of the woods yet where GVI was concerned, but thanks to Jana's help with Don Martin this evening—on so many fronts—it soon might be. "Your business partners will be all right with you inventing a new position for Don?"

"I'm the primary stakeholder in the company," Jana said as if announcing the weather. "Makes me a little difficult to say no to." She lifted her head, smiled into the sky. "Besides, it makes sense to have someone on the payroll who can see opportunities we can't or that we might be missing out on. Trust me, this is as much a benefit to HyperNova as it is to Don. What you asked Mano. About Freya." She shifted her gaze to his. "You've been planning that for a while, haven't you?"

He shrugged. "Like Remy, he's a good man, and he is so good with her, with who she is. He doesn't want to change her, he wants her to be the best she can be as she is. Why wouldn't I want him in my daughter's life on a more permanent basis?"

"Mmm-hmm." She smiled and it lit up his heart. "What a lucky little girl she is."

"Yeah, well, just wait until Mano gets another taste of a Freya tantrum. He might change his mind."

"Doubtful. She's his Ohana. So are you. Neither of you are going anywhere."

"What about you?"

"What about me?"

He'd been rehearsing this for a while, but now

that the moment had arrived the script he'd written in his head vanished. "You said your time in Nalani was open-ended. Have you thought about when you might be going home?"

"I've been distracted lately," she joked. "Haven't really given it much thought."

His heart pounded faster. "You've considered staying, though, haven't you?" He stopped walking, turned her to face him. "If you haven't, I'm just going to say it. I want you to stay. I want to see…" His mind raced. "I meant what I said before, Jana. I'm falling in love with you. I would very much like to see where things go between us."

He recognized her quick blinking as her processing new information. He hoped it wasn't confusing, because—

"I…" She frowned, shook her head as if to clear it. "At dinner the other evening I said I couldn't understand how one can fall for someone so fast but…" She sighed, as if surrendering. "You've proven me wrong, haven't you?"

He put a hand to her cheek, took comfort in how she closed her eyes and leaned into his touch. He stroked her skin, knowing how he was feeling was due to her entirely. "We're going to give this a go?"

She nodded, and after a moment opened her eyes again. "I've never felt like this before, Silas." When she met his gaze he saw fear there, but also promise. "I don't really know what to do with it?"

"Here's one thing." He kissed her. Softly, almost reverently, all the while mindful of the sound of crashing waves. The warm breeze felt protective of all that could be. All he wanted to be. When he lifted his head and looked at her warm expression, he smiled. "I'll take that as a yes about your feelings."

Her eyes shifted as if taking all of him in, as if committing the image of him to her memory. "When I came here, I told myself to take chances. To do things that scare me." She rested her hand against his chest. "I'm not sure anything feels quite so frightening as falling in love with you, Silas. But I'm also not sure I care."

His entire system jolted, her words rebooting his heart that had, until now, only beat for his daughter. Now it beat twice as fast. Twice as hard. For Jana.

"So, what do we do now?" Her question struck him as so practical, so logical, he couldn't help but laugh.

"Well, how about we start with you coming with me to pick Freya up from school tomorrow. I'd like you there when I talk to her about moving to Nalani."

"I'd like that, too." She rose up on tiptoe and kissed him again. "I'd like that very much."

JANA WAS MORE than used to not sleeping. What she wasn't used to was being happy about it.

Standing on her front porch, her hair still damp from the swim she'd taken shortly after sunrise, she sipped tea and looked out at the ocean, allowing the peace to engulf her. She'd come here to heal. To recover. To reset. And somehow...

Somehow, she'd found love.

Befuddled at the notion that Silas Garwood had somehow settled into her heart to the point it would probably forget how to beat without him, she realized no one had ever looked at her the way Silas did. Very few had paid attention to her outside of work. And she'd been okay with that. With spending the rest of her life alone.

She put a hand to her chest.

Funny how the universe had other plans.

"Uh-oh." A glance at her watch reminded her she hadn't charged it since yesterday. She headed inside to plug it in. "And this." She laughed since it hadn't occurred to her to turn her phone back on after last night—she'd been too happy to think of anything else.

Silas loved her.

She tightened her shoulders, let out a tiny squeal of excitement, then chuckled at herself. How lovely it felt to be utterly and completely giddy.

After switching on her phone, she set it aside and started scrounging in the kitchen for leftovers, which were sparse. But it would give her something to do this morning. She'd head into town and stock up. Maybe she'd stop in at Luanda's and see if they could order her art supplies for the painting she'd been "hired" to do.

"This place really is magic." Everything in her life had changed since she'd come here. Now, for the first time in a very long time, things felt perfect.

Her phone chimed. Chimed again as alerts filtered in, stacking on top of one another. She could feel that anxious sensation in her stomach, a sensation that had been constant back home. She had to be sure to thank Daphne for insisting she tune out and turn off her cell yesterday. The silence and preoccupation had done her good.

Putting the kettle on for another cup of tea, she sighed and retrieved her phone, scanned through the list of emails she could thankfully avoid. The four text messages from her assistant, Connie, confirmed that plans were in place for the travel version of the WonderBubble and their engineers were already hard at work to get them out the door well before the holiday season. Her lawyer had emailed to say he'd completed the paperwork she'd requested. And...

Three voice mail messages.

"Strange." Everyone she knew was well aware she preferred email or text. The number wasn't familiar, but whoever it was had called three times in two hours last evening. It was either a very determined spam caller or...

"Better find out." She tapped the play icon on

the first message, turned the speaker on while she went to get more tea.

"Jana, it's Dr. Myers."

Jana froze at the familiar female voice.

"You probably aren't answering because you don't recognize my personal cell number. I'm on vacation with my family, but I just got a look at your latest lab tests." The slight pause left Jana's hands trembling. "I need you to call me back at this number when you can, please. I'll have my phone on."

Jana's chest hurt. Every breath was an effort. Her entire body went cold as she tried to stop the spinning in her head. Everything around her came to a screeching halt, but she forced herself to take one step, then another until she stood over her phone. She stared down at the screen for a long moment.

That pit she'd been dragging, clawing herself out of for the past few months re-formed around her and threatened to draw her back into despair. Into fear. Into...

Nothing other than panic seemed to be at hand, but she had to focus. Had to...

"Call. You have to call." She tapped the number, turned off the speaker and lifted the cell to her ear.

"Knock-knock."

Jana looked up from the kitchen table where her suitcase was open and most of her clothes had been stashed. Noodles sat on the ledge of the open windowsill, chomping away on a bit of left-over papaya. "Hey, Sydney." Jana pushed open the screen door and waved her inside.

"This was delivered by courier to the Ohana office." Sydney handed her the overnight envelope.

"Thanks." Jana set the envelope aside for later. "I didn't know the address for the cottage."

"No problem. Chopper's getting some maintenance work done, so I have the day off. From flying, anyway." Sydney pointed at the suitcase. Then at Jana. "What's going on?"

Jana knew the second she stopped to have a conversation she could very well fall apart. "I was going to come by the office in a little while. I'm sorry, but I need to—"

"What's wrong?"

Jana tried to hold on to what control she had left. "It's nothing. It's…" Her throat thickened. "I don't know that anything's wrong, but I need to get back home. My doctor called." She took a deep breath. She had to face someone about this sometime. "The lab work I had done before I came here showed something off. My doctor isn't sure what's going on, but I need to get back."

"Why?" Sydney's question struck Jana as odd.

"Because my cancer might be back." She hadn't wanted to say it. Now that she had…she felt sick. "Because—"

"No." Sydney's voice dropped, and her face

310 THE SINGLE DAD'S PROMISE

grew determined. "I mean why do you have to go all the way home for the new blood tests?"

Jana had been struggling with that question since she'd hung up the phone.

"Hilo Medical Center is the best in all the islands," Sydney said with assurance. "Unless your doctor specifically told you to come back—"

"She didn't," Jana murmured. "She's not even there. She's in Portugal with her family."

"Then maybe you should stay here with yours."

"But." The sentiment brought tears to her eyes. "I've already booked a standby flight. I've got—"

"What about Silas and Freya?"

Shame swamped her. Home was where she knew how to cope with this. She didn't want this, want a possible recurrence to be anywhere near Silas or Freya. "I'll say goodbye." Somehow. Someway.

"But you aren't going to tell them why, are you?" Sydney stalked away, started to pace. She stopped once, started again, trying to figure out how to process that which Jana couldn't.

"I'm not doing this again," Sydney said finally. "I'm not losing someone else I care about to silence or distance. Remy did this to me. To all of us. He didn't tell anyone he was sick, that there were issues, and the next thing we knew…" Tears exploded into her eyes. "You are not going through this alone."

"Sydney." Jana froze. She had never had any-

ANNA J. STEWART   311

one stand up for her like this before. "There's nothing any of you can do."

"We can be there for you. Whatever the tests say." She pulled out her phone, held it up as if wielding a weapon. "I will drive you to Hilo myself. No one else has to know until there's something to know. Please." Sydney swallowed hard. "I don't know how else to convince you that you aren't alone this time, Jana. Ohana is more than laughing at the good times. It's about support when things get rough. I promise," Sydney whispered, "I've got you. We've got you."

Jana understood that in theory. And it had sounded lovely. Wonderful even. But in practice?

"What tests did they order?" Sydney asked.

"Um." Capitulating, Jana picked up her cell, accessed her health app and opened her lab folder. She turned the phone around so Sydney could read it. "These."

"Okay." She sounded relieved as she took Jana's phone and dialed from her own. "Don't... Just stay right there, okay?" She gestured to one of the kitchen chairs. "I'm not letting you out of my sight until... Hey, Doc? Hey, it's Sydney. Yeah, I'm doing okay, but I need your help with something. You have admitting rights at Hilo Medical Center, right? I have a friend who needs some emergency lab work done. Can you—?"

Jana took Sydney's outstretched hand.

And finally breathed.

SILAS SPENT MOST of the day watching the clock. He didn't know what to do with himself without Freya around. He hadn't been without her this long since she'd been born, since those long days she'd spent in the NICU. He missed her so much he ached, but that ache was tempered by his replaying his walk back last night with Jana. She hadn't said the words, but he knew she was thinking them. Had to be. There was no other explanation for the shock on her face. Her beautiful, exquisite face.

Finally, he'd gotten so fidgety hanging around the cottage he went to hers, but no one answered when he knocked. Huh. Strange. She hadn't mentioned going anywhere.

He almost called Tehani to see what Jana might have scheduled with Ohana, but that seemed too… He didn't want to come across as possessive or as if he needed to spend every waking second with her. Despite the fact he really, really wanted to.

He checked his watch. She'd be back, he told himself, in time to pick Freya up from school. In the meantime, he headed into town.

How had this happened? How had he gone from rarely thinking about dating to falling head over heels for a woman he'd only met because the universe had put her in his path? Fate had never been on his radar before, but what were the odds that Jana would be in Nalani at the same time Silas finally decided to return?

He didn't want to calculate them, but he would thank them.

Nalani had been a respite for him years ago. Clearly it hadn't stopped being one. Everything he needed, everything he wanted, was right here. Where Remy Calvert had always told him it was.

If only he'd listened sooner.

No. That was wrong. If he had, then he never would have met Jana. *All things happen in the time they're meant to.* Something else Remy had often said.

Remy.

Silas stopped, found himself at the entry to the beach, the arched palm trees covering the path from land to sea. He waved at Maru, who was instructing Lani on how to pack up the now empty malasada boxes.

Across the street, in front of Luanda's, a middle-aged woman sat behind a small table making beautiful hibiscus leis. He walked over, bought one of the pure white ones, chatted with the woman for a while before he headed for the shore.

This part of the year the crowds were light. The smattering of beachgoers were far enough away that he could make his way to the water without any hindrance. He kicked off his slippahs, waded in calf-deep.

The way the ocean stretched out in front of

314 THE SINGLE DAD'S PROMISE

him, like endless possibilities, eased whatever leftover trepidation he still possessed. Any question his mind posed, he had an answer. Any concern or worry he dwelled on was easily solved. And everything had the same answers. Jana. And Nalani.

He crouched, the cool water lapping up around his waist as he set the lei into the waves. He watched as the tide carried it back and forth. Back and forth. Until the wind blew and took it toward the far depths. Toward where Remy had been lain to rest.

"I'm sorry it took me so long to come back," he told his friend. "But I'm here now. And I'm not going anywhere. You got your wish. Finally. Feel free to say I told you so."

When Silas finally made his way out of the water and back up the beach toward his and Jana's cottages, he knew, without a doubt, his life had absolutely changed for the better. He couldn't wait to see what happened next.

"WE'LL HAVE THE results soon." Sydney tapped a hand against the steering wheel of the Ohana Odysseys jeep. With the open top and warm wind, it wasn't easy to hear her. But Jana did. Mainly because it was the third time Sydney had said those words since they'd gotten into the car. "It's going to be fine. Everything will be fine."

Jana pressed her lips together, looked out her

nonexistent window, squeezed her eyes shut. She didn't want this. She didn't want anyone worrying over her, worrying about anything they had no control over. What she had no control over.

But that didn't mean she shouldn't be grateful. "Thank you." Jana raised her voice over the wind. "For calling your doctor friend." She knew from experience the blood work took anywhere from a few days to a week. Now all she had to do was wait.

"He was happy to help." Sydney caught her flyaway hair and shoved it off her face. "How are you doing?"

"I'm fine." She'd gone from panicked to being numb. There didn't seem to be any in between for her. "You're right. I need to talk to Silas." Even as she said it, the nerves grabbed hold. "You didn't call him, did you?"

"I did not." Sydney changed lanes beneath the turnoff sign for Nalani. "But I'm glad you're going to. He'll probably be ticked I'm the one who took you and not him."

It was a sweet thought to entertain. She glanced at her watch. "Freya gets out of school in about an hour."

"We're almost there." Sure enough, five minutes later, Sydney pulled the jeep to a stop in front of Jana's rented cottage. "You want me to stick around?"

"No, thanks." She needed to do this part her-

316 THE SINGLE DAD'S PROMISE

self. "I'm going right over. I need you to hear me this time, Sydney. I've made a decision and I'm not going to change my mind."

"What decision?" Sydney frowned.

"I'm grateful for your help and your support, but I can't do this again here. In Nalani. I just… can't." She started to get out of the jeep. "I have to do this alone. Please, Sydney. Just accept my thanks for today and understand I have to do this my way."

"Friends never have to say thank you." Sydney told her.

"Yeah." She smiled through a sheen of tears. "I know that now." She followed the path to the front door of the cottage. She came up short, startled to find Silas sitting on the top porch step, scrolling through his cell.

How he smiled when he saw her made her heart weep. "There you are. You disappeared on me."

"Yeah, sorry about that." She walked past him, opened her door and, leaning in, grabbed the envelope Sydney had dropped off earlier. "I had something come up."

"Everything okay?"

The concern she saw in his eyes was the deciding factor. She didn't want him concerned. She didn't want him worried. Or fretting or…or or or.

"I wanted to give this to you before I left."

"Before you…" He set his cell down with a

clunk. "What are you talking about? I thought you could stay as long as you wanted."

"I can. But something's...come up." Why was this so hard? She ripped open the envelope, pulled out the documents her lawyer had sent and sat beside him. "This is for you and Freya." She handed him the papers, explained as he read. "The other day, when we were talking about how you couldn't bring Freya's WonderBubble with you on vacation because it didn't fit in your suitcase, it inspired me, I guess you could say. We're in the process of designing a new portable unit specifically for travel." She forced a smile. "We're calling it the Freya."

He balked, the shock on his face the perfect expression to make her feel lighter. "It's an offshoot of the original model, but it's still new. I've signed over all my proceeds from it to Freya. My attorney has set up a trust account that you can access at any time for her education. She's going to need it sooner than eighteen," she said. "I'd anticipate her being ready for college by fifteen, sixteen at the latest."

"I don't—" Silas set the papers aside. "Jana, this is beyond generous and completely unnecessary."

"Like I said, she, you, inspired me. I've made plenty of investments in stocks and businesses and...now I'm investing in Freya." It was, she knew without a doubt, the best one she could ever make. "I'm sorry, Silas. But I don't think—"

"Don't." He sat forward, grabbed her hands, the panic in his eyes the same panic she'd been trying to quell for the entire day. "Don't tell me you're walking away from this. Don't tell me I scared you off last night."

"It's not you." She couldn't resist. She lifted a hand to his cheek. "I promise, it's not you, Silas. I…" She owed it to him, owed it to herself to speak the truth at least once. "I love you. Beyond logic and reason and science, I think I fell in love with you the moment I first met you." She couldn't stop the tears that filled her eyes. "But I don't want you trapped in a life of worry and fear because of me."

"What on earth are you talking about?" The confusion on his face made her hurt more. "Where is all this coming from? What's changed since last night?"

Sydney was right. She owed him the truth. "My, um—" She had to clear her throat. "My doctor called, said there was something off with my last set of lab tests."

She saw the instant he understood. There was an emptiness at first, followed by the sympathy, then concern she never wanted to see.

"It's possible my cancer's back. That's where I was earlier. Sydney took me to Hilo to get some follow-up labs done."

"Okay." He caught her hand in his, held on so tight she couldn't help but think he'd never let her go. "Okay, so when do you get the results?"

"Could take up to a week. Could be sooner. Hopefully it will be." She took a deep breath. "But it doesn't matter what they say."

"Of course it matters." The disbelief in his voice was harsh. "It's the only thing that matters."

"But that's just it," she whispered. "I don't want it to. I do not want you living a life of uncertainty. Of waiting for this horrible ball to drop again. Because it can, Silas. And the odds are it will. It might have already. I will not have you and Freya going through this." She drew in a breath along with her courage.

"I love you." He caught her face in his hands, his gaze boring into her. "We love you, Jana."

"I know." And that alone was going to have to get her through when she was home, alone again. She already knew, whatever the results said, she was going home. "I need you to let me go, Silas. Whatever's coming—"

"We can handle it together."

She tried to shake her head but he wouldn't let her. "Silas." His name was a whisper on her lips. "Why don't you understand? I don't want that for you."

"Too bad." There was no anger in his voice, only resolve. "Being with you is my choice, Jana. And I do choose you, along with whatever comes

320 THE SINGLE DAD'S PROMISE

with it. One day, one year, a lifetime, I'll take everything I can get."

He couldn't mean that. He just couldn't. But, oh, how she wanted to believe.

"I can't give you any more children, Silas."

"I know." He frowned, as if he hadn't remembered what she'd told him. "That didn't change anything before. Why would that matter now?"

"Because—"

"I, *we* have Freya. And I want her to have you. She's enough, believe me," he added on a weak laugh. "And if we decide she's not, there are plenty of options. There's nothing you can throw at me that I'm not going to dodge," he said firmly. "I love you. Whatever those tests reveal, nothing is going to change the fact that I love you and I want to be with you."

She could feel her resolve crumbling, like a rock face tumbling into the ocean. She clung to it desperately, even as her hold weakened.

"You said you love me, Jana."

"I do." If he believed nothing else, she hoped he believed that.

"Then trust me. You're not alone anymore. You haven't been since Freya and I saw you out in the water that day. Our mermaid." He pressed his forehead against hers, still holding her face. "My mermaid. You're all I want. Please." He stared deep into her eyes. "Trust me. I won't walk away, even if you leave. We'll follow you. Wherever you go, we will be there, too."

She squeezed her eyes shut. Tears trickled down her cheeks. "This isn't rational."

"Neither is this." He kissed her and she felt every ounce of love he had for her coursing through her system. Like a balm soothing the rough edges of her fear and doubt. "Don't run away from me, Jana. Please."

Something Daphne had said to her at dinner the other night rang in her mind. That Daphne admired her because she'd run toward something instead of running away. She'd never really had anything to run toward before. But now?

She trembled in his arms as he wrapped her in an embrace she never wanted to leave. "All right." Even as she started to speak, she could feel the fear evaporating like droplets of water beneath the sun. "You win." Surrender, she realized, had never felt so utterly sweet. "I'll stay."

"Yeah?" She heard the smile in his voice and prayed she'd never have to see the worry and fear. "Yes."

"Well, it's a good thing you made that decision now." He stepped back and pointed to the small group of people headed in their direction. "You were aware Sydney is incapable of keeping a secret, weren't you?"

She laughed, wiped at the tears on her cheeks. "I had heard something to that effect." Sure enough,

322 THE SINGLE DAD'S PROMISE

Sydney led the pack consisting of Keane, Marella, Tehani, Wyatt, Daphne, Griff and Marella. There was no mistaking that determined stride and she steeled herself for an onslaught of unexpected emotion.

"Stand down!" Silas yelled when they got within earshot. "She's staying."

"You are?" Sydney didn't look convinced. "I thought you said nothing was going to change your mind."

"Silas is harder to say no to you than you are." Jana actually smiled even as her heart continued to pound with suppressed worry and fear. "I'm staying."

Tehani raced forward as Jana and Silas held hands. The next thing Jana knew, she was caught up in an unending series of hugs that could very well last her a lifetime.

"I knew it," Daphne whispered in her ear as she held on tight. "I knew you and Silas could make this work." She then rested her hands on Jana's shoulders and looked her in the eye. "We're waiting with you tomorrow, or whenever, for the test results. You aren't going to hear them alone, Jana."

"I know." And she did. For the first time in her life she knew, without a doubt, she'd never be alone again.

SILAS STOOD ON the back porch of Daphne and Griff's home a week later, looking out at the lush garden that had been tended to with the meticulous care of one with multiple green thumbs. Beneath a large arbor—hand-constructed by Wyatt—sat a trio of benches currently occupied by Jana, Marella, Daphne and Sydney. Tehani paced nearby, trying to calm a rather cranky Kai.

"You holding up all right?" Mano came up behind him, handed him a cold bottle of beer and took the empty one.

"Longest seven days of my life." He checked his watch for the millionth time. He'd put every distraction into place, not only for Jana, but for himself as well. Freya's new school routine had helped. Jana had smiled and laughed convincingly enough that she was coming around to the idea that whatever the results might be, they were going to be okay. And their friends, their Ohana.

They couldn't have asked for more support.

Despite Freya's excitement about her new school routine, they'd made the decision together—all of them—to keep the children home today so that Jana was surrounded by family. As the days had passed without any word, Sydney had finally called the doctor again to confirm the results would be in today. Now that they knew that for certain, the waiting had become even more excruciating.

"Jana and I talked to Freya last night," Silas told Mano as Keane joined them. "We didn't give

324 THE SINGLE DAD'S PROMISE

her all the details, but told her we were waiting on some news about Jana's health."

"Is that why she's sticking close by today?" Keane asked as they looked to where Freya sat tucked tightly against Jana on one of the benches.

"Yes." It had also been the reason the little girl couldn't sleep last night. She was worried because she could tell Jana was.

"When are you going to tell Freya about moving here?" Mano asked.

"Once we're on the other side of this," Silas replied. "And you can stop smirking like that, Mano," he added. "Your plan worked. Revel in silence, please."

As if on cue, Freya jumped up from her seat and ran over to them. She threw herself against Silas. "Daddy, what time is it?"

"Five minutes past the last time you asked me." He bent down, tugged on her braid. "I have another surprise for you."

"What is it?" Freya demanded.

"You can call Mr. Mano Uncle Mano from now own." He'd purposely waited until Mano was here before he'd shared that. "He's your godfather now."

"Like Uncle Remy was?" Freya's eyes went wide. "I get another one?"

"I think you're probably going to end up with a few of them, actually," Silas said as he toasted Keane.

"Yay!" Freya abandoned Silas when Mano held out his arms to scoop her up. She laughed and hugged him tight around his neck. "I can call you Uncle Mano?"

"Uncle is fine." Mano shifted her to his side, held her with one arm as she reached into the front pocket of her bright yellow shorts. "What's this?" He pointed to the piece of fabric in her hand.

"It's Jana's Bee Brave badge." She handed it to him. "Her mommy and daddy made it for her. She gave it to me when I got scared and ran away." Freya looked over at Silas. "Maybe I should give it back."

"That's a nice idea," Silas confirmed.

She wiggled out of Mano's arms, raced across the yard.

Silas watched, his heart in his throat, as Freya climbed into Jana's lap and pushed the badge into Jana's hand. Across the distance, Jana met Silas's gaze before hugging Freya so lovingly his daughter's happy squeals echoed.

Conversation stopped when Jana's phone rang.

Silas pushed his beer into Mano's hands, hurried over as Jana leaned forward to pick her cell phone up off the table.

He stood behind her, looked down at the number on her screen. "Whatever it is, we're here."

Jana nodded. "I know. Okay. Here goes." She answered the phone. "Hi, Dr. Myers."

The silence pressed in on him, pressed in on all of them. Silas looked around the group, the group that had closed in like troops defending their general. Hands reached for one another, breathing stopped as Jana nodded and responded to questions and statements.

"Daddy?" Freya was not a fan of the tension; she stood up on the bench, held out her arms to him, and he picked her up. "I'm scared," she whispered in his ear.

"Me, too." He kissed her cheek.

When Jana hung up, she sat there for a moment, her hands trembling. "The tests were normal," she said. "Whatever abnormality they saw before, wasn't there this time. I'm okay." She dropped her phone in her lap, covered her mouth as she sobbed. "I'm okay."

The cheers of joy and relief that resulted filled the last empty space in Silas's heart. He circled around, Freya still in his arms, as Jana stood and reached out for him. For them. Freya patted Jana's back with such care Silas worried he'd lose it himself.

When she took a step, she turned to look at all of them, just as Silas did. Looked at the amazing people she'd met in Nalani. The friends she'd made. The friends he'd never lost.

The Ohana they'd found.

EPILOGUE

"Did you see? Did you see that, Jana?" Freya ran up the beach to where Jana sat, the girl's legs pumping hard in the sand. Her arms were stretched out mainly due to the floaties. "Daddy didn't have to hold me up so much!"

"I definitely saw." Jana shielded her eyes as Freya stopped in front of her, kicking sand onto the towel. "You're getting better at swimming every day."

"I love the water so much!" Freya twirled before she tumbled onto the towel, narrowly missing the plastic containers of fresh fruit and misubi, Jana's new favorite island snack. "I never ever want to leave the ocean!" She rolled onto her back, stared up at the passing clouds. Behind them, the guest cottage Silas and Freya had been calling home was cast in late morning rays, shimmering thanks to the beautiful island sun.

"Kid is wearing me out." Silas joined them, sweeping his wet hair out of his face.

The mere sight of him was enough to switch Jana's heart to fluttering. How had she found her-

328 THE SINGLE DAD'S PROMISE

self in the right place at the right moment, she wondered for the millionth time. Island magic, she reminded herself. It was the only explanation she would ever accept.

"Might be time to take Jordan up on her offer for private swimming lessons for Freya," Silas announced.

Freya sat right up. "Jordan and her cat? Will her cat help me learn how to swim?"

"Wouldn't bet against it." Silas's bright gaze wasn't lost on Jana. It had been two solid weeks since her retested blood samples had come back clear. Two solid weeks where they had spent evenings discussing everything from her latest diagrams for the portable WonderBubble to where they might want to live here in Nalani to...

How to broach the topic of their move and progressing relationship to Freya? They'd agreed to wait until the right moment. The perfect moment.

Silas inclined his head in a way that she now recognized was him silently asking the question. She smiled even as anticipation rose in her chest.

"Freya, Jana and I have made a couple of decisions." Silas sat beside his daughter as she neatly arranged the seashells she'd been collecting all morning. "Freya." Silas touched her arm. "Can you please pay attention?"

"Uh-huh." Freya shifted one shell to the side, then turned her focus on him.

"You know how you and I talked about moving here to Nalani. So I can work for Uncle Mano and you can go to school with Cammie."

"Uh-huh." Panic appeared in the girl's eyes. "I can still do that, can't I?"

"Of course." Silas winced, looking to Jana for help. "I thought I'd worked up a script." He shook his head. "Freya, I was thinking maybe it wouldn't just be the two of us anymore. What do you think if Jana comes to live with us?" He held out his hand for Jana's. "We'd like for the three of us to be a family."

"Another Ohana?" Freya's eyes cleared before they went wide. "Can I have more than one?"

"There's only one Ohana," Jana said quietly, entwining her fingers through Silas's. "It only ever grows bigger."

Freya bit her lower lip, her brow furrowing. "Would this mean…?" She took a deep breath. "If you come to live with us, can I call you Mama?"

Jana's throat tightened even as her heart swelled to the size of the ocean. "If you want to." It was a subject she had yet to bring up, that if Silas was amenable, she'd very much like to legally become Freya's mother, when the time was right. "That part's up to you."

Freya took an extra beat before she shifted to her knees and scooted over to Jana. She locked her arms around Jana's neck and squeezed. It wasn't until she felt the tears drop onto her bare shoulder that she eased back.

330 THE SINGLE DAD'S PROMISE

"Is that a yes?" Jana swiped her thumbs across the girl's freckled cheeks.

"Yes. Mama." Freya threw herself back into her father's arms. "Daddy, Jana said I can call her Mama."

"I heard." Silas scooped her into his arms and hoisted her over his shoulder.

Freya's giggles erased whatever trepidation or concern Jana had. About anything. The only thing she could feel now was hope. And love. So much love.

Silas retook her hand and pulled Jana to her feet. "I think this deserves another swim, don't you?" He tugged her to her feet and the three of them walked to the edge of the shore.

Freya kicked and Silas set her back down, barely able to catch up, as they followed Freya into the water.

"Look at her go," Jana whispered. Silas wrapped an arm around her shoulders and pulled her close. "She's a mermaid."

"Yes, she is," Silas agreed, and pressed a kiss against her temple. "Just like her mom."

* * * * *

*For more great romances in the
Hawaiian Reunions miniseries from
Anna J. Stewart and Harlequin Heartwarming,
visit www.Harlequin.com today!*

Harlequin® Reader Service

Enjoyed your book?

Try the perfect subscription for Romance readers and get more great books like this delivered right to your door.

See why over 10+ million readers have tried Harlequin Reader Service.

Start with a Free Welcome Collection with free books and a gift—valued over $20.

Choose any series in print or ebook.
See website for details and order today:

TryReaderService.com/subscriptions